LANDCASTER PRESS

# Crazy Eddie

## Thomas G. Jewusiak

# Crazy Eddie

Jacket Design by Thomas G. Jewusiak

Cover Painting by Thomas G. Jewusiak

Printed by J. Hand, LLC on the Outer Banks

*Wolf, Saints Out of Charlatans, We All Tell Stories, Jon Breedlove Panders, Panders Senior, Peterson, Megalomaniacally Holding Forth, One Very Old Woman, Jackie Gleason, Hemingway, Paul Tripp, John Dean?* were published previously as chapters in a novel entitled *The Great Landzman* (©2015) of which they form an indissoluble and essential part. They are reprinted here with the permission of the publisher, Landcaster Press.

First Paperback Edition

26th Printing

Jewusiak, Thomas G.

# Crazy Eddie

ISBN-10:0-9970967-7-2

ISBN-13:978-0-9970967-7-4

Parts of this work were written in old growth ancient virgin forests. While the author was living in the woods, he hurt no old trees in any way. The paper in this book was made from the pulp of fallen trees. No live trees were cut-down. Only hand tools were used to cut and gather the fallen trees. Only horse and oxen drawn vehicles were used. The Humane Society monitored all animals, one monitor per animal. The linen fiber in the paper was recycled from the white linen suits originally worn by Spanish grandees in pre-revolutionary Cuba; subsequently executed by firing squad, by Fidel Castro.

**LANDCASTER PRESS**
West Palm Beach
LandcasterPress.com
LandcasterPress@aol.com

"If people bring so much courage to this world the world has to kill them to break them, so of course it kills them. The world breaks every one and afterward many are strong at the broken places. But those that will not break it kills. It kills the very good and the very gentle and the very brave impartially. If you are none of these you can be sure it will kill you too but there will be no special hurry."
— **Ernest Hemingway**

# Prologue

## We All Tell Stories

We all tell stories and listen to each other's; the deal we conceive and call a compact; we hush and nod enthusiastic approval to each other's lies, shoring up the ruins which we are. We reinforce, bolster the mutual hallucination we persist in calling reality, against every shred of hard evidence. We could not survive a clear glimpse at things as they are.

Those who claim stories are a worthless mind sop are clueless, ensnared in an involuted whorl. What clear-eyed business type doesn't ambition to be a raconteur, the lifeblood of the party; the orator spellbinding at the fire; the high priest in holy robes intoning the magic words? It is the word that is magic, summoning forth the demons and the angels to frolic with; or war to the death with.

The God of the Jews existed in the word and through the word; images were blasphemy. The "Second Commandment" reads: "Thou shalt not make unto thee any graven image or any likeness of anything that is in heaven above, or that is in the earth beneath, or that is in the water under the earth."

The word held sway long before universal literacy or literacy at all; the word is not dead; if it dies, we die. The word creates us, keeps us alive as humans. Poetry isn't some trickey verse; it is the word's consummation, it's ultimate elevation. Of poetry, James Dickey wrote: "It's language itself, which is a miraculous medium which makes everything else that man has ever done possible."

Whether we read is largely irrelevant, especially, the mindless pap served up to us, which mostly is not worth the vegetative death or the momentary flicker of dancing electrons on a fading Kindle screen. Print is not the word it is merely the medium. How many third-rate films are momentarily redeemed by a well-crafted speech mouthed by an inferior actor entirely out of his league, oblivious to its meaning?

But: "The written word is far more powerful than simply a reminder: it recreates the past in the present, and gives us, not the familiar remembered thing, but the glittering intensity of the summoned-up hallucination." Or so said Northrop Frye, at least, who concocted an elaborate theory to rationalize his singular, problematic literary conclusions.

It has been suggested that the written word is not merely an echo of a speaking voice but another kind of voice altogether, a magician's trick of the very highest order. But, in "freezing" the spoken word, (an unfortunate word choice), is that not taking the life out of it? "Words are meant to be spoken and lie dead on the printed page until resurrected, or resuscitated, or merely shaken awake with a new oration."

The Egyptian god Thoth, who is reputed to have brought writing to the king, Thamus, was also the god of magic.

We love stories; we live for them; they soothe; they comfort; they lull us into a running catatonia from which we never wish to wake or a fever pitch of unconsciousness; or stark, blatant consciousness; they keep the wolf at bay and mock the bull into a tango of death, taunted by the preposterous executioner in tight pants and dancing slippers. They fashion order out of the chaos and impose order and meaning where there is neither. And some, the best, rouse us from our stupor.

Frye said that every human society possesses a mythology which is inherited, transmitted, and diversified by [its] "literature". He might also have added that myth can just as easily be embodied in the lowest of its popular culture or erroneously claimed by pop culture. Too often old worn out cliches endlessly repeated, or mere tropes are given a false dignity and appropriated as "myth". The very idea has been contaminated, denigrated.

Myth is the story that vibrates in and strums our soul and plumbs our depths.

Myth is a culturally authorized and endorsed propaganda using images with universal reverberations and ordinarily recognized meanings to communicate to individuals what and how to feel about being human. This is what Barthe said or something close to it.

Jacques Barzun wrote that figures, whether of fact or fiction, insofar as they express destinies, aspirations, attitudes typical of man or particular groups, are invested with a mythical character. Jay Gatsby and James Gatsby both fit the bill.

But it is rarely that our myths rise to literature and that literature just as often demolishes those myths, those childlike, elemental storybook stories; the myths that once ruled and sometimes imprisoned our primitive psyches.

The lower social classes, even those with money, and heaps of worthless things, that they are suffocating in, have no interest in and indeed are threatened to the quick, frightened by any knowledge of experience beyond their own everyday preoccupations. Literature, art, is despised by them, regarded as a dangerous threat because it will blow apart their hovels, no matter how grand, where they eat and sleep, and make a mockery of how they comfortably conceive of themselves.

But inexorably assaulting high culture and swapping-it-out with the low, which they claim is the genuine, authentic culture, has become the peculiar relentless rallying cause of high IQ stupid people; a means of assailing and reviling, the standards and values of mean-old mommy and daddy.


It is a consummate irony that the Anglo-Saxon has internalized and made a core value of what is essentially an impoverished class's value system. For the Anglo-Saxon "soul searching" is undignified and unmanly; the examined life is a fool's life; not worth living and it is that very examination that makes it so.

No whining, no complaining, stiff upper lip, no inerasable stigma of the malcontent:

> Theirs not to make reply,
> Theirs not to reason why,
> Theirs but to do and die

While proclaiming their own love of freedom, this is a self-imposed slavery more appropriate to a totalitarian slave state, requiring its citizens to march lock-step to their own unquestioning slaughter. How supremely ironic that Shakespeare, with his quintessential Hamlet, should perfect and write in the language of these constricted English.

There is myth that is art and myth that is anti-art, kitsch.

Myth, in contemporary culture, often kitsch, is simultaneously a simplified explanation of human experience and a mask protecting everyday humanity from the despairing, existential depths of that experience. Myth is indispensable and destructive at the same time; necessary because it keeps humanity from full consciousness of the dangers associated with the blacker side by offering palatable explanations and dangerous because it keeps humanity from full consciousness of the hazards associated with the more "realistic" view.

Popular escape novels, even if gussied up in faux intellectual trappings, are destructive of the human condition. They are the translation of the stupidity of received ideas into the language of beauty and feeling thus moving us to tears of self-pity for the utter banality of what we think and feel. Milan Kundera said this or something very like it. True literature sharpens the focus on reality even if it means evisceration.

Pauline Kael insisted that trash gives us an appetite for art. She was dead wrong; it stifles any possibility of recognizing art when we see it, much less the possibility of appreciating it or being ennobled by it. Human appreciation of artistic beauty, of literature, is cruelly, irreparably distorted and ruined by the requirements of mass culture, pop culture, and the mud gods it constrains us to kneel before and offer obeisance to.

But Kael did finally acknowledge the fundamental error of her ways, acknowledging that although the previous generation was persuaded to disdain trash, the newer generation, with the media and schools in hot pursuit, had begun to talk about trash as if it were serious art. But worse, still, these new cheerleaders for trash, on a raucous joyride in the stolen car of self-inflating egos, having killed off the Master in the big house and his lovely wife and all his beautiful children, Anastasia, too, and the babies, too; became the new Vandals with empty credentials, attacking not just the Anglo-Saxons but all European White Men, Jews especially included, bursting open the treasure house to toss the riches to the clawing, trampling multitude, grinning cannibals in top hats from the explorers that they ate, picking human flesh from their teeth with pilfered gold toothpicks.

The great museums and the great books are not just vaults to preserve the past, or monuments to edited histories; they are a storehouse of collected human genius; they preserve the possibility of our future, if we are to have any future worth living.

Pauline Kael called movies a tawdry corrupt art for a tawdry corrupt world and if we don't learn to indulge in great trash, and there is great trash, what movies shall we see or books read? Movies are so rarely great art, that if we cannot appreciate their great trashiness, we have very little reason to be interested in them; or so she dangerously pontificated; though she may be right.

Indulging in trash is going to an Irish wake for the death of souls; having such a grand old time that you forget entirely about the corpse stinking up the room or the flies blotting out the light and clogging your nose, much less the quintessential tragedy of death.

I remember guiltily reading the works of a particular author deeply ashamed of my self-indulgence. I read all of him, but he leads me to question what a good writer is; with his appallingly mediocre prose and second-rate intellect, no-doubt tailored to mesh with his freshman English class, which he dare not educate, if he even knows how, lest they threaten his precious tenure, which he wore out his knees licking ass for. (But F. Scott Fitzgerald had a second-rate intellect and wrote luminous, if studied, prose, marred by an ill-used thesaurus. His gift with language is inexplicable; this man was so dumb and stupid [read a hundred or two of his letters, if you doubt it] that he can only be explained as a kind-of idiot savant, although true "idiot savants" are never creative.)

11

One critic warned that too many bad writers write to settle old scores. But good writers do, too. Only the best, stand back and refrain from judgement. It is not the writer's job to forgive, to assume such god-like conceit, the ultimate condescension. You want to forgive, that's fine, that's personal, your own business; but you have no right to forgive for all mankind, certainly not in the name of God, that's blasphemy, that's obscene, criminal; the racket of priests and "holy-men", the currency of conmen and bad writers. Forgiveness is abrogation, the easy way out; the cop-out; the pivotal act of spinelessness; or sheer lethargy; the oppressive duty shucked. It is not for nothing that we love revenge movies.

But this writer of whom I speak: why does he not hold this bum, his father, to account? I ran into this author's Daddy's ilk; you couldn't avoid collision; the old decaying cities were swarming, seething with them; left-over men; the saloons swamped, slopping over with them; ignorant, arrogant men, quarrelsome, confrontational, who bellowed, sober or drunk that "my opinion is as good as any man's". And this has nothing to do with "class" or money. I knew families without two nickels who scrimped every penny; and nurtured, I mean cherished their children. And this poor dumb writer was constricted, shackled by the milieu he was born into. I was always optimistically bemused with what incredible and graceful ease the movie and TV generation slipped out of their backward social bonds; an ample number demarked themselves by the English they clearly enunciated; more Gregory Peck than their janitor father; and only the markedly ignorant, eager to wallow with the hoi polloi, mocked, "their clipped, Anglophile stage speech". We should bear-in-mind that the Lone Ranger spoke perfectly enunciated English without slang, twang, or slur. (The writer's character description was set-down, inviolable canon, and ruled the show.)

But this particular, poor schlep writer can't shake off his Daddy, who clutches tenaciously to his wounded, bleeding, psyche; who, no doubt, reading only the lines he wrote: this father was a mean, vicious, lazy, drunken bum, in real-life, unalloyed city white trash, who abandoned his son, responsibility and everything else that mattered; and this poor dumb writer returns the favor, as so many crippled children are masochistically compelled to do, by magically turning his Daddy into a fantasy hero worthy of Disney, salt of the earth, an aching wish fulfillment made into fictional flesh. And he does it again and again and again. The effect is compelling; his pipedreams talk and walk and seem to have a human face and smile at you and sit with you late into the night, hold on tight and won't let you go. They gave him the Pulitzer (he beat out Franzen) for this intoxicating kind of shit; which shit is subversive. It is every bit as subversive as Mailer or Coppola and Scorsese. And he's doing the exact same thing; pandering to the throng, watching, a self-congratulatory voyeur, as they lap-it-up, dogs wolfing-down their own vomit, creating culture heroes out of garbage.

Northerners like to mollify themselves with the fairytale that Tobacco Road was a rutted dirt track in poverty stricken rural Georgia, when in fact it is a highway running right straight through the American heart; nor was it isolated in the ribbed north end of Jersey, nor in the pine barrens, nor the western counties, either, nor on the banks of the Cahulawassee River; no need to hike deep into the backwoods; the demons lurk just outside your door, and are knocking at it; take a casual twilight stroll into Morningside Park, if you doubt it. The impure products of the American magnet were crazy and cracked long before, devoid of any peasant traditions to give them character. Lehane feels these people deep in his bones, in Boston, more than a half century later. Instead, we fancy writers who spoon-feed us expedient lies, emasculating us in the process. We are enthralled by the utter stupidity of received, accepted ideas transmuted into the language of beauty and feeling, moving us to tears of self-pity for the utter banality of what we think and feel (Milan Kundera, again). We refuse to admit that we crawled out of a communal cesspit; though, how much more noble and empowering that confession would be. We are anxious that people will distinguish the inerasable aroma of shit, even after years of conscientious scrubbing; as if we must forever carry our father's sins and the sins of our neighborhood. We conspire to pretend that the corner working man's saloon is a Socratic academy instead of a sounding board for loud, belligerent, lazy drunks, convinced that their dumb, ignorant, illiterate opinion is as good as any man's.

I would leave him be, this writer of ours, a good, if seditious, storyteller, more than good; isn't that enough? *Even-though he adds absolutely nothing to our understanding of the human condition.*

I remember my son getting a gift of a set of recordings of Appalachian storytellers, who had memorized their stories and carried on a long ancient, oral tradition of live performance; their stories, never told exactly-the-same way twice, and my son was mesmerized by them; and what's wrong with that?

Hemingway, a literary writer, at his best, liked to don the bogus anti-intellectual mantle, an armor or screen, phony peasant clothes adorned with intricately crafted patches, a silly getup in which he fancied himself, and pretended to be, a mere story-teller, an old-timer reigning at the campfire:

> "There are many kinds of stories in this book. I hope that you will find some that you like.... I would like to live long enough to write... twenty-five more stories. I know some pretty good ones."

But our particular writer's arrogance is inexplicable, and jarring, grating, infuriating, but mostly merely irritating. He repeatedly, deludedly, refers to his work as art and himself as artist. "Have you no shame?" Even Thomas Hardy, the better writer, was astute enough to be discomfited by his novels (serialized in the newspapers) which he openly admitted were popular pulp, even though they were something more than that. Hardy tried to redeem himself with his poetry, which he did consider literature but which ironically and sadly was not very good. But at least Hardy's heart was in the right place. Even Graham Greene drew a strict distinction between his pulp or "entertainments" and his literary works, until finally in his latter years, throwing up his hands, as if in surrender, comprehending that his pulp was sometimes "better" than his more ambitious literary work, he simply stopped "dividing" his work. In the end he singled out only two of his novels as worthy with perhaps an additional third. And make-no-mistake, I often prefer high-level trash to the often-excruciating tedium of low-level literature. John Grisham, fully acknowledging that he wrote pop trash, said: "So I decided a long time ago, I'll take the money and run. You talk about legacy? I don't care. I'm going to be dead and gone." You've got to love that kind of brutal honesty.

Samuel Clemens loathed Mark Twain; so do I. Twain was his idiot, demented twin who was invited into his house as a guest, and took title to it; Clemens became powerless to control or exorcize Twain and became his avatar victim; his Hyde had expropriated, usurped, enslaved and humiliated him and made him astoundingly rich which clinched the imprisonment with gold shackles. Clemens fought a culture-war inside his own head. He bankrupted himself just to break free, to make a living as a businessman which he didn't have in him. But the slighted Twain came-back with a vengeance, infecting Clemens's brain, eating it from the inside out, exacting retribution for the attempted expulsion. The exultant buffoon, Twain, donned his preposterous Oxford academic robes at his daughter's own wedding; talk about having to be the bride at every wedding. His daughter was mortified. She loved her father but hated Twain; but Twain would eventually corrupt that love of her father. What Clemens knew in his bones is, that America loved idiots and buffoons; we elect them to public office; we worship them as culture-heroes. Dare we even whisper that Samuel Clemens was writing a derisive satire at Mark Twain's expense when he wrote *The Adventures of Huckleberry Finn*? Huckleberry Finn isn't seven years old, as he seems; he's fourteen years old, and dare we use the word, quite obviously, mentally-retarded, and the pathetic victim of one Clemens joke after another, all cheap and low. Finn is the Forest Gump of his day. The author of the book the Gump movie is *based* on, Winston Groom, in his early interviews made clear that the book was a biting satire, repeatedly referring to Gump as a moron. It didn't take Groom long to see the hand-writing-on-the-wall and that the gross misunderstanding and misrepresentation of his book would pay-the-rent in perpetuity. His book would sell one million, seven hundred thousand copies based on a misinterpretation. In later interviews Groom changed-his-tune and went along with the gag, much as Clemens must have done. The present-day writers who inexplicably admire Twain also find it sidesplitting to mock the crippled or the speech impaired.

If Finn is a gross caricature, Jim is worse; the most brazen over-the-top exaggeration of even the cruelest racial trope. Was it really-necessary to call him N***** Jim; wouldn't Black Jim do the trick? Oh, but it wouldn't have been as funny, would it? The demon Twain in respectable Clemens could never pass up a crude joke; and Twain reveled in that word, wallowed in it, using it every chance he got.

Not-withstanding-this, our preposterously smug author, of-which-we-speak, has his cartoonish

17

boogeymen, who he foists upon us, the reader, which boogeyman distracts him and us from the greater evil under his very nose.

His is a dream that will put you to sleep at the wheel. And when your head cracks open like an egg crashing through the windshield, who do you blame? Oh, you won't blame anybody because you'll be dead; you stupid fuck.

Popular pulp fiction, trash, even when bleak evades and denies reality, partly to avoid the stain and stigma of infuriation and skepticism. Instead of telling a story of desperate survival and perhaps even triumph of a kind, it wallows in a fantasy of benign rescue. It makes us eager collaborators in our own emasculation and devitalization. We're waiting for superman to fly in or our ships to come in, or the Fairytale Prince to gallop in on his white charger, or the king's golden-haired daughter to come down from her tower, or the homicidal idiot locked-up in the cellar next-door to abscond to save us in the nick-of-time; same as Kemo Sabe; or the cavalry; or Hani Pasha; or Abel Magwitch; or the all-seeing eye in the sky, which is not god, but now-and-again pretends to be. ... To be plucked from jeopardy or obscurity or poverty or disgrace by a magic mentor or an astonishing savior or a quirk of fate.

Vargas Llosa said that one of the most important functions of literature is to remind us that however firm the ground we walk on appears and however brightly the city we live in shines, there are demons lurking everywhere; and I would add, the most dangerous demons are in the garb of saints wanting to lead us by the hand enthusiastically to our own damnation by means of sugar sweet persuasion.

But the demons also lurk within us needing only an urging, or some primordial hint to leap suddenly to life or sneak out at night. Hegel was wrong: Macbeth didn't step out of nature to cling to alien beings; the alien beings sprung out whole from Macbeth's own soul and weren't alien at all. It's like meeting your double in the street and failing to recognize it for what it is and flailing at it uselessly with an old buggy whip or asking it to afternoon tea, which is worse.

By educating and sharpening critical perception, the accepted and revered works of high culture seek to subject any conventionally accepted canon to a withering barrage of truth, to pull down the idols, demythologize the established pieties, a sharp stiletto point to burst the pompous, bloated and pretentious. It is the great equalizer.

In a world of universal deceit unveiling the truth is an act of revolution or revulsion or pure mindless anarchy.

I disliked popular fiction as a child and still do; and regarded it as a kind of cataleptic undeath, an escape to a la la land, a total and absolute waste. There is nothing wrong with escape in its place and some children, especially those of adult age, need this protective cocoon, a deep, supposedly healing sleep until the deadly fever of their childhood has past; but the time comes to wake up, to leave sleep behind, not to worship the bronzed baby shoes which bound and crippled our little feet or to gild our old wooden crutches like holy trophies but which made our legs withered and weak, or to keep our antiquated iron lung like a consecrated precious object in the middle of the living room to ooh and aah over but which still secretly sucks the air out of us and the entire room.

I listen to these poor fools today in astonishment as they wax nostalgically ecstatic about the novels they loved, which they pretended to be literature. Even the language these ninnies use is self-indulgent, effete, weak, languishing, masturbatory: "a hot bath, a glass of wine and a good book", or "I like to curl up with a good book." These dupes will pleasure, masturbate themselves to death, all the while convincing themselves that they are the "so brave" pursuers of ultimate truth. Orwell got it all wrong. Big Brother is obsolete, a Stalinist state quaintly antiquated, at least in the United States. We are Las Vegas. We have Oprah to teach us to eat our own brains out, and trade recipes for the perpetual pig-out, the phallic-less circle-jerk, all-you-can-eat buffet. We are our own most efficient enslavers. We throw ever-more exotic lynching parties in which, we ourselves, are our own hanging trophy. Auto-erotic asphyxiation is emblematic and symbolic of our much self-lauded, self-celebrated, "enlightened western world". We don't even know enough to cut the corpse down, but are mesmerized, intoxicated, tanked-up by its stench, swaying in the stagnant air, metronomic, thumping in time the tune of our ruin, our shambles.

True literature engages the mind at its highest, most rigorous, arduous level; it's excruciating, if rewarding work; more like aerial combat on a high wire than it is a hot bath. And if you can't even get through *Moby Dick,* why bother reading anything else; why don't you just go and blow yourself up and give us all a break, and don't, don't dare to write; you haven't earned the right. Even when these ninnies do adopt true literature, they misinterpret and corrupt it and twist it into their own mind's watery mush.

*The Great Gatsby* is not a romance, as they would have you believe, but the most corrosive, bitter indictment of the American Dream, in which Fitzgerald, for just once, resurrected himself to a self-knowledge and a wisdom he, pathetically, did not, or could not, profit from. Daisy, the sad retard, is Gatsby's destroyer; whether she leaves him or not is largely irrelevant. If you think this stuff is glamorous you've missed the entire point. Fitzgerald knows he has been seduced and ruined and seems powerless to do anything about it, except to write a literary masterpiece, and slog headlong, straightaway, to ignore its warnings.

"You must read... read... read." What? to have ill-conceived words tumble through your brain like an adulterated street drug, that leaves only a throbbing hangover in your dulled-down damaged psyche? Most so-called educated people read too much. I am especially blessed in having regarded shit as shit; and to quote Emily Dickenson: "... then discovered Shakespeare. Why is any other book needed?"

"Reading, after a certain age, diverts the mind too much from its creative pursuits. Any man who reads too much and uses his own brain too little falls into lazy habits of thinking." Albert Einstein.

We are addicted to trash: the smothering, suffocating big tit that squashes against our face and blocks our nose and kills the air; that we can't wean ourselves from, that we're stuck to with a mawkish glue.

Pauline Kael, though wildly opinionated, contrarian and downright wacky, was: incendiary, provocative and at times enlightening, if most often wrong; worshipping at the feet of problematic actors and directors, as a form of sadistic masochism, foisting them upon the credulous, gullible public, who pant and crave to bond with the self-appointed literati. Kael's was a tribal revenge, of the disqualified, excluded, omitted. She lionized the purveyors who ushered in a procession of psychopaths; which pimps are, unaccountably, inexplicably, venerated to this day, a new sacred canon to entomb us in slop.

Coppola didn't "write" accurately or naturalistically but rather, persuasively, entertainingly, hilariously; a great showman not an artist or reporter; his prodigious gift was insurrectionary, subversive. The Mafiosi learned more about being Mafiosi from Coppola and Scorsese than the directors did from the Mafiosi; they studied the films, the role-models, to get the lingo down and perfect the attitude, becoming more engaging, amusing, and effective murderers. These directors, in effect, invented them, conceived them, invigorated, and exploited them, and gleefully loosed them upon the world. Theirs is no more authentic than Jack Abbott's capable book, a synthetic, made-up, purely "literary" construct tailored to seduce and manipulate naïve, credulous literary types; little sissies who adore and glamorize the toughs who bully and beat them up; pawns in a logical extension of a criminal career. But with Coppola and Scorsese, this is doubly subversive; the illiterate lazy psychopaths channeling through these talented creators, who tirelessly do *their* dirty work. One might seriously ask the question whether these epicene men, by laying themselves open, being thrilled by, and glorifying and romanticizing these much more formidable, definitive men, aren't engaging in a rape fantasy with themselves as squealing, wiggling, ecstatic victim.

It's as if Norman Mailer concocted *In the Belly of the Beast* to make *his* own anarchic case, (confused mishmash of Marx, Sartre, and Jean Genet), foisting it upon us, as Abbott's; who is no more than Mailer's willing avatar. Mailer is more guilty of murder than Abbot is; he wound him up and let him loose to wreak-havoc, which was inevitable; or at least predictable. Are Coppola, Scorsese and Michael Mann murderers, too? Mailer was a creative innocent in comparison to these three. Are we really so removed from those heady days gone by when giddy Radcliff girls flocked to Attica to line-up to fuck murderers and suck the pricks of various assorted psychopaths; remember the cry, or howl: "all crime is political"; or, unbeknownst, was it always embedded deep in the American psyche? Waspy Kay Adams is Coppola's wet-dream. Neil McCauley is a holy icon on Michael Mann's bed-chamber wall. (As a "youth" Mann attempted to burn down his father's new competitor; but more revealing is, he is not afraid to tell us about it; no

23

embarrassment; in-fact he is bragging. He isn't stealing food for his family; he's a "businessman" trying to put his father's legitimate competitor out of business. Lucky for us all, he is such a very little man and not cut-out for a life of more blatant, barefaced crime.)

My half-brother married a woman, who was born in Italy, and had denied vehemently that the Mafia even existed, considering it no more than an American fabrication to purposely put-down the Italians: that is until the movie, *The Godfather*. She had absorbed whole scenes out of it and would act them out by heart. She was especially orgasmicly thrilled by the scene where Corleone, back in Italy, kills Don Ciccio:

> Have him come nearer. I can't see him so good. What is your father's name?
>
> My father's name is Antonio Andolini.
>
> Come closer. I can't hear so good.
>
> Antonio Andolini. And this is for you.

She performed the whole scene, including the knife thrust with its upward gutting, quivering with unrestrained glee, all the while protesting what horrors they were, while glancing with utter disdain at her castrata marriage partner, who piously said the rosary with her every single night; and dutifully, meekly journeyed to novenas with her. Granted, this was a consummate scene by superb showmen and the revenge was perfect, sweet, and righteous, and that's exactly what makes it so subversive. The devil, himself, couldn't have crafted better.

This garbage gorges upon itself, self-replicates and takes on an independent life all its own. Henry Hill's book and the movie based upon it owes much more to the movies than to his real life, which was mind-numbingly dull, as was he.

*Madmen* takes place on a planet far, far away from earth in another galaxy or alternate reality, an hallucination or delusion, concocted by a self-absorbed, narcissistic writer who claims to have done research but was actually locked away, ensconced in the upper stacks compulsively masturbating. Anyone who has lived through the Sixties or seen the countless movies and books that more accurately portrays this era, knows what a wildly entertaining but dangerous crock-a-shit *Madmen* is. But as we said, life imitates art much more than the other-way-around.

It becomes especially treacherous when a self-intoxicated president who speaks nothing but clichéd gobbledygook, takes it as a life-lesson for the me-too movement and the scandalous past treatment of the womenfolk. This president, a contrived, fabricated grandee of minimal gifts, foisted upon us by our *betters*, who hunkers-down in a darkened closet, flying high, deep breathing, in timed exercises, his own flatulence, which is accumulated, magnified, and cherished by his over-paid keepers, who themselves partake, and pump it in and distill it into a marketable essence, is not one to bestow wise counsel.

*Madmen* is saved by its actors who harken back to the thrilling days of yesteryear, of cigarette and whiskey-soaked Hollywood leading-men who were – men: Bogart, Mitchum, William Holden. It also taps into the self-creation myths of the American Dream, our founding if corrosive on-going saga. The Jon Hamm character is Jay Gatsby "on-steroids", to exploit that unbeautified, vile chestnut.

Pauline Kael was a barn-burner with a match. She tweaked the great beast to bring it to its knees and humiliate it, a wiseass delinquent schoolgirl who aced the finals and received a special dispensation from the principal. Out of pure spite, she usurped, displanted, an Anglo-Saxon movie icon and idol (Orson Wells) with a third-rate, alcoholic hack (Herman Mankiewicz). She must have thought this was one hell-of-a joke.

Kael may have justifiably reviled smaltz but as a spurious alternative, became enamored of excrement which she misguidedly imagined was its opposite.

But, in her defense, she had some idea what she was doing; and was more attuned to what constituted high culture, art, than clogged, constipated wags like Eliot could even conceive; who never saw the imminent onslaught of pop-trash "culture"; much-less its ascendency.

More "humanity" will die in this war, and make-no-mistake, it is war, and it is death, and this is not just metaphoric, more death than in any other war, or all the wars together.

What reviewer today would acknowledge, even to themselves, that 99% of what they review is pure garbage? They haven't got a clue.

Kael, speaking of trash movies might just as well have been speaking about trash books:

> Movies are our cheap and easy expression, the sullen art of displaced persons. Because we feel low, we sink in the boredom, relax in the irresponsibility.

"The sullen art of displaced persons", a line worth repeating and posting on every theater marquee and on every video recording right before the FBI warning and on the cover of every pulp book which books are now printed on fine paper, lodged in libraries instead of newsstands, the-better-to lure, trick and ensnare us.

Trash opens-up the soul to raw sewage; it can taint whatever purity that soul might have possessed, cheapening existence, disconnecting us from any struggle to come to terms with reality or in any way ameliorating it. Most popularly acclaimed writers, best sellers, hawk a kind of mawkish barely sentient death and a special place in hell will be reserved for these money whores who sell themselves to the public taste and have the gall to call their academically embellished garbage literature. They diminish our righteous rage and lull us into a self-induced narcolepsy. They are minutely skilled gilders of shit. They hollow out our cores with a skillfully wielded razor knife and reduce us to servile cowards submitting to a puerile fantasy of external intervention.

We are reduced to facing down the homicidal apathy of the fat girl serving-up candy bars to the morbidly obese on silver platters at state dinners.

If anything, it is literature that will save us; literature, which is a matter of life and death. But even true literature is habitually ruined by being entrusted into the wrong hands, desiccated school-marms, shrunken and shriveled, male and female, who suck the life-blood out of it. The schools and Universities are a death-trap.

If someone came from another world and wanted to know the truth about what it was to be human, what and who we are, quintessentially, he should not waste his time reading our history or science books; looking at our great construction projects or our scientific achievements will only reduce him to laughter or tears. Rather, he should learn our languages and read our great books, of literature, which, if he has a soul himself, will reveal to him the soul of man, both the good and the bad of it; that we are brothers under the skin. And if the visitor does have a soul, what he sees of us will not save us; quite the contrary it will sign our death decree; only these few great books will grant us a reprieve from that doom of certain annihilation.

> *In the annals of ancient civilizations, there existed a remarkable practice—one that diverged from the usual clash of swords and shields. These people, upon encountering a stranger, would temporarily suspend their animosity and engage in a different kind of combat: the exchange of stories.*

*In the past, the echoes of these storytellers still resonate:*

1. *Mesopotamians: In the fertile lands between the Tigris and Euphrates rivers, the Mesopotamians recognized the power of narratives. Amidst the ziggurats and bustling markets, they would sit cross-legged, their eyes alight with curiosity, and share tales of gods, epic battles, and the mundane struggles of daily life. Violence could wait; stories were the currency of connection.*

2. *Ancient Greeks: Beneath the olive trees and beside the agora, the Greeks reveled in their oral tradition. Whether in Athens or Sparta, they understood that stories wove the fabric of humanity. So, when a stranger arrived, they'd set aside their spears and invite them to recount their adventures—their odysseys across stormy seas, encounters with mythical creatures, and the trials that shaped their souls.*

3. *Indigenous Tribes: Across continents, from the vast plains of North America to the dense jungles of South America, indigenous tribes practiced this art of narrative diplomacy. They'd gather around campfires, and listen intently. The stranger's tale might reveal shared ancestors, common spirits, or the whisper of a forgotten kinship.*

4. *Silk Road Traders: Along the ancient Silk Road, where caravans carried silks, spices, and dreams, merchants from diverse lands converged. They'd halt at oases, their camels laden with treasures, and sit in the shade. Instead of haggling over goods, they'd exchange stories—their silk roads intersecting in the tapestry of human experience.*

5. *Polynesians: On their voyages across the vast Pacific, Polynesian navigators would steer their outrigger canoes toward distant islands. When they encountered other seafarers, they'd anchor their vessels and share legends of celestial navigation, ocean currents, and the stars that guided them. The waves listened, and so did the strangers.*

*These ancient custodians of stories understood that violence could be deferred, that swords could rest in their scabbards while words poured like rivers. For in those moments of storytelling, they glimpsed the common threads binding humanity—a shared longing for meaning, adventure, and connection.*

*And so, around campfires, under temple arches, and amidst humming marketplaces, they wove a fragile peace—one spun not from treaties, but from stories.*

......

The trashing of so-called high culture and all its accoutrements is not without cause. It has been the culture appropriated as the defining feature by an upper class, an aristocracy, a self-appointed, abusive intelligentsia, a bunch of stuffed shirts full only of their own hollow selves.

But it can be more universally defined as a storehouse of a broader enriching knowledge, an avenue to transcend and abolish the strict boundaries of any entrenched class system.

High culture has been exploited as an instrument of exclusion; a club to beat down the aspiring, clutching masses; formal dress to the opera. But opera was at one time popular entertainment considered in some of its forms, decadent by the keepers-of-the-flame, with its shamelessly hokey melodrama. Literary Romanticism revalued and seriously reconsidered the "low culture" previously disparaged in medieval romances. The trash of one era becomes the treasure of another without ever ceasing to be trash; only the perception changes, the softness of age and an enriching patina masks the rank smell.

Shakespeare was a journeyman playwright, the son of a glover, ever-mindful of making a buck, peddling cheap humor to the groundlings. I'm always humorously struck by the self-proclaimed literati decked protectively, demarking themselves in evening dress, hee-hawing hilariously at his lowest jokes, gags that must have stuck sharp in his throat; a source of embarrassment to a creator who balanced dexterously on the taut hanging rope between trash and the best combinations of words ever put down on paper.

There is a pathetic tendency for individuals of ostensible intelligence to pay homage, toadying to the multitudes, as if to gain favor when the anticipated upheaval comes, offering obeisance, even, to popularly worshipped dregs of the promulgated media culture. It's like raising a baby chimpanzee, nurturing it, pretending and truly believing in your heart that it is a gifted child only to have it grow up and eat your face off with a knife and the proper fork; and your hands; and finally, your testicles, in pooled blood on a white porcelain dish, for dessert. Kael, one of those devoted flacks for trash, a pop culture oracle as someone labeled her, belatedly remarked to a friend:

> "When we championed trash culture, we had no idea it would become the only culture."

People find a commonality of blood, a brotherhood, bonding of the dumbest in their basest, most vulgar and most prurient interests; low culture, pop culture, a natural herding instinct, getting high sniffing each other's armpits, inhaling each other's flatulence and wallowing ecstatically in each other's shit.

. . . .

Some lewd ditty warbled by an old whore in the streets inspired politicians to glory. We have the very word of martyrs and patriots that it was the forbidden music insinuating itself from the magic west misconstrued as celestial harmony which helped bring down the Communist monolith. We have the word of Vaclav Havel for this. The music critic for the New York Times equated *Elinor Rigby* with Beethoven's Fifth, which leads me to suspect she was 13, flying high on LSD with her best buddy, when she first heard the Beatle's little ditty.

Esteemed jurists and competent lawyers claimed to have been inspired by a fanciful fabrication, in what is no more than a wildly popular little girl's book, made more saleable by another author of genuine gifts who rewrote it as a goof, repaying his childhood friend who did yeoman's service as his amanuensis and gofer. He may have proved the academic point in his head about making kitsch marketable but didn't want his name associated with it and he didn't laugh last; he stopped laughing completely. His little joke became a gargantuan beast he had unwittingly unleashed and lost control of, which haunted him. Even the putative author, no fool herself, was ashamed of her currying favor with the gullible, ignorant multitude yearning for its pap:

> "I wonder what their reaction would have been if [the book] had been complex, sour, unsentimental, racially unpaternalistic because Atticus was a bastard."

There is no end to the self-indulgent melodrama that we ourselves love to wallow in. We cry real tears for fake concoctions which mock us mercilessly by their gross stupidity.

. . . .

I think of talk show hosts fawning over the dredged up resuscitated corpses of old Hollywood, huffing and puffing mightily to blow life into the very dead carcasses; Victorian post-mortem photography or memorial portraiture as they euphemistically advertised it with the added kick of a real live ventriloquist bobbing the desiccated head like a grotesque hand puppet. This particular late-night host was an unabashed pusher of poshlost. It was not enough that a previous age had its worthless icons to worship at. He had this malignant requisite to resurrect the discarded refuse, so a clean, new age could kiss their putrid clay feet. I dare you: try to sit through Charlie Chaplin, Buster Keaton, the Marx

Brothers, Laurel and Hardy or the Three Stooges. And if you think this dreck is genius then you're an idiot, plain and simple.

. . . .

Although there may be as much to be learned from a soap advertisement as from a pensée by Pascal it does not follow that they have the equivalent value. I can see the usefulness of analyzing pulp, pop entertainment, and other societal out-growths; a fascinating, colorful fungus growing out of the heat of decaying compost; an intriguing jungle of life in a toxic bubbling brew of pond scum. This detritus can divulge much that is critical to the survival of the greater civilization, but only on the level of an archeologist deftly sifting through the dumps and latrines of a long-lost people; or the CIA cutting open the drains of the Soviet premier's hotel rooms a floor beneath to collect his excrement and thus determine the state of his physical wellbeing and the continued possibility of our own.

# Megalomaniacally Holding Forth

Leslie A. Fiedler, megalomaniacally holding forth, on Rip Van Winkle and Huckleberry Finn:

> "The typical male protagonist of our [American] fiction has been a man on the run, harried into the forest and out to sea, down the river or into combat — anywhere to avoid 'civilization,' .... One of the factors that determine theme and form in our great books is this strategy of evasion, this retreat to nature and childhood which makes our literature (and life!) so charmingly and infuriatingly 'boyish.'"

I think Fiedler got it absolutely, totally wrong, like he did most things. It is the stodgy prigs entrenched in their routine, mind numbing, status quo, their appallingly normal surrender, which they doggedly proclaim a life, the staunch defenders of the soul rot they are mired in; these are the walking, putrefying dead men who fail to sniff out their own stink, who complement themselves as "adults", as mature.

It was Aleksandr Solzhenitsyn, [not American] no boyish dilettante running away to the woods, who said, that at all costs, he structured his life to avoid a tedious everyday existence, the penitentiary of ennui, life as the-vast-majority-of people lived it. One gets the feeling that even the gulag was preferable, was in some sense a choice, an alternative; he wasn't talking about escaping Communism but about life itself, or what we call life, civilization, if you will, what life has degenerated into; the dropping into unconsciousness, into rote, doing what everyone expects you to do, what they do, the default settings, the cop-out, the rat's-race, the endless, self-defeating, mindless pursuit of nothing worth anything, the gnawing, corrosive sense of having held it in your hand, having been distracted for just an instant and lost, some infinitely fine and infinitely wonderful thing.

It is Holden Caulfield who refuses to enter the world; call it the "adult" world if you like, a world that Caulfield considers unethical, a fraud, a pack of lies, a world of self-deceptions and pretentious bad taste; and there is a moral dimension to bad taste; "poshlost":

> America is awash in poshlost... sinking... drowning in poshlost... base self-satisfied vulgarity... highfalutin banal superficiality... taste so bad that it becomes more than an esthetic offence and becomes a moral obscenity... complacent hackneyed mediocrity curdling into moral degeneracy... Dostoyevsky applied the word to the Devil... smug narcissistic inferiority... not only the obviously trashy but the falsely important, the falsely beautiful, the falsely clever... corny, treacly trash, cutsypie clichés... the sentimental... the saccharine... the mawkish and maudlin. Philistinism in all its phases, bogus profundities, crude, moronic dishonest pseudo-literature parading as the real thing, stealing away the souls of the gullible, parading up and down decked out, garbed in garbage.

Salinger became incensed when one potential editor suggested that Holden is crazy. Holden isn't crazy; the world is crazy; and if Holden becomes unhinged it is the crazy world that unhinged him. Caulfield is Huck Finn, with intelligence, whose innocence and down to earth decency contrasts with the corruption and hypocrisy of the ~~adult~~ world. Everyone wants Holden to learn to play the game, to adapt to the world as it is, to find his place. In one of the most misunderstood quotes in literature, Holden quotes one of his teachers who quotes Wilhelm Stekel:

> "The mark of the immature man is that he wants to die nobly for a cause, while the mark of the mature man is that he wants to live humbly for one."

This kind of a "mature" man, the kind Stekel is talking about, lives an existence of quiet, cowardly desperation. There are things we must be prepared to die for or life is not worth living.

# Brides of Christ

The nuns were the true brides of Christ; of this they had utterly convinced themselves. In their own minds they were God's chosen ones; to use the jargon they lived by: they had a vocation. Of vocations the nuns spoke incessantly; not of their own vocation, this would be too obviously proud, but of the vocations that we might have. They were always on the lookout, checking us out, nosing about. We were always being reminded that we too could be one of them, one of the chosen ones. We must look within ourselves, wrack our souls for the signs that God would send us. Of course, the nuns and priests, being chosen themselves, were especially adept at recognizing the telltale signs in those whom God had singled out for his special service. One sure sign was an absolute, total, obedience, and reverence for those who already convinced themselves that they had been chosen. Therefore, those most obsequious would be guaranteed a first place in line. In this way the nuns and priests exercised full control over those who would join their ranks and succeed them. Many a young boy or girl would run home ecstatic with the news:

> "Sister James Marie says that she sees signs of a vocation in me."

My sister came running home in reverie, tears welling in her eyes, with just such news, only to have the mark of God rescinded a week later: "Sister says she was mistaken in thinking I might have been chosen"; this for some imagined or perceived infraction, failing to lick sister's ass with sufficient enthusiasm; reducing my sister to all-out panic; for being kicked out of heaven. This is how the nuns sadistically toyed with their charges; the cat with its pathetic, alacritous mouse.

The concept itself was a skillful conscripting tool. To recognize the hand of God in the form of the nuns' boney fingers digging into your shoulder blade was a mixed blessing; much like that famous poster of Uncle Sam, his finger pointing, dagger-like, his determined glare; but many a time a steadfast death's head peeked through the cadaverous skin, exfoliating, even as it pinned you to the wall like a benumbed specimen. It all depended on whether you shared the nun's twisted sentiment. We were admonished repeatedly, that to be presented with this gift, this holy vocation, and not to march after it, was a damnable sin. The much bigger sin, of course, was to claim that you had such a vocation, to perpetrate a fraud, when the finger of God did not alight. This was the most terrible sin of pride, to think that you were one of God's chosen ones when He in fact had passed you by.

Without quite realizing it, more than anything, the nuns hated intelligence. Having a good memory could be useful, as-long-as it was used to parrot back the simplistic answers in the catechism which shrunk the world to a pat load, the universe stuffed into a nutshell; or to recollect what the priests and nuns had commanded you to do and how they commanded you to do it. But genuine intelligence, the ability to think critically, to examine and question, this was assessed with nothing less than horror. It was treated like a rank weed to be extirpated by any means. Critical thinking rocked their power structure to its core, shook them from the cozy niche from which they exercised their power so absolutely. And that is what they craved, power, the ability to strike fear by their very look, like a beast craves its carrion. They were always ever vigilant for the signs of a quick, enquiring mind, ready to pounce, to crush, to annihilate.

With the nuns, obedience by itself was never enough; without a truly humble heart the obedience was merely a hollow act which thereby mocked them with its counterfeit show. It was fundamental to acquiesce with the correct mindset. Attitude was penultimate. In order to prove that your heart belonged to the nuns and thereby god, you were expected to master the intricate rituals of the kowtow with meticulous precision. It necessitated that you carry yourself with a decorous countenance and modest comportment, that you cringe perceptibly as they materialized, always quick to avert your glance, submitting yourself to full inspection, as if there was fire in their eyes and they could burn you with their mere glance. Your subservience had to be communicated by the very angle of your head; you must be bent slightly as if constantly bowing and scraping. Even though afraid, (they wanted you to be afraid), you were required to wear a bright open expression on your face as if your very being were justified only by their next commandment. But most of all there must be love in your eyes, for the nuns demanded love, from the very ones they tormented, because they tormented you for your own good. They stipulated that that smile of love brighten even as the screws tightened. This was the world of the master and the slave. They were doing God's work. God hated pride. In-order-to be worthy in God's eyes you must be meek, self-effacing, entirely devoid of any sense of self.

I, myself, was never quite successful in summoning forth the proper beatific look of complete surrender. And so, sitting peacefully, unaware of any impending catastrophe, I would be jolted by the banshee scream:

"Wipe that look off your face"

Followed by the whack from the back of their hand. I had no idea what condemnable look had invaded my face; could it be the truth staring out naked for all to see? They were forever monitoring our faces, our expressions; the unacceptable look was enough to convict; deeds weren't needed; the look alone would be succeeded by a welt.

The nuns loved and favored those values, if you can call them values, which Americans love least: humility, poverty, and obedience. One must be careful to understand that the nuns never wanted to cure poverty. They were in no sense philanthropists or social-workers. Rather, they wanted to minister to poverty, to feed it and feed off it. Poverty was their bread and butter. If you took the values they professed and took them as your own, you too would be subjected to a life of abject poverty, and this served their circumstances perfectly. They loathed the entrepreneurial spirit; that was for the loathed

41

Protestants and Jews. Their paradigm was the humble char woman, swinging her mop late into the night in hospitals and banks, denying herself and her own, denying even sustenance, picking through heaps of clothes for her kids at the rag shop so she could scrape her pennies together to furnish the priest, so he could swill down his fine Irish whiskey and bellow from the pulpit how we must be humble of spirit and "give 'till we suffer."

Humility was the ultimate value, humility in the sense of self-abnegation, denial of self so severe that you fade into oblivion. They were ever vigilant to distinguish want of humility in others, especially those left in their charge. Absence of humility must be eradicated, crushed, obliterated wherever it could be ferreted out. Their preferred blunt implement was humiliation, which they utilized with an enthusiasm approaching ardor. Ridicule, ridicule that was ego demolishing that could cut down its victims into a quivering mass of fear and self-loathing, squashed into a smudge so dilute not even a memory of existence persisted. To call them sadists is inaccurate, much too pat. The formal study of psychology views sadism as a deviation, a sickness. The nuns regard the infliction of suffering as the center of their system of values. To bring the proud to heel, to teach them humility, to make them humble in God's eyes is God's work in their demented judgements. Suffering is good for the soul they truly believed and they would be instruments of God's will. The irony is that these so-called religious aggrandized themselves in their god's pursuits. The more suffering they inflicted the more their egos swelled. You could catch it in their eyes. They loved it. They gloried in it. The more humiliation they could mete out the larger they were magnified in the eyes of their cruel god. They were like the savages who would spend weeks torturing their victims, growing ever more magnificent the longer they could make their quarries linger and stretch the torture out.

The most loved of these nuns was Sister Margaret George who was famous among the children for her little acts of mercy. And to speak truly, she was the best of them; a sentient, conscious being while the other nuns were mindless drones; and because of this very fact she was the guiltiest. She was the only one who rose to any moral level at all; she earned her evil. The most staggering thing is how the tormented fell in love with their tormentors. Any minor act of minimal human decency was seized upon, dwelled upon, and clutched to the bosom, to sleep with, to suck sustenance from. When you are reduced to a level of abject fear and powerlessness you grasp at and magnify mere phantasms of grace.

Sister Margaret George gave food scraps to the trapped, the incarcerated. She was the guard at the concentration camp who scrounged food morsels for the inmates and lead them in nightly prayer, against all rules. Sister Margaret George was of Italian descent, which reduced her to untouchable status in the caste system of the Irish nuns. They watched like cats their prey as if she were some kind of spy or worse yet the pathfinder for more of her kind. They intruded upon her class with impunity and corrected her in front of her pupils. This church and its school were theirs; they owned it and they knew it.

There was one particularly dim-witted lad by the name of Fitzgerald, whose face was nothing but a misshapen, dispersed, splotched mass of disgusting poo-colored pigment in a sea of albino pastiness, dog diarrhea floating in spoilt milk emptied into the gutter, (it is astonishing that deformity can be hoisted to a hallucination of beauty by those so afflicted) who insisted on pronouncing oil as erl; toil, soil as, terl and serl; proclaiming disdainfully and obstinately that this is the way his father said it and his father couldn't be wrong. When Sister Margaret George gently asserted that the correct pronunciation was oil, the dim-witted lad stomped out of the class, grumbling noisily, straight to the principal's office. He returned shortly, reclaimed his seat as if he owned it, and trained a self-satisfied, withering stare at Sister Margaret George. He was followed by the principal herself, who positively swaggered into the room and called out the sister as if she were a disobedient child, who followed the principal into the hall like a beaten dog. Although inconceivable, I heard what sounded like a beating but I must have been mistaken. After some time, Sister Margaret George returned, shaken, but fully intending to ignore the subject at hand. But the dull lad, pumped up by the principal, wouldn't let it be and in steadily swelling volume, repeated over and over and over: erl, erl, erl. He wouldn't shut up until she finally said the magic words: "yes, 'erl', erl is correct; I was mistaken." These Irish nuns and lay teachers were so astoundingly ignorant and stupid that what they imparted was a kind of anti-knowledge.

A week later, one of the children asked whether "Negroes" can go to heaven. The sister paused for a few seconds, as if to choose her words carefully. But before she got the chance to answer, good-old Fitzgerald, without following the accepted protocols of hand-raising: "N***** can't get into heaven because they don't have souls. My father says they're not human. They're half-way between monkeys and us." The good-sister, taken aback, sidestepped the issue by remonstrating in a calm, school-teacherly voice: "It is not proper to use that term in the classroom. The term we use is 'Negro'". Before the sister could even finish: "My father calls them n***** and that's what I call them. That's what everybody calls them, n*****." Fitzgerald had his point. In his neighborhood, if you used the term Negro, you would be subject to unrelenting ridicule and maybe worse: "Aren't we fancy-schmancy. What, are you a n***** lover or something?" It should be noted that sister emphasized, "in the classroom". She was beyond trying to redeem the outside world. Fitzgerald had only one word in reply: "N*****". And here the sister took a terrible chance, in an act, she, no-doubt considered, an achievement of supreme courage: "I'm afraid I can't allow you to use that term in my classroom. If you have a problem with that, I suggest you take it up with the principal." And with that Fitzgerald stomped out of the classroom fully expecting a replay of previous events. The sister remained in a state of controlled panic, eyes repeatedly darting toward the door in anticipation, throughout the rest of the school day. But the principal didn't swagger in, and call her to task like a beaten dog. Whether the principal ever broached the subject with her in private, I don't know. Fitzgerald was transferred to another class, to an Irish lay-teacher who presumably wasn't a n*****-lover. Fitzgerald bragged to the other kids about his victory in getting transferred, but it was more like a standoff.

The next school-day Sister Margaret George fully intended to avoid the subject, but she was blind-sided. A girl who had never raised her hand before, poked-up her hand tentatively, wiggled it a little, then lost her nerve, and quickly retracted it, pretending she never raised it. The sister never suspected what was coming: "Yes, Sharon, did you have your hand up?" She half-expected Sharon to retreat into her anonymity and remain forever silent throughout the rest of her school career; but instead, as if jarred awake from a deep sleep, she screwed up her nerve, piped up in an angelic little voice: "My mother says that colored people can get into heaven, but God has to change them into white people first, as a reward, if they were good, otherwise white people wouldn't want to go to heaven with colored people there." Of course, they would have to be Catholic, because only Catholics can get into heaven. By the time Sharon finished speaking, she was out of breath, depleted and in a fright. She was incapable of saying anymore or entering into any discussion of the matter. Sister Margaret George was pressed into a corner and tried to wrangle her way out, explaining: "that only our souls go to heaven so it doesn't matter whether you are white or black because your soul has no color." But, even so, Negroes have their own heaven, separate from white people. Notice, she didn't address the questions directly. The nun's grasp of basic Catholic theology was tenuous at best, failing to take into consideration a prayer she recited mindlessly every day by rote but was too impenetrable to listen to herself or understand the meaning of what she was saying. The definitive enunciation of Catholic doctrine, the so-called Apostles' Creed: "I believe in the resurrection of the body, in the communion of saints." That means, quite clearly, that the corporeal body of those who are "saved" ascends into heaven and joins together into a community with all those in heaven and who will go to heaven.

It might seem that Fitzgerald's is the view of some isolated inbred underclass, of troglodytes, which may accurately describe him, but that isn't entirely the case. Today, people have absolutely no perception of how far we have come. The discussion wasn't whether we should integrate the schools or allow Black people to vote; the much darker more fundamental question was whether they were fully human or not. David Brinkley, on national, network television, in the late fifties, interviewed a politician who proudly boasted of the progress we had made toward integration by explaining that he and members of his class, not too long ago, did not regard "Negroes" as human "but as a superior kind of chimpanzee".

Some poor, half- demented, old man, who grew up in the late forties and early fifties lets slip the word n***** and we excoriate and denounce him, drag him through the mud and set him in the stocks. This was the language of the time, the first language he learned; it's wired deep inside his brain and cannot so easily be expunged, no matter whether he tries. Like someone born in a foreign country, who has lived here seventy years, who grasps for a word and clutches his original mother tongue, involuntarily, in default-mode; and only after uttering it, realizes too late, that it is now obscene and a capital offence. For anyone born before 1950 the question: "Have you ever used the 'N' word" is a weapon to pummel him with, not a genuine inquiry; it is meant not to enquire, but to penalize, not only the individual, but, rather, the world he came from and to make him guilty for all of his father's sins and his father's father's sins.

. . . .

The Irish boys got away with murder, literally. The Italian boys, however, were held to a stricter yardstick. In fact, they were singled out for a vicious form of boot camp style verbal and physical abuse that only the nuns could engineer in their distilled cruelty. Like so many of the children, they seemed to have an enthusiasm, a natural love for life that exuberantly burst out of the chains the dark nuns tried to wrap them in. But Sister Margaret George was even tougher on the Italians than her Irish fellow sisters.

I don't include the girls in any of this because the girls seemed to have been immune to the myriad evils the boys were drowning in. The most blatant and obvious of these was the need to urinate. Only the filthy little boys needed to do this on a regular basis. The little girls "knew how to control themselves", so did the good little boys. The fact that the boys needed to touch themselves while performing the dirty deed compounded the infraction. I believe the nuns suspected that it was only to touch the forbidden, awful organ that the boys needed to relieve themselves so often. This is why the whole business so disgusted the nuns. You could see it on their faces every time you raised your hand to be excused.

"What, again? I'm on to you."

They constantly pointed to the girls as paragons of pure virtue, wiggling in their little seats with faces beatific, but agonized with the pain of their held in pee.

There was an unwritten rule that you never raised your hand to be excused during the recitation of prayers. Prayers punctuated the day, starting it, marking recess and lunch and then tying it up. If you didn't get your hand recognized before the start of prayers you were out of luck. The nuns observed this rule rigidly and were particularly skillful at having the supplicant boy vaporize before their very eyes, if the time approached too close to the magical cut off point. The etiquette of hand raising must also be tightly observed. You were required to raise the hand straight up, as if it were a salute, and stiff, no wiggling, no moving, no waving it around. To wave your hand around was tantamount to shouting out loud, like screaming at the good sister and this could bring down the heavens for the gesture alone.

Robert Fote was of Italian heritage and for that very reason was singled out for especial persecution by this Italian nun. Robert Fote didn't know this nun was Italian and, being of a generally good nature, never suspected that this was the reason she was always on his case. He would have naturally figured that if she was Italian, she'd be nicer to him, which would have made sense to him, and me. Sister Margaret George never even whispered about her heritage; it was a deep dark secret. I don't think there was anything in her vows preventing her from speaking about it; the Irish nuns were forever carrying on about the Irish and Ireland until you became nauseatingly sick of it. Perhaps she thought it would compromise her standing with the other nuns, the Irish. From what I could see she needn't waste her time; her standing with the Irish nuns didn't exist.

The only reason I knew she was an Italian is because she divulged it to one of the other boys in strictest confidence, exacting a solemn pledge of absolute secrecy. John Mele was bragging expansively about Italian mobsters and their deeds of derring-do; about Al Capone and two or three other names he rattled off that I'd never heard of. He was quoting his father who obviously had enormous admiration for these men; speaking of Capone:

"He showed them a thing or two."

The nun, overhearing this appalling speech, called John over, not for the usual slapping or a dressing down or for the other often exotic punishments the nuns seemed to live for, but rather for a heartfelt attempt at instilling proper national pride in a shared extraction. When the nun was through with him, I was curious because of the length of the speech, which was highly unusual since the nun had never-before taken a student aside for such an extended heart-to-heart. John paused momentarily, because of the solemn sworn oath of secrecy he had taken, and then spilled it out about how she told him that she also was an Italian and that he should not be proud of murderers and gangsters. She told him all about Leonardo Da Vinci and Michael Angelo and Columbus, all of which he referred to variously as a bunch of crap and horse shit. I think he resented this speech; after all, it did make his father, who he seemed to revere, out to be more than mistaken and he remained entirely unconvinced. When the nun saw me speaking to John at such length, she called me over to find out if he had revealed the confidence. She asked me about ten times as if I wasn't telling the truth, reminding me that it was a sin to lie and a more grievous sin still to lie to a nun. She seemed to think that if she kept asking me over and over, I would finally break down. If I had broken down John would have wished that he'd never heard of Italy. My greatest fear was that John would wither and crack under the barrage of the incessant questioning, the third degree, that he was sure to face over the next week or two; and spill his guts; then I would be the liar. But John, bless his soul, stuck to his guns, for which I will be eternally grateful.

Why she singled out the Italian boys and called them to a sterner standard is more sinister. No doubt she wanted to prove they were just as good as the Irish and therefore they must perform in superior fashion (by which she meant humble and obedient) to prove themselves beyond question. There was also an animus involved against those of her own who didn't quite measure up to her warped standards, who, she was convinced, dragged down all Italians by their failings. I think if she could she would make them not exist, these, the ones who gave Italians such a bad name and made it so much more grueling for her to ever be accepted by the Irish. She reminded me of the sergeant in the movie *A Soldier's Story*: a vicious, pathetic soldier who is a self-hating Negro, bringing down destruction on those Negroes who didn't measure up. But Sister Margaret George did this under the veil of kindness and concern, more in tune with Nurse Ratched. I think she seriously misjudged the situation, because even if she came from a superior race descended directly from heaven these Irish nuns wouldn't have given her the correct time of day.

I think in a moment of frustration she might have let slip a racial epithet, for these young boys so full of themselves, who just couldn't be squeezed into the Irish nun's mold. If she did let it slip, I heard it only once.

Robert Fote was my friend, taller by a head than all the other kids in the third grade, a friendly, gleeful, warm-hearted kid. Robert was poor in the days before the Great Society's welfare state; this was the early Fifties, a time when getting clean, decent clothes together so as not to be too embarrassed to come to school was a major accomplishment for some families.

Robert Fote raised his hand a good five minutes before the scheduled prayer recitation, high, still and straight, exactly as the rules dictate. He kept his hand up, high, still and straight for three minutes and then he made a grave, grave mistake. It was not unusual for the nun to keep us waiting a few minutes, with our hand saluting the heavens; it was the price you had to pay, to keep it high, still and straight, waiting to hear your name expectorated like a curse; this for the unforgivable crime of needing to perform a completely natural bodily function. Robert began moving his hand back and forth in the air under the mistaken impression that the nun had not seen his hand. He did not mean it as the act of gross insubordination. She seethed, a volcano about to explode. The more he waved it the more she pointedly ignored him, all the while glowering, smoke pouring from her ears. As we all stood and the praying began Robert started pleading mournfully, out loud, another grave infraction:

"Please sister, please, please, may I be excused."

And as the nun droned on in her dead sing song voice ignoring the pathetic, plaintive accompaniment:

"Please, sister, please."

Try as hard as he might, Robert couldn't hold out any longer and he let go with a torrent, saturating his patched pant legs, soaking both his shoes. Robert stood stunned, paralyzed. The nun, facing front, clutching her prayer book, eyes glued to the tortured, dead Christ nailed to her beloved cross, turned, and flew into a rage, took dead aim, and hurled her prayer book at Robert, striking him square in the head; that he should dare to piss while she was proclaiming the word of God, her words, she regarded as nothing less than sacrilege. Robert, frozen, just stood there, and looked down at his only shoes, sodden, spoiled with urine.

"Get out. Get out. Get out."

the nun screamed like the true secret maniac she disclosed herself to be.

Robert couldn't move, continued to convulse in dry heaving sobs, transfixed by the sight of his ruined shoes in the expanding yellow pool; he was drowning in that pool. In a way we all drowned in that pool that day.

"Sister, you don't understand. You don't understand. These are my only shoes."

I would love to report that our hearts all went out to Robert, in solidarity; but you know that isn't the case. These kids were so punch drunk with the nun's incessant abuse that I think they actually-took pleasure in watching their classmates suffer at the nun's hand, just so glad, so incredibly relieved, that it wasn't one of them. They had long ago become enthusiastic co-conspirators in the nun's dark, demonic pleasures.

As he tried to get out of the room, clomp, clomping, his shoes heavy, clumsy with saturated urine, making a squishing sound, as if his feet were toilet plungers, sticking. He finally made it to the door, which seemed forever, but which wouldn't open for him. I could feel a bomb explode as the class detonated as one, in an obscene peal of uncontrollable laughter. It enveloped me, the concussion, as it struck Robert down with a thud more powerful than the prayer book. This was the third grade and Robert was a boy, the tallest in our class and boys in the third grade weren't supposed to wet their pants and boys in the third grade weren't supposed to cry.

Just before he let loose with his cries, holding the tears back, he gazed searchingly around the class to see if he could find one sympathetic set of eyes. If he had found just one person with some Christian compassion, he might have steeled himself, stanched the flow of tears and braved it out. Boys didn't cry. He had caught my eye with an infinitely hopeful look, as if I was his only friend in the whole wide world; but he misunderstood. I was on his side. But I, too, misunderstood, completely. I was absolutely triumphant. More than anything I wanted to scream out:

"Let's all piss all over her stinking floor. Flood the place."

If only he could have saved his shoes. I think if all of us urinated on the floor, together, at that moment, in unison, especially including the girls, it would have been one of those defining moments, redemptive and regenerative and sacred, even. We would have earned a perfect place in heaven. It would have been a holy day, of obligation, a day of saints. Although I don't think it would have made the church calendar, it certainly would have been a banner day in my life and all my life from that day forward would have been different, better. And it may sound stupid, but I think the world would have been different, better.

Robert didn't come back that day. The rumor was he was expelled. He didn't come back for three weeks, perhaps because he had no shoes. When he did come back, he wasn't quite the same person. Whether he was altered by the mortification or the perceived betrayal, I can't say which. He was okay, but changed, somehow, not so friendly, not so trusting, more subdued. He didn't smile anymore. He moved the next month, to a new city, a new school. I prayed to God that it wasn't a Catholic School.

What is it that drags me unwilling down this venomous road of wistfulness, of poisonous nostalgia? I was content to disremember or neglect, but am buttonholed by the morning paper, or should I say dragooned, fetching me the news that Sister Margaret George is now and forever "Blessed", the Holy See's exclusive recognition of a dead person's entrance into Heaven; beatification, set on her sure path to canonization. The observant faithful, encouraged now to pray to her, the intercessor, encouraged also to come forth and swear testimony to the miracles she's famously performed. How many pure souls did she warp, crush or forever disfigure? The monster maker, the evil creator. "She's up in heaven now, watching over us." So, say the "faithful".

# Cardinal Mackinson

The pastor of our church was a decrepit, senile old man named Mackinson, Monsignor Mackinson. They would trot out the beloved Monsignor for display every few weeks and the parishioners would go wild with thunderous applause, cheering, accompanied by a rhythmic stomping of feet that was really alarming in the usually deathly quiet church. The dust would rise and the children, stuck lower to the floor, would cough alarmingly. The hung-over ushers, booze-hounds the night before, faces turning beet red from the unaccustomed exertion of stomping, their wicker baskets bopping up and down on the long poles (for the four collections of money) and their beer bellies flopping outside their pants, would fart uncontrollably. The trouble was they never thought to explain to the school children that the old priest had not always been a slobbering, demented fool. The effect was highly subversive. Perhaps the older parishioners didn't want to admit what had become of their revered pastor and convinced themselves that he stood there before them in his former glory, presuming he possessed a former glory.

Most of the children bought into this charade and saw exactly what their parents wanted to see and wanted them to see. But there were some who had to summon every ounce of whatever will persisted after determined religious pummeling to keep from busting a gut. The nuns would eye us warily, like cats their prey, eager to pounce, just praying, knuckles white, that we would crack a smile so they could take us out, drum us senseless, ever fervent to fulfill their God-given mission, as Brides of Christ, to annihilate any vestige of critical thinking.

The scene was hilarious. Here was this idiot led down the center isle by his two keepers, the subordinate priests, one at each elbow. He seemed to be decked out in the full regalia of a cardinal. I suspect that they had convinced the old man that he was a cardinal, to make him happy, to keep him under control. Some of the beaten down kids insisted that a monsignor outranked a cardinal, ignorant of the intricacies of church hierarchy much as their parents were. It was only years later that I discovered that the rank of monsignor was archaic, with little real significance, an empty title, bestowed on ecclesiastical sycophants. It could be seen clearly during his parade that the Monsignor was imperfectly shaven, with bits of missed stubble and nicks all over his sunken, cadaverous face. And his face was full of slobber that he had regurgitated. I suspect that his two keepers, who always looked extremely pissed off, purposely left the slobber on his face, which they easily could have mopped off. Mean spirited alcoholics, among other vices, (who were sent off periodically to that special place, the Congregation of the Servants of the Paraclete), they never got applause like this and never would. The getup he wore didn't fit right. He was stooped over, wasted, emaciated, from improper feeding. The vestments hung below his hands and dragged under his feet, like Mickey Mouse in The Sorcerer's Apprentice. He would giggle like a child, his eyes wide, racing from side to side like Harpo Marx with a captive audience, only funnier.

Once he pulled out a squeeze horn, (the kind the nuns used to use to end recess) that he had secreted under his vestments. His keepers tried to wrestle it from him but to no avail since they weren't prepared to beat up the old man, not in front of the whole parish. (They would frisk him from that day on.) He fought them like a tiger until it was they who acquiesced and then he continued to merrily honk his horn for the rest of his parade. One would have expected this to have been disconcerting to the parishioners, but it wasn't, not in the least. It was as if the squeeze horn had been part of a new revised Latin rite handed down directly from Rome with the Pope's blessing. Some had actually complained when they didn't hear the honking horn the next time the Monsignor made an appearance. They thought the old Monsignor had played it like a virtuoso, a sure sign that he hadn't lost his deft touch.

The old man finally gave up the ghost, what little was left, not without a good fight I suspect. The party was over. There would be no more cheering in church. I half expected them to carry the old Monsignor's mummified corpse in a sedan chair, in procession round and round, years after he was dead, pretending he was still alive, with his two keepers getting ever better at the art of ventriloquism, even more pissed off, bobbing his old head up and down. But they had the decency to stick him in the ground. It was as if Jesus himself had died again, with the crying and wailing but no stomping of feet this time.

# Crazy Eddie

Eddie found a couple of dozen gallon cans of old, half-used paint piled by the side of the garbage and determined in a moment of inspiration to become an artist. His first canvas was the sidewalk in front of the slum he inhabited. He poured swirls of multicolored paint with a manic glee approaching frenzy. People passing by, inadvertently stepping into his creation and getting paint on their shoes, tried to dissuade Eddie from his crazed expression, but to no use; Eddie was in a state of artistic ecstasy, deaf to all but the insistent voices of his own wacky muse.

A distinguished looking gentleman pulled up in a polished, long black car, double parked carefully and approached Eddie with an air of infinite patience. He was wearing a beautiful dark suit, a pure white shirt and a rich, modest silk tie. A gentleman, rare in these parts, stood out from the local inhabitants. At first, I thought he was lost and indeed he was, it turned out. I didn't know it at the time but this was the new landlord of Eddie's apartment house. A savvy investor in commercial real estate, he had recently bought these buildings (a short walk to the Hudson Tubes and then ten minutes to Wall Street) at the insistence of his well-meaning wife, with the notion of renovation and "giving back". They were the worst slums in the neighborhood and Eddie's art work didn't quite fit the new decorating scheme.

He approached, tall, regal in bearing, and spoke to Eddie in a measured, clear, authoritative voice, but kind, which seemed to have the effect of rousing Eddie to new heights, a whirling dervish, armed with bent containers of color. He shook Eddie gently by the shoulder and got swirls of paint on his shiny black, expensive shoes and swirls of paint on his beautifully tailored suit. And he made what proved to be a fatal mistake. He slapped Eddie across the face with his open hand which had the unintended effect of flipping a hidden switch deep inside Eddie's cracked brain which shifted him into an even higher gear. And with his open hand he slapped Eddie again and the Landlord never saw it coming, never saw the toothless Beetricks in the red fright wig which was her natural dyed hair bearing down upon him from behind in her grease soiled canvas shoes, and her speedy legs, hair covered, thick as fur; stealthy as an alley cat, well oiled, deep into her third quart of Piels beer.

The Landlord never heard the whoosh of the baseball bat bear down upon his carefully coiffed head. Whether he actually heard the crack of bone and the splash of blood I don't know. But the blood swirled on his polished shoes commingling with the paint and swirled on his once beautiful suit, beyond salvaging, onto the filth encrusted sidewalk enhancing the color mix of Eddie's demoniac creation. From the second blow the landlord dropped to his knees as if his legs were kicked out, a trick stool, sinking to meet a dirty trick of fate, arms outstretched in greeting, sacrificial. And just as his blood splashed into Beetrick's face she spewed out:

"You filthy kike."

If she had introduced the assault with this screaming epithet the landlord might have been forewarned, sidestepped, and so saved himself; but it was "his dirty blood" spurting on to her that provoked Bectricks, beyond patience, eliciting the obscene outburst.

There were hungry looking women hanging out the windows, screeching at Beetricks, Eddie's mother, as if it was witch's day at some crackbrained ball game, bases loaded, players too. Back before the downtrodden possessed TVs to vegetate before, before food stamps and the universal predilections for gorging confections, they hung out the windows for entertainment, like there was a show on the street, and they set to swoop and land on their feet, just like Beetricks when she spotted it coming, the unprovoked attack on her baby. She could divine the future as the car pulled up. Whether these crones were egging her on, cheering for her team, or trying to warn her that the cops were coming, already in sight, is a subject of discussion.

Eddie, entirely oblivious to these goings on, was building to his head of steam. Beetricks, without missing a beat, dropped the bat and laid into crazy Eddie with renewed enthusiasm, feeding on the blood of the previous slaughter. She never hesitated to beat Eddie. She beat him often and hard but like any good mother she drew the line at a stranger budding into her exclusive parental prerogative:

"Who the fuck did this Jew think he was?"

Beetricks laid Eddie out with a series of swift, deft blows from her boney fist, opening up his upper and lower lips, closing his eye with swelling black, contributing more blood to the prospect. By this time the police were piling out of cruisers blocking the street with impunity, called, no doubt, by pedestrians who didn't like getting paint on their shoes. The ambulance would take its sweet time, as the landlord lay in-the-midst of Eddie's masterpiece, becoming, as the minutes past, an intrinsic part of it. It seemed as if the police were selling tickets to the spectacle, as to an art exhibition, unenergetically trying to push the curious back. The police at work at a crime scene or an accident, their ice cold, almost studied indifference, their graveyard humor can be more jarring than the carnage at their feet. They seemed reluctant to move the wounded landlord, as if moving him was an act of desecration, whether of the art or the sacrifice, I don't know which; to preserve the crime scene at all costs. So, he lay there in his own ever widening pool of thickening blood. They didn't so much as place a rag beneath, to cushion his wounded head on the unclean concrete. If they cared a whit, they concealed it cunningly with a staccato of wisecracks for the amusement of their cop buddies guffawing like dumb beasts.

It took three cops to hold Beetricks down, another couple to extricate the bloody weapon from her bony grip while she spewed forth a barrage of venomous obscenities centering especially on what the mothers and wives of the cops liked to do in back alleys for minimal payment. She was hauled off in cuffs screaming hysterically:

"He beat my baby; he beat my baby."

The cops spent some time looking for the baby, questioning bystanders, thinking it might have crawled off somewhere.

After a day and a half had elapsed Beetricks was back, ensconced in her old familiar habitat, her kitchen table with the greasy oil cloth cover, impatient to wolf down her unfinished quart of Piels beer, (saved in the refrigerator with a cork) with renewed gusto and break open two more to make a fiesta. The neighbors, hanging out the windows, witness to the event, came forward to do their civic duty, unanimously declaring their willingness to swear on a stack of bibles that Beetricks was only protecting her beloved son from a crazy man:

> "...who appeared outa nowhere... like a fucking spirit."

Who would, no doubt, have massacred poor Eddie if not miraculously stopped in his tracks by the well-aimed blows from the now famous baseball bat. They appeared at her door, bearing condolences, the mob spilling in the street with bowls of macaroni and cheese, pork and beans, potato chips, pretzels, oreo cookies, the baked ziti Mrs. Martini was famous for in these parts, a small keg of cheap beer sent over by the saloon across the street, the Eelight (spelled Elite) "with all due respect" and a full carton of Chesterfield cigarettes, (Beetrick's favorite) asking politely after Eddie in hushed tones:

> "...after the health he was in."

I, also, stood witness, just to the side as events unfolded themselves with an over-lit cinematic precision. I told my story. But by this time Beetricks had been elevated, beatified, if you will, the beneficiary of the great big lie, the essential myths by which we survive and console ourselves. My mother couldn't admit that her only daughter Janey was best friends with people the other kids were warned not to go near. Was it for the love of Janey that my mother jumped for this diabolic ride; was she cracking up herself and was Janey just the occasion for the dive? Was it liberating, like suicide? There was nothing else to lose, no lower to go than Beetricks and her brood. Beneath were the bums, only, that slept in doorways reeking of their vomit and piss.

As the mother of Janey's only true friend, Beetricks was reinvented as the proverbial whore with the heart of gold:

> "Her door was always open and a hot meal for anyone who needed it."

As I remember it, before my mother's largess, her kids subsisted mainly on spaghetti soaked in cheap margarine. No longer a "foulmouthed piece of trash", Beetricks became a "genuine original," a master of colorful idiom and the picaresque, peppering her speech with piquant colloquialisms. Her idiom was:

> "fuck, goddamn, prick, cunt, cocksucker, motherfucker, shit, frig, jesuschris."

interspersed with a litany of banalities, clichés my mother, for mysterious reasons, found hilarious. They were hackneyed; used by the illiterate all over America in a cheesy simulation of down to earth wittiness:

> "Back when Christ was a corporal, I coulda shit a pickle, or canary, I had a kitten, up shit creek without a paddle, go pound salt up your ass, let's not and say we did, I don't know whether to shit or go blind, wouldn't say shit if he had a mouthful. Why don't you go play in traffic, Happy as a pig in shit, I'm free, white, and twenty-one, wouldn't know whether to cat, shit, chase rabbits or howl at the moon, And, if he hadn't stopped to shit the bear woulda caught the rabbit. Jesus H. Christ."

"What are we having to eat, Mom?" "Shit on a shingle", cackling like the virago she was. There were no more than fifty of these shopworn quips, certain to crack up dumb drunks collapsing off their stools in cheap saloons. But by these platitudes she rose in stature. She was the "salt of the earth", a noble savage who had my mother "on the floor" "in stitches."

Janey cried hysterically, when I testified, calling my truth "a pack of lies". "I love Beetricks" she heart-achingly proclaimed. I would put her best friend's mom behind bars. She told me that she would tell the police I made it all up, to hurt Beetricks.

My mother by this time had been regularly subsidizing the Beetricks household. In the beginning she had been giving them money; but Gwunnie complained to Janey:

> "It's all your mother's fault."

66

The money, it seemed, had allowed Beetricks to dramatically increase her Piels beer consumption, making living conditions worse, which was inconceivable. So, my mother would show up weighed down with bags of groceries like their trusty servant, leading to more recriminations.

"Who the hell does that fucking bitch think she is?"

Beetricks would bellow as soon as my mother had left. Besides, all the brands were wrong. It seems that Beetricks and company were real connoisseurs and had very particular brand preferences.

"We don't drink Chock full o' Nuts coffee. Our brand is Maxwell House."

My mother jotted down a comprehensive list of their favorites like an obedient amanuensis. But nothing was ever right; the meat had too much marbling or didn't taste fresh. They claimed to be getting sick from what they judged were cut rate provisions. Or so Gwunnie would confide to Janey under a vow of the strictest secrecy and Janey would race to my mother shaking with tears.

Above all else Beetricks hated anyone she suspected was "conceited" or putting on airs, which meant anyone above Beetricks, which meant the better part of the world population. They were phonies, bogus, every damned one of them, conniving to make her feel little and stupid. She would not believe that some people naturally spoke standard English or were polite or soft spoken. She was convinced it was an act; if you shook them out of a sleep in the middle of night, they would be loud and vulgar, uttering the same illiterate patois as she.

Once a long time ago she worked in a great house, high up on the hill in Englewood as a charwoman-scullery maid, taken in reluctantly as an act of charity through church auspices, cinched by a late-night call direct from Father Mulrooney himself, the saint, selfless mentor to so many young boys. She was fresh off the work rolls, young and only marginally presentable as a back room domestic. Her black rotting teeth were making a last ditch stand in her stinking mouth, before being yanked out. She complained bitterly about how these rich-folk would:

> "...look through me like I wasn't even there, like I was fucking air."

Never acknowledging, it seems, that she even existed; never once inviting her to sit down for tea and finger sandwiches.

She got back in a manner she never tired of recounting in every disgusting detail; how she would contaminate her hands and then contaminate the food she helped prepare. It was a large family, the paterfamilias a prominent physician of some renown, with many young children whom he loved dearly.

> "He's a donkey just like me. Who the fuck does he think he is...?

> "Those fucking little bastards and that cunt, their mother, in their fancy clothes, with their snooty manners, their fucking books, their

fucking fancy china and their hoity-toity talk. I didn't know half the words they said, I got no idea what they're talking about; looking down their fucking noses.

"Who the fuck do they think they are?"

She would scream triumphantly. She saved her most poisonous spite for the near at hand, who she was certain sought to put on airs. She particularly loathed a girl who dwelled over the bar in a filthy estaminet across the street, over the "Ee-light", Ginny, whose father, a bartender, an amiable man who greeted all the children with a beaming sinister smile, friendlier when lit, which was always. Ginny read books, studied school books and wrote stories and spoke a form of practiced English, beautifully enunciated and elocuted, that made her stand out and Beetricks's blood boil over. It was back in the days when people practiced how to speak, took elocution in the public schools, whose Anglo-Saxon spinster teachers spoke mid-Atlantic English and memorized vocabulary lists from the Reader's Digest. Ginny's own Irish-Catholic teachers spoke an illiterate bog lingo that she was just smart enough not to imitate. Ginny's favorite book was *A Tree Grows in Brooklyn*, a mirror to her own stunted soul. She read books, lots of books, smaltzy books she would have been better off not reading, better off not reading anything at all for that matter. She fancied herself a writer; the nuns, from her all-girls uniformed Catholic high school, pumped her up, murmuring in her ear she'd be a celebrated writer someday; doled out easy As for all her empty sentences. She read aloud to the gathered multitude of selected street kids; the

69

name of the story was "Man in a Hurry" which she believed to be mostly true. It was about one of our neighbors who lived in the building I lived in; a big man, in no more than his early thirties who was always rushing for work; who lived on the third floor of our unelevatored "walkup". He would jump down the stairs, an entire flight (half a story) at a time, hooting and hollering so loud that he woke the whole building, and proceeded to wake the whole neighborhood, running and screaming like a wild man, right past Ginny's filthy estaminet on the corner, above the working man's saloon with fouled sawdust on its floor. What Ginny didn't make clear was the especially high spirits Mr. Kanutte was always in. She wrote about how he said hello to all the kids and talked to them, addressing them by name; how he horned in on their games and played in the street with them and how his wife, after calling after him, tried to drag him, resisting, by the hand from his beloved stickball game. Ginny embellished this with many hilarious details, many untrue, which made him out to be a particular fool. The gang of kids laughed and laughed, all the while telling Ginny what a wonderful story teller she was. Tears welled in my eyes; my sister attacked me viciously: "Can't you see it's funny; everybody thinks it's funny; everybody but you. You idiot; you have no sense of humor."

But, alas, Ginny would never be a writer; not a good one, not even a decent one. But, curiously, there was a story here, a good story, a true story, a story I took for granted everybody knew. The adults spoke in front of the kids like they didn't exist; so being a kid was like being a spy, right out in the open, nonexistent, a fly on the wall, swatted often. Perhaps Ginny, closed off in her books, just didn't listen or knew too much to care; she read lots of books, you know; insulated from life by sentimental, mawkish, claptrap, revered as "literature" by little girls forever stuck in grown-up bodies. Who can say how many lives have been ruined by silly books? What Ginny didn't seem to understand was that Mr. Kanutte came from a very wealthy business family; he worked in the stock room traveling to the family business every morning, catching the tubes, always on time, to Manhattan. He never missed a day. This was back in the day, the Fifties, when people like Mr. Kanutte were often locked away; institutionalized I guess you'd say. But the family resisted, determined to find a place, a normal place, but far enough away, to avoid discomfiture, for everyone including him.    They found him a bride, a little more intelligent than he was, who they hoped could watch over him; they had a child together. But his wife couldn't handle him. She would come down to the street begging him to come in, crying uncontrollably, that dinner was getting cold and that he was embarrassing them. Finally, one of the onlooking older men would intervene and take Mr. Kanutte firmly by the arm:

> "It's time to go, your family's waiting dinner and your little girl is crying. It's time to go. Come on Buddy, game's over".

To this day I have no idea what Ginny found so hilarious; or the kids, who should have known better.

Ginny went to confession every single Friday without fail and Mass every Sunday and took the consecrated wafer into her open, inviting wet mouth from the fingers of the priest's hand, and carefully scrutinized *The Advocate*, the Catholic newspaper, for its list of dirty movies that Catholics were forbidden to see on pain of mortal sin and everlasting damnation in the fires of hell. Ginny unsuccessfully solicited me to picket *The Moon is Blue* with her, which the Catholic Legion of Decency had marked with a "C", for "Condemned"; the Stanley Theater, reputedly owned by Jews, was boycotted, by enraged, epithet hurling parishioners who spit on ushers jostling past; the theater closed, the film seized by armed men sent by Boss Kenny's successor, Bernard Berry, who banned rock and roll, calling it "N***** Music promoted by Jews to ruin our children"; blocked Bill Haley and the Comets from Roosevelt Stadium, city-owned. Was this all a charade, a smokescreen to shield the priests? (I was always catching the priest of Saint John the Baptist, Roman Catholic Church, the dumpy squat obese little priest, who squeezed like grease from the Tubes in civilian dress, almost daily, disguised, with his boys trailing after him at a decorous distance. For some reason, more than any other person on earth that I had met or ever would meet, I regarded this personage, viscerally, perhaps irrationally, as quintessentially evil, an almost demonic presence.)

I guess, the nuns were not quite specific enough in the enumeration of particular sins. So, Ginny gave blowjobs to boys in the neighborhood, those she could chase down and catch. Ginny was fat with a pretty face, framed by a tangle of golden ringlets untouched by brush and the kids chased after her and my sister, her friend, screaming "piggy", "piggy", "oink, oink, oink". But I've found old photographs and what was fat then, what we all thought was so incredibly fat, wouldn't even be noticed today; no more than fifteen pounds over the then very lean norm. (I am told Ginny is a three hundred pounder today, a "social-worker", which makes perfect sense: an overread, overreaching postulant disseminating her ineffectual erudition, browbeating the downtrodden, adding to their exploitation; bloodless; ink seeping out of her leaking varicose veins.)

This is back in the day when people were especially lean; when men were, what would be called gaunt today, but muscular; wiry they called it; and they were strong, stronger than the bulging, pumped-up muscle men who clog the fancy "gyms" today. Ginny did corral a "boyfriend", of sorts; skinny, unmuscled, and a head shorter, who bragged about the blowjobs; she blew him every chance she got; (he would complain bitterly that Ginny couldn't give proper blowjobs and should take lessons from his mentors in the Village.) Ginny seems to have been obliviously proud, a feather in her cap. She sucked him off in the bushes while hiding for hide-and-go-seek; so that she was sure to be caught and caught she was, by the "nosey" superintendent of our building, "sticking her nose where it didn't belong", who was just as sure to spread the word. I suspect that Ginny's mother knew precisely what mischief her little girl was getting into; one wonders where Ginny learned to love to suck dick with such boundless enthusiasm; perhaps Ginny had been schooled at home, at her mother's knee. The mother, when she heard about the superintendent spreading the news, threatened the woman with bloody murder, who believed every word of it and shut her mouth tight, thereafter.

"Seaburglar", that's the beau, that's what they called him; the kind of character that makes for bad fiction, a black and white world of good versus evil. Seaburglar, fourteen, was a whore, a hustler who took the tubes to New York, Greenwich Village and sold himself to the highest bidder; but he was also an entrepreneur, a procurer, a pimp, a talent scout who would ingratiate himself to beautiful young boys, treat them to hot dogs and earn a commission. The Hudson Tubes were an open highway to hell; ten minutes under the river, an open sewer; no police manned the gates; nobody stopped an entourage of young boys. Seaburglar made a killing.

Seaburglar did manage to recruit Crazy Eddie, who admitted he did it for the money, $25 in 1958, when he was thirteen; a princely sum back then, to let a grown man perform oral sex on him. They told him to lose weight and lift weights, to up the ante to $50 or even higher; the sky's the limit. I forgot to say that Eddie was good-looking. He said I might get $100; I lifted weights. But Eddie warned me that Seaburglar was targeting me, and not, under any circumstances, to go, no matter what he offered me. Eddie was comparatively lean and didn't need to lose any weight at all, except to thrill these old homosexuals, who loved to watch the muscle stand out hard through paper thin skin; who truly horrified and demoralized Eddie. He didn't need a priest to tell him this was a "mortal" sin, soul killing. He clutched it gnawing deep-rooted in his substance. Eddie didn't go to church, though hypothetically Catholic, which probably saved him, at least from the priests, who would have normalized the horror and made his whole life a living nightmare. But Eddie cared nothing for morality or ethics. This was a matter of esthetics. The act so revolted him because it deeply violated his sense of himself, his manhood. And, in-spite-of what he said, he didn't do it for the money; that was a cover, an excuse. He did it to bond with Seaburglar, his pimp, a sadistic little street thug, who he worshipped, who he thought was fearless but he wasn't. I saw him whither and fold once when confronted by a bully much tougher than he was.

Eddie told me later in life that that this one single act obsessed and haunted him, "imprinted" him (though he did not use that word, that's what he meant); the hallucinatory nightmare vision of this man "sucking him off" with such gusto. This visceral loathing of the homosexual act by "straight" men is not some societal construct or the result of conditioning; it is inborn. "He pawed me like I was a dog and drooled over me like I was a girl." His saliva running into Eddie's pubic hair was a particular detail I didn't need to hear, or envision. Did he want to bring me in, imprison me in his own personal nightmare, by sharing it? I can never un-think the image. This single seminal act impeded Eddie's conjugal duties; the vomit would rise in the back of his throat, sometimes, just before orgasm; how charming for his wife; who was not beautiful, but might have been. Eddie settled. She was devoted, which was better. Eddie never went back. Did he quit the race? When he told me all this, his voice broke and he was broken too.

I forgot to tell you: Eddie never did turn into a criminal; I think his fear saved him. Courage is morally neutral but not over-rated. What did Thomas Eliot say?

> Think neither fear nor courage saves us. Unnatural vices are fathered by our heroism.

Eliot is disqualified to speak disinterestedly on the subject, since he had a dog in the fight, so to speak. Eliot, by accounts, was wanting in that very attribute of which he so eloquently expounds, and thus surrenders the earned privilege to hold forth on the subject so brazenly. Most honest men are honest out of fear, timidity, hesitancy, laziness; not, definitely not, out of goodness. The meek will not inherit the earth; nor should they, nor will they try, nor even ask for a reading of the will; they will bow-out by Tuesday and feign graciousness, magnanimity, saintliness; a face-saving, tactical cover for cowardice. Most criminals I've known are absolutely fearless. Is it conceivable that we lock-up our bravest men out of fear of them; in penitentiaries in which they decline to do penance or crook the knee? Some are intelligent which is a dangerous, incendiary mix. More than anything, please God, keep them locked up.

Jack Abbott's *In the Belly of the Beast* is a synthetic, made-up, purely literary construct tailored to seduce and manipulate naïve, credulous literary types; little sissies who adore and glamorize the toughs who bully and beat them up; pawns in Abbott's logical extension of his criminal career. You can doll Abbott up in a bespoke suit but his fangs are a smile away.

But Ginny had other attachments besides Seaburglar. She paid to watch; watch Georgie Schwann have sex with an eight-year-old boy. She wanted me to watch with her, offered to pay my way, my admission, like it was a Saturday movie matinee, probably with popcorn, too. But Georgie loved his privacy and put a stop to putting on a show; to Ginny's chagrin. But this little boy of his was no innocent cherub; he, too, was a hustler, aggressively offering his services to the older boys, taunting them if they resisted, teasing that they couldn't get it up yet. In a case of misplaced benevolence, I tried to give him two dollars once, a deluded act of supposed Christian charity. He spit at me and crumpled the money to the ground: "I don't take no hand-outs ... I earn my money."

I listen to people wax nostalgic, about the old neighborhood, the innocent Fifties and I wonder what planet they were on. This was a priest-ridden hell. All the people in power were perfect clones of Fred Mertz from *I Love Lucy*; stupid, fat, ugly, mean and drunk; stumbling and smiling; god did they smile and smile; men, who through the gross corruption of power, clambered up way beyond their only obvious talent, that of barkeeps in cheap corner saloons. The firemen from *Ragtime* had ascended to obscene dominion, taken over the town by default.

. . . .

My mother, rolling in my dead father's hard-earned loot, (handed it out like it was left-over party-favors); easy to toss-away what she hadn't earned or in-any-way merited. Early death was her benefactor. She searched out mansions in the suburbs every weekend, wearing out Realtors; but my dumb sister wouldn't budge, wouldn't even look; cared not a whit for white mansions with wide lawns; devoted to, constricted by, her ever beloved Ginny, and Gwunnie; subsisted in La La Land; came squealing home years later, ecstatic with news that Gwunnie had been invited to the prom by no less than the inimitable Georgie Schwann.

Ginny's father, who loved his little girl, and she returned the favor by reinventing him into a character in a little girl's fiction book, (one might say that Ginnie's life was ruined by bad fiction) slid her a secret stipend of $25 a week, a meager week's pay for a working man in the early fifties, better than the one he got as bartender. But this was a time after the war when men who had never had a dime found their pockets full, became alarmed, and quickly emptied them out at the corner saloons, doing a land office business, spilling their regulars into the streets, with the police coming by to shout "take your beer inside", "but there ain't no room inside"; not even elbow room and the spigots stayed open 'til the kegs ran dry. The proprietors, pulling in money hand over fist, couldn't count it and so $25 a week wasn't missed. But Ginny didn't know what to do with it either, except for Georgie Schwann; and Seaburglar, whose way she paid like he was a fancy man; so, she doled it out to other kids in the neighborhood as a kind of sub allowance. She and my sister would raid the corner bakery clutching their dollars and make their getaway with shopping bags full of confections, jelly donuts, crumb buns and éclairs and seven-layer cakes, to gorge themselves. Both grew fatter. Beetricks wouldn't let her daughter talk to Ginny, and Gwunnie listened; Gwunnie always listened.

There was a scary thing about Ginny, who herself emerged clean enough and decently enough in boyish dress. Beetrick's three room flat had linoleum floors mopped weekly with a pungent antiseptic smelling pine disinfectant, the kind they used to use in hospitals and prisons. I went to Ginny's looking for my sister with a sense of foreboding. Until then I had no conception of such squalor. I had this uncontrollable desire to bolt for the door, teetering on the verge of panic. I came to the not entirely rational conclusion that if these people lived like this, they were capable of abominable crimes, of cutting me into little pieces and devouring me on the spot. There were abandoned spider webs hanging down from the ceiling in profusion, saturated with black grease, elongating like pendulums dangling into the sink, seeding it with the detritus grabbed from the thick air, the sink caked with putrescence and piled with crusted dishes and dented blackened pots. The linoleum was curled and worn in spots with the rough splintered wood showing through, grabbing tightly to the sweepings, an overwhelming fecal smell as if the toilets had been backing up for weeks, or as if the toilets were ripped out and sold on the street and the inhabitants now just relieved themselves in the corners whenever they wished. There was an ancient senile woman moving every which way, obviously incontinent, spreading her scent cautiously throughout the habitation. The amazing thing is that Ginny had no embarrassment about this establishment she managed to crawl out from under.  My sister was not embarrassed for her friend.  In fact, she laid into me as soon as we left:

> "You embarrassed me.  Don't you have any manners? You were staring all over the place."

But Gwunnie was different. It wasn't that Gwunnie was like her mother, she wasn't, not in the least, not at first. She was a charming, bright, sweet child who lived entirely in a world of her own, uncontaminated by her mother's taint. She floated in the air, impossibly, a feat of magic, that she could navigate so closely without her feet ever touching the filthy ground surrounding her.  How she managed this miracle is a mystery to me. There was always the school, public school, blessedly. Her teachers loved her. She was an excellent, obsequious student. If only she could have stayed in school. Gwunnie was a cut above my sister and my mother knew this without admitting it. She had been a substitute teacher and had "the pleasure of teaching Gwunnie" for a week, examining her comprehensive record which revealed straight As and a 110 IQ. Poor, dumb Janey had only been able to eke out an 85 (around the same IQ as half her "idiot" half-brothers so loathed by her mother) and barely squeaked by. My mother was convinced this was some big mistake:

> "Janey doesn't do well on tests. Janey gets nervous.

> "The tests are designed wrong. They can't really measure intelligence."

on and on. My mother, indoctrinated in the Normal Schools of her day, deep down believed fervently in these tests in spite of what she said. Being a woman of only average intelligence, she was always putting a number on people's heads, estimating their IQ. She was in love with the idea of intelligence without being able to recognize it or in any way share in it. She showed extraordinary deference toward those she suspected possessed it, people in positions of power, who in fact were no more intelligent than she was. The experience with her first husband's "idiot" children had been withering. The principal's:

> "Madam, these children are doing as well... better than could be expected... unfortunately they are all borderline morons."

But Gwunnie was a revelation, a miracle crawling out of a sewer.

> "Gwunnie is a sweet child who has a marvelous influence on Janey"

My mother pronounced with her best school-teacherly inflection. And she was right. Gwunnie was a devoted friend who never looked down on Janey as the other kids did. Janey would have given anything to be friends. The other kids sensed her extreme neediness and shunned her for that very reason. As a child Jane was perfectly generous with her "friends" without expecting anything in return except perhaps a kind word. The other kids would grab and grab and then run and taunt her for her stupidity in being so big-hearted.

One Easter Janey cried so hard that my mother bought her this huge chocolate Easter bunny. Jane could barely carry it. I must have been four feet high in this fancy gold box with a cellophane window tied with a big red ribbon. My mother let Jane stay down stairs in front of the apartment building so she could be with the other children. Jane opened the box, so ecstatically happy to be able to share with her "friends", carefully untying the ribbon as if she were presenting them all with a very special gift and she started giving out the pieces and the kids started grabbing, tearing apart the bunny rabbit in what appeared to be, from a distance, a ritual slaughter, devouring it until there was nothing left, not one morsel for Jane. She hadn't even tasted it. She never even got it upstairs; even the beautiful box was torn to shreds. And when it was all gone and she could give them no more they began mocking her and pelting her with the bits of chocolate they were too stuffed to force down their throats, until her pretty new dress and face were smeared with chocolate and tears.

Gwunnie had been able to reach Jane, to teach her things that nobody else could. I remember trying to explain to Jane that our grandmother came from Austria not Australia. But Jane became vicious as if I were poking fun at her or trying to prove how much smarter I was. I tried to explain that the Boston Tea Party was not actually a party, but to no avail; all irony and humor was entirely foreign to grim, sullen Janey. Jane trusted Gwunnie and with good reason. Gwunnie was the best friend that Jane would ever have. Jane would never love anyone as much as Gwunnie, nor would she be as loved. (Years later Janey threw this girl away like a bag of garbage. I remember Gwunnie sitting at Janey's wedding, passed over as a bride's maid, supplanted by especially brainless lassies from the Catholic girls finishing school that passed itself off as a college; that her mother bribed the nuns to get her into; devoted Gwunnie now totally ignored by her once best friend, the tears welling, asking me why. I couldn't tell her why.)

Gwunnie managed to hang on for a while. She was able to float above the filth in her own world, a fantasy. However, it's as if the moment her feet met the ground, she formed an unholy union with the sticky filth she touched, as if her being curdled from contact. At the age of fifteen she erupted as the spitting image of her mother. Her pretty face became grotesque as if a wicked spell had been cast. She plucked her eyebrows and painted in a whorish, rakish arch where bare skin had been. Her dainty nose seemed to bust out, outlandish like her mother's and her hair, with much work, became inflated, puffed and teased. When she was sixteen she found a boyfriend, Ferguson, who fucked her good, initiated her into the mysteries, jailhouse style; she would drop to her knees to kiss him good night, just the way he liked it, outside her doorway in the filthy urine soaked hallway; fifteen years her senior, trained in reform school and drilled in the prison system, a real charmer who would regale anyone who would listen with his felonious exploits and Gwunnie would gaze up in awe, eyes wide, lips parted, her soul connected to his direct wire transmitting demonic scripture in a Tom Sawyer voice. He would make his rap sheet sound like a story book escapade, with a sick twist, like the caper that sent him back to hard time for three years:

> "I'm walking down the street minding my own business...happy as a fucking lark... about to get into my Chevy that I just made a deal on when I see this cellar door is open... the kind with two metal doors opening out of the sidewalk... and the door is open and nobody's around. I look in and the cellar is stacked with cases of booze. So, I say to myself.... this is likc a gift. Somebody up there is watching over me. So... I go down to the basement, grab a case of scotch whiskey, climb up these real steep stairs and put it into my trunk. And I look around, still nobody. I'm thinking this is too good to be true, my lucky day. I go down get another case, of gin, and put that into my trunk, and I'm thinking I better go and get myself a fucking truck. And I go down and get my third case, this time J& B and as I'm coming up the stairs and there's this big ugly sonofabitch standing at the top of the stairs with a fucking shotgun, telling me to put up my hands or he will fucking blow my head off. And so, I drop the J&B, crash, push past him and start running down the street like a bat out of hell and the shotgun goes off, boom and I can feel the blast raise the hair on the top of my head and I drop down and I can hear the sirens coming closer and this maniac's screaming, 'freeze you motherfucker' and poking me hard in the back of the head with the shotgun and I laid so still you woulda thought I was dead."

Sounds like a riot. Beetricks was ecstatic. Ferguson was always popping in at odd hours so weighed down with swag he couldn't walk straight and Beetricks just fancied him, a dream-catch. This is what she ambitioned for her daughter, a monotonous replay of the debacle that was her own brutish biography. She forced Gwunnie to quit school at sixteen so she could "earn her keep" and before that, secretarial courses, no college prep for her.

> "You better an me? You think you're better an me?"

She screamed drunkenly when Gwunnie begged to graduate. She wouldn't have her daughter putting on "false airs", in front of her own mother, "thinkin she was better".

. . . .

In what for me was a small act of valor, but a defining one, I walked up all alone to the police station weeks after the assault on the landlord. What, after all, was the Landlord to me? They wouldn't listen. I was nine at the time. Not unreasonably, they told me to come back with my parents. What parents?

My mother forgot what I told her or didn't hear it, refused to hear it. And I think she really believed it when she spoke of Beetricks and grew misty:

> "What a wonderful mother... She'd die to protect her young."

Yeh, like a mother wolf.

Beetricks was like the Mother Teresa of the slums long before anyone knew who Mother Teresa was. Beetricks thrived in her own element, enamored of the squalor. I always marveled at why Janey loved her so. Beetricks simply acknowledged that Janey existed. Like any minimally canny merchant she returned service for payment and my mother paid dearly. The remarkable thing is that none of the many others, taking much more money from my mother, felt the least obligation to treat her children, even, decently. In fact, quite the opposite; they took their resentments out on her children. The more money my mother gave them, the more they needed to grovel, the meaner they were toward her children, because they could; get away with it, that is.

Northerners like to mollify themselves with the fairytale that Tobacco Road was a rutted dirt track in poverty stricken rural Georgia, when in fact it is a highway running right straight through the American heart; nor was it isolated in the ribbed north end of Jersey, nor the pine lands nor the western counties, either. The impure products of the American magnet were crazy and cracked long before, devoid of any peasant traditions to give them character. Lehane feels these people deep in his bones, in Boston, more than a half century later. Instead, we fancy writers who spoon feed us expedient lies, emasculating us in the process. We are enthralled by the utter stupidity of received, accepted ideas transmuted into the language of beauty and feeling; moving us to tears of self-pity for the utter banality of what we think and feel. We refuse to admit that we crawled out of a cesspit; though how much more noble and empowering that would be. We are anxious that people will distinguish the inerasable aroma of shit, even after years of conscientious scrubbing; as if we must carry our father's sins. We conspire to pretend that the corner working man's saloon is a Socratic academy instead of a sounding board for loud, belligerent, lazy drunks, convinced that their dumb, ignorant opinion is as good as any man's.

Lost, I came looking for my family once, at the Beetrick's slum, which they seem to gravitate toward like it held a wicked spell; down the long urine-soaked hallway, my stomach contents rising in my throat from the stench. The door creaked open to reveal a vision, or revelation, a young girl squatting at the kitchen table across from Beetricks, not much older than myself, maybe eleven or twelve. It was as if they were scheming strategy together. She was pretty and I approached her with my warmest smile saying how glad I was to meet her and taking her hand in mine as if I were about to kiss it and then realizing too late, my gross, gross mistake. Her smile broadened ironically to meet mine (as if she could take a joke) to uncover two rotten molars in the back of her head and the breath to match. Beetricks cackled, baring her wet glistening gums:

"You don't have to talk fancy to Chickee."

Beetricks, infinitely amused. I couldn't bring myself to call anybody "Chickee"; the name is preposterous and would stick in my throat. I think it was the mockery of her smile, her hand, moist and clammy, as if it had been in unclean places, which made me drop it, just prematurely, at the name, at the touch, at the rotting mouth, the smell and the jarring recognition, her expression which screamed:

"Ya moron, don't cha recanize me?"

Like we were old buddies. Her face was scrubbed raw of its heavy makeup, exposing that it had been carefully beaten, regularly, green through black and blue. I had seen her almost daily, (looking much older to me now that the recognition dawned), pounding her beat, up at Journal Square, between Nedicks and the Hudson Tubes, looked after by an older man, following behind by other even older men up the stairs in the hallway between the stores where the bompies slept, getting into a police car every day or two, only to return an hour later. I looked down now at Beetricks's soiled oilcloth covered table, at its half-finished glasses of Piels beer going flat, reluctantly relinquishing the last of its bubbles, at the thick overcooked spaghetti clumped together, drowned in vegetable fat, littered with its unmelted globs and pools of fake yellow. Sick, I left without saying another word.

Beetricks was always feeding margarine drenched spaghetti to those less fortunate; she fed off her gifts to these people, like a sick beast off carrion. This was her element. She reigned here.

I never saw the landlord again. I learned later that his name was Lancaster or McMasters. He was not a Jew but a dying remnant of the old moneyed Anglo-Saxon elite, rare in this neck of the woods, a breed unknown to Beetricks. To Beetricks if you had money, you were a Jew. There were rumors he was in a coma for weeks, that he "came back from the dead" after three days, but was "never the same man" that his wife felt responsible and was "heart sick" and sat by his bed crying. It was she that persuaded him to buy these buildings:

> "...to pay back the community from which you have derived so very much."

He found it easier to go along with his wife's silliness. He found her language bizarre and was reluctant to give voice... that "these people were a part of no community that he was in any way connected to and that none of his hard-earned wealth was in any way derived from these people who he considered essentially unconnected, outcasts." It was his wife's fancy that "slumlords created slums" and that it was "his bounden duty to raise these people up" by "shoveling his hard-earned cash into the holes in which they dwelt".

His apartment houses were liquidated a few months after the "incident", snapped up by an ex-handyman rising in the world, who unblocked his own toilets and found any notion about renovation beyond ridiculous, a philosopher who would pontificate:

> "Poor people have to have some place to live... that's what slums are for. If I fix-em-up they won't be able to come up with the money to pay me my rent."

He had his point, feeling right at home in possession of the worst slums in the neighborhood. Eddie's creation lived on, remaining visible for years, along with the blood, which immediately surrendered its bright red blush. Nobody tried to scrub it clean, not the new landlord, who was, more than anything, transported by the fire sale price he had forked over.

Eddie, in 1963, at the age of eighteen, with heartfelt patriotism and the insistent urging of a local judge, joined the United States Marines. Eddie, it turns out was no idiot, as universally believed; Beetricks, freely admitting that she herself had also been totally fooled. It seems he tested "way above average" on the tests they administered. The tests were not foolproof. In no time Eddie "broke down mentally"; he went berserk, attacked his drill sergeant:

> "...pummeling him repeatedly with a heavy metal object about the head... with particular viciousness".

Of course, it was necessary for him to sneak up from behind, stealthily, like an alley cat; if he had taken the sergeant head on, this tough Marine would have killed him, hands down, which once and for all would have put an end to the bloodshed which continued to drown down the years. This caper earned Eddie an immediate psychiatric discharge with only a minimal sentence in the stockade, just in time to escape Viet Nam, which blew the face off his best friend.

# Master Carpenter of Holy Name Church

When I was twelve years old, I was given the news that a great opportunity would be presented to me. I would be allowed to watch at the elbow of a great master carpenter, to learn his secret art, to study right there at his side. It would be as if Michael Angelo were alive and I could bear witness as he plunged his chisel into the beautiful, soft marble. George Matter was his name. He was the master cabinet maker at Holy Name Church, busy these many years plying his magic art on church pews and ornate confessionals and grand pulpits from which the priests spoke. George was going to build a recreation room in our basement and I was to be his assistant.

The commission was arranged by his brother, Steve Matter who had married my father's sister, Helen. Helen had been devoted to my father, now dead, and had acted as his housekeeper, and cared, in her attenuated, limited way, for his many more limited children, while his first wife remained sealed off in her room, bedridden with her myriad illnesses, consoling herself with her Christian Science faith right up until the moment of her awaited death. After my father had remarried a healthy young bride, my mother, it was expedient that other arrangements should be made for Helen. Helen no longer wished to be an old maid, nor to scrub the kitchen for her brother's brand-new bride. For appearance's sake a husband was found, a marginal man of limited intelligence and fewer prospects, who moved in with Helen, into her mother's house, into the third best bedroom without the full benefit of conjugal rights. My father was grateful for her many years of dedication, although it was whispered by many that it was he who had reluctantly supported his spinster sister and her services were no longer convenient.

Since Steve Matter was only sporadically employed, my father thought it expedient to purchase for him a permanent job, with a solid future, as a city fireman, for the rather princely sum, in nineteen forty-three, of five thousand dollars. This would have the unintended effect of christening him with an ineradicable name. From that day forward he would always be the "Five Thousand Dollar Beauty". Steve Matter was and would forever be a joke.

Shortly after the deal had been struck my father got a panicky call and a request for a sit down, with all humble apologies, from the venal politician. The old politico slid the envelope re-stuffed with cash across the table as if it were sticking to his fingers, protesting that he couldn't, in all honesty, keep it. It seems Steve Matter didn't have the common sense or the necessary physical stamina to pour water on a fire.

I'm sorry, a deal's a deal my father protested. It's too late, much too late. Arrangements have been made.

Matter, in residence at my father's mother's house as a kind of glorified janitor, was swift to sweep the first snowflakes off the front steps, lickety-split. He proved invaluable in keeping the halls spick-and-span and sat happy as an engorged flea side by side with the proprietors taking dinner at the main table. This was back in the old days when a crooked deal made was a crooked deal kept.

The old ward heeler slinked off, mightily pissed, loot bulging, stuffed in his coat pocket, recognizing that he had been had, and that my father, a man of some influence, could not be crossed with impunity. The compact was kept by all sides. Steve Matter had the distinction of being the only firemen in the history of Bayonne who would never fight a fire. He became the big chief's gofer, his boy Friday, his chauffeur, slow of foot factotum. As the years past Steve Matter forgot how really stupid he was and assumed a grim arrogance only the very dumb are capable of. He even pretended to own his mother-in-law's house, which the landlords went along with:

> "...seeing as how he kept the lawns so neatly trimmed."

In the beginning Steve Matter entertained the preposterous prospect that there might be the possibility of consummating the marriage, sexually, that is. But Helen was having none of it, keeping her own room's dead bolt safely secured at night. Steve would come knocking. She got one look at the offending organ and suggested an operation. For a man his age circumcision required a hospital stay in those days. When she got another look, she had another better lock installed. Rumor had it that she wished him to have a further more drastic procedure. Steve Matter drew the line. There would be no more knocking.

As far as his brother, George Matter, the master carpenter and the cellar work, since this was a family affair no contract was signed and no price agreed upon; whether flat fee or hourly wage remained untouched upon. No design was submitted and George Matter was simply let loose to use his utter discretion. He made a showing whenever he pleased and a job that should have taken a month wound up taking more than a year. He protested that he had other pressing work and had accepted the basement with the understanding that he could squeeze it in, at his convenience, between other previous, much more important commitments. Of course, no such thing had ever been agreed upon.

What nobody seemed to notice, except for me, was that when George did show up, he was seriously intoxicated. He wasn't falling down drunk but his eyes were glazed and his pupils dilated and he was in particularly high spirits but clumsy, all thumbs. He was what was called a functioning alcoholic, although he "functioned" only minimally. When he wasn't drunk, he was morose and irritable and would work for less than an hour. In fact, George was so unpleasant when he was sober that I actually came to prefer him drunk, which was almost always. When sufficiently oiled he could eke out three hours of sporadic labor. I say sporadic because George was incapable of sustained, concentrated effort. He would stand for ten minutes on end in a trance like state, as if frozen or in a state of suspended animation. At first, I would shake him gently:

"Are you all right, George?"

And he would get very annoyed as if I were breaking his concentration, ruining some brilliant idea.

> "I'm planning my next move. What the matter with you... Can't you see?"

He would protest in dead earnest. I learned not to break into these reveries, which to be honest were a welcomed retreat from his wood work which often seemed to be clueless and downright dangerous. At first, he used no power tools, which was for the best. However, his brother would butt in every so often with a shiny new power tool straight out of the box, encouraging his brother to try it out, a golden opportunity, forgetting I was listening. I think the noise rattled George; his nerves shattered. Whether using a power saw or hand saw, George could not cut the true measurement on the first shot, which meant a lot of ruined wood. George, at first, would smuggle it out, usually under his coat, when it would fit. Other times he would simply say that he had to take it to his shop at the church to either plane or sand it because he didn't have the proper tools with him. He summoned up this vision of his shop as a state-of-the-art working place, with the most expensive European tools collected over a life time. George never had the right tool with him, of course, most were at the shop.

Once when George was near to declaring the basement finished, he surfaced with his brother Steve and his son. All were armed with borrowed power vibratory sanders with the intent of putting in a marathon session. George's son was a "college man", as George proudly called him; unlike his father in every way, sober, clean cut, deferential, capable of sustained endeavor. Before quitting George drove himself for five continuous hours accomplishing more than he usually did in ten sessions. It was touching to see father and son work together, to see the father work more than he had ever worked, and the son asking with genuine tenderness:

"Are you all right Dad? Are you all right?"

George, not a well man, hung from the end of his tether.

After George hadn't been around for a long while, he would show up at day break but never to work. He'd be especially besotted, loaded down with enough bakery sweets for three days and he'd sit down for an hour. He was a sweet man in his own way and we all enjoyed his company at the breakfast table. My mother was extremely impressed by his generosity. It never did dawn on her that the jelly donuts and crumb buns were costing her a hundred dollars apiece.

"Are you going to work today, George?"

She would ask.

"Not today, Anna."

George would say and smile as if this were the silliest question in the world. Of course, he wasn't going to work, suggesting that he had piles of work lined up all over the place infinitely more important than our basement.

George was floundering. The little he did was third rate at best. But unbeknownst to himself he had a rather profound effect, on me. Without suspecting it he drove me to the library to study and master my first subject. I began to haunt construction sites, to watch. And I did master this subject. I became a carpenter before I became anything else. Watching George inspired in me the inevitable question:

"This can't be right. This can't be right."

He would also bring home to me firsthand the realization that experience has its limitations. Someone can do something for forty years and do it badly and wrong for every one of those years. It wasn't a lack of intelligence, particularly. There were fine craftsmen who weren't particularly bright. It had to do with a fundamental laziness, a refusal to discipline one's self, to summon forth the necessary concentration to do something with excellence, a lack of pride and sense of one's self as capable of excellence. These were the shiftless, marginal men. They did it wrong and badly with an orneriness and conviction almost. Somewhere in their years of doing the same thing over and over they must have seen someone do it right; they must have had a boss who walked them through the steps. I would come to witness such useless attempts and the inevitable response would be: "You gotta be kiddin." The required absorption, the attention to detail, the meticulousness is just inconceivable to them; something for suckers, to work so hard when it can be done so easily, like falling off a log. These men, forever, go through the motions. Although they put in the time they don't work in any

97

real sense of that word. They never work a day in their lives.

Originally, I had concluded that George through alcoholic self-abuse had lost the superior gifts he had once possessed; after all he was the cabinet maker of Holy Name Church. My mother never once referred to him as a carpenter. He was always the master carpenter. All of his flaws committed to wood seemed magically invisible to her; the power of mind control. There came a time when the master carpenter didn't show up for six weeks and we were genuinely worried about him. My mother didn't dare call her sister-in-law, Helen. This would have been a serious breach in etiquette. And it was reasonable to assume that his brother and his brother's wife supposed that George had been putting in his time, that my mother instinctively understood that in calling them she would be telling tales out of school. I assumed that Steve Matter, fully acquainted with his brother, was fully aware that he was drunk most of the time.

And so, I took it upon myself to travel by bicycle to Holy Name Church, eight miles away in the neighboring town. Besides, I was anxious to see the wonderful woodworking shop that George was always talking about, that I "would have to see some day." The church was a Catholic church, more a cathedral really, taking up almost a whole city block. I walked around the church with its high black, wrought iron gates and its many ancillary buildings to see if I could locate what looked to be a shop.

I stopped to ask a couple of street kids, punks, a little older than myself to see if they knew where I could find George Matter, adding with a certain pride, the church cabinet maker. They said they never heard of him. Perhaps a little too insistent I said:

> "You must have heard of him because he's the craftsman who built the carved confessionals... the pews... the pulpits.

I must have sounded like an idiot.

They told me the pews and pulpits had been finished back "centuries ago" and a church as a work in progress sounded hilarious to them. They got nasty:

> "We don't know no George, 'the church cabinet maker' and we don't know about no wood working shop. The only George around here is George the Rummy, who mops up. Sometimes you can find the old boozer sleeping off a drunk out back."

They pointed to a stone building the size of a shack. I forced the door with a certain trepidation, believing that I must have the wrong church, that maybe there was another Holy Name. The door was half coming off with one of the hinges gone and I had to use the applied momentum of my shoulders and the weight of my whole body. The door finally gave in to a room that measured no more than ten feet by twelve feet. There were rickety shelves piled with cans of old dried out paint and on the beat-up work bench cans of dried turpentine with old paint brushes permanently stuck like dead trees in the mud. There came an overwhelming mildew stink from the slop sink, a wet filthy mop fermenting in its own puddle with its stick protruding like a weapon ready to catch the unwary in the eye. The light was dim and I was more convinced, this couldn't be the right place, until I spied the beat-up canvas army cot. Underneath the cot pushed way back, almost out of sight, were brand new power-tools re-stuffed into their original boxes that seem to have been hidden there. They looked like the ones Steve Matter had brought to his big brother with such impossible expectations. (I had, in fact, unearthed George's flop, which doubled as the janitor's closet, used when he was too drunk and ashamed to stumble home to his neat little house where his wife abided, exhausted from her long hours scrubbing floors for the city at good steady pay.)

I never told a single soul that I had gone on a hunt for old George, the Master Carpenter. He finally did make an appearance a week or so later and eventually he did bring the work to a less than final conclusion. Without tying up the loose ends, he simply, without warning, declared it complete, by presenting a statement of account for services rendered, as if the paper magically made it so. When my mother got the bill, unfolding it at the kitchen table, she cried for a full hour staring at the wet disintegrating paper. It was typed out neatly on a piece of blank stationery with George Matter's name typed at the top and the title Master Carpenter, which he seemed to have no embarrassment about committing to ink. The description of the work said simply:

Basement Recreation Room -Knotty Pine $3,000.

The price was beyond exorbitant. I said:

> "Don't pay it. The fact that there's no contract works both ways. Have a reputable contractor come in and estimate the value of the work and pay that."

> "I can't do that. I have to live with these people."

my mother pleaded.

> "But you don't have to live with these people at all. This is your chance... your excuse... to make a clean break."

It had occurred to me that having a reputable contractor check it out might not be such a good idea. He might insist on ripping the whole thing out and start from scratch or call in the building inspectors; there was no permit; how could there be. In that case my mother would have to present George with a bill and that wasn't in the cards. She had been referring to the fact that the bill in reality came not just from George Matter but also from Steve Matter and Helen Matter, his wife. This, after all, was a family affair. They were all in on the shake-down and knowing my mother, knew what an easy mark she was and that she would pay. She would cry, for a full hour, but she would pay. They knew that; they could take it to the bank.

The rec room was only four hundred square feet, only about thirty percent of the basement area. The house cost $26,000 dollars in 1956 only a year before. The value of the rec room was no more than five hundred dollars. It had a cheap asphalt tile floor and a cheap acoustical tile ceiling. There wasn't even a lavatory installed.

Many years later and a world far away I escorted my mother through a house that I had built. She admired the fine cabinetry, running her hands across the finely rubbed mahogany:

> "You learned from a master carpenter. Do you remember?"

Struck, but without missing a beat, I replied:

> "How could I ever forget... the Master Carpenter of Holy Name Church."

# Sheeny Rosenbaum or 23andMe

There are stories that people tell over and over, never too embarrassed to repeat themselves, pretending to be gifted raconteurs, but most, at best, have a limited trove they're forever rifling through, like reaching into a beat-up trunk. Self-important literary types have proclaimed that the informal stories told to groups always translates into bad literature. This only proves that there are too many bad raconteurs; that good spoken story telling is a lost art.

My mother's brother told a story he thought hilarious, and never tired of repeating with slight variations. George professed to despise Jews which was ironic; if anything, he learned this hatred in America from his beloved Irish nuns and priests who hated everyone except their own inbred tribe. Racial epithets may have been loosely dropped but there was no enmity, not from my grandmother. These people, while separate, had lived in the same neighborhoods, come from the same villages in Europe. According to my grandmother the unterlander Jews of the Carpathian Rus lived with them in idyllic harmony; no doubt another fairytale. But my mother's mother in-spite-of the words she used admired the Jews, while recognizing them as in some ways entirely different. She would carry-on unendingly in her own Yiddish to the Rag Man, like an old friend from the old country, who called on her religiously. George never spoke of his father except in this one story. It was about a man that was always hanging around and George's father would complain:

"What the hell is Sheeny Rosenbaum doing here all the time?"

It was always Sheeny Rosenbaum, Sheeny Rosenbaum. In a variation I heard only a couple of times Sheeny Rosenbaum would bring George little gifts and gifts for his mother. And although George would never admit it, he formed a genuine bond with this stranger.

George was different from his brothers and sister, an entirely different class of being. Although the youngest, fifteen years younger than his sister, he completely dominated them. He was intelligent, certainly more intelligent than they were. They would defer to his knowledge, asking him questions as if he were a walking encyclopedia Britannica. George was always quick with the answer; what he didn't know he made up and they lapped it up. His answers were at times ridiculous and if caught in an obvious fabrication he would laugh uproariously as if it were all part of this big joke. He read little but was brazenly, contentedly ignorant as so many intelligent people are. With the help of the Irish nuns, he did manage to get a full scholarship to a Catholic high school and then a small Catholic college.

George was like one of those cuckoos you see in nature documentaries, ridiculously large, hogging the whole nest, ignorantly being fed by the stupid mother bird while the smaller weaker birds starve to death or get pushed out of the nest. The difference was that George's mother knew exactly who he was, that he was bigger and stronger and smarter than the others; and if the other children had been younger and, in any way, posed a threat, she would have gleefully starved them all to death to make room for George. She was an old European schooled in the brutal need to nurture the strongest and the best; this was a survival instinct. But the others were actually older and helped in his support. He looked nothing like his siblings, but they looked nothing like each other. Not a bad looking man, handsome in his own way; he had this gigantic nose, a good nose; which noses are disparaged by those who lack them. He was taller by a half a head than his brothers. And he would lead you to believe that he was afraid of nothing.

George always persisted in his staunch Catholicism. In his own mind there seemed to be no inconsistency between being a gifted fabricator and his religious piety. But there is never any doubt that being a deceiver was his true religion. Perhaps his devotion to the Irish nuns derived from the fact that they were the first ones he could fool so totally.

But getting back to where we started with Mr. Rosenbaum, the kind stranger who visited so often. Little George not knowing any better, hearing him called "Sheeny Rosenbaum" so many times took this to be the man's given name, and when he showed up for one of his customary visits young George yelled out in enthusiastic greeting:

"Hello, Sheeny Rosenbaum."

And of course, Mr. Rosenbaum, his feelings deeply wounded, never came back again, and the louder George laughed the sadder I believed it to be.

# (POSTSCRIPT)

Disregard everything you just read. I got it wrong. I misunderstood. I couldn't see.

Almost seventy years later and a world away, thanks to science and technology, the story has clarified itself and not at all to my liking. The most elaborate stories we tell ourselves are often self-serving. I liked the old story much better; although my suspicions were not without foundation. I believe my grandmother brazenly and underhandedly deceived Mr. Rosenbaum into thinking he might be George's father. And me? I, too, was deceived. I liked the idea of bringing a Jew into the family, even if sideways. I'd always heard that my father's family were Jews. I'd heard it whispered. They were rich; at least by the humble standards of the day. If you were rich, you were suspect. I embraced the rumors. I imagined a Jewish grandfather who converted to infiltrate, like a spy, and would reveal himself one day, if even from the grave, in all his glory. How we romanticize life.

I was disappointed when 23andMe told me I was .3 percent Ashkenazi Jewish and even more disappointed when they revised it, without so much as an apology, to zero percent, in one of those cataclysmic miniscule shifts which moves continents.

. . . .

There was a time in my life when I was touched by profound evil, demonic evil. It was profound because I was so vulnerable, so young, less than five. I was saved from this seemingly cosmic evil by a humble housekeeper, like in a child's storybook; a woman I had never seen before or if I had seen her did not recognize her; nor did I ever see her again; although perhaps I wiped her out of my mind. She risked everything for me or at least I think she did, certainly her job, and "betrayed" the man she worked for; in his own constricted, inbred, degenerate way, an incredibly powerful man. How many other little boys had she been able to save or more to the point, how many could she not save. Sometime after it happened, after I had managed to make some-kind-of sense of it all, I supposed her to be an angel of God manifesting itself in a humble housekeeper, as angels were disposed to do, I suspected. I believed in angels back then. To this day I do not rule out the possibility of some sort of supernatural intervention which is, in-itself, a leap of faith. If not for this woman I would not have survived, not in any real sense. She didn't necessarily save my life but she did save my soul. It might have been the most important moment of my life.

Back in 1950 when I was not yet five years old it was not uncommon to let children roam on their own. Boys who were blessed with parents who hovered over them protectively were bullied and ridiculed by their peers. But at less than five I stayed pretty-close to trusted adults. My grandmother, who I was staying with, who would often "mind me", suggested that I play outside on the sidewalk right below her third-floor window on Hudson Boulevard, a hundred feet north of Newark Avenue and just a short block South from Saint John the Baptist Roman Catholic Church. Although my grandmother was technically a Catholic, under the pope of Rome, she belonged to an Eastern Orthodox

Greek Catholic Church whose priests married, though forbidden by the iron hand of Rome. She never set foot inside the church on the corner, which she referred to invariably as the Irish church, no more than she would set foot inside a church that sacrificed young children to some unnamable demon, and devoured the leavings for communal lunch.

Although I had no particular desire to play on the sidewalk outside my grandmother's window, this was not a particularly rare request on my grandmother's part, so, given little choice, I acquiesced. Even to a young child the whole process seemed to be contrived and suspect.

So, trying to be a good boy, I played on the sidewalk, looking up to the window for my grandmother every minute or so. A man came up to me and asked if I knew who he was. I didn't answer. I looked up to the window but my grandmother wasn't there.

> "You go to mass at Saint John's Church, don't you? I know... I've seen you."

I nodded, yes? He looked like someone I had seen before, at my grandmothers, often; but I had never been able to figure out exactly what he was doing there.

> "I'm a priest at Saint John's Church. I say the mass. Do you recognize me now?"

I nodded, yes. I didn't recognize him without his priestly vestments and never before connected him to the man who visited my grandmother without his Roman collar.

"I want you to follow me. I have something I want to give to you, a gift, something very special, very valuable".

I told him I would have to get permission from my grandmother.

"I spoke to your grandmother. I know your grandmother. She wants you to go with me. She wants me to look after you... she had somewhere to go."

I told him that I couldn't go unless I got permission from my grandmother. How naïve and trusting I was. He repeated once again that he had gotten permission from my grandmother, but this time, firmly, as if I had been accusing him. He said a priest never lies. He asked me if I believed in God and whether I knew that priests were directly chosen by God and that it was a sin to disobey a priest. I kept looking up at the window for my grandmother, but she wasn't there. I would conclude, only much later, that there may have been a limit to her collusion, that she would go only so far, that she would refuse to witness it with her own eyes. The priest asked me if I knew what a mortal sin was and if I knew what the punishment was for committing such a sin; if I knew about the eternal fires of hell. He was commanding me now, or at least attempting to.

"You must follow, but at a distance. I can't be seen to be playing favorites. You must not be seen with me... otherwise I won't be able to give you the gift... You must follow me at a distance... into the church. I will leave the rectory door open for you and you must follow me in. You know what a rectory is... where the priests live. The door is inside the church, you will see it... it will be left open... close it after you enter."

I don't think at any time, either before or since, that I felt myself in such a palpable, unnerving presence. I had no rational reason back then to believe he was evil. No rational reason that is, but there was something. He was a priest after all, chosen by God. All priests, I was continually told, were chosen by God. God was good. He was, wasn't he? So, like a good little Catholic boy I followed the priest; like all good little Catholic boys do. He didn't look back; he knew I would follow; they always did, every last one of them. He paused briefly at the top of the church steps and then went in.

I dutifully followed, down the block, into the church, a cathedral really, worthy of any medieval European city. (How many charwomen let their families go hungry to build this exquisite pile of stone; scraping their nickels and dimes together?) And true to his word the rectory door was left wide open, with a dim light shining from inside. I had been in the church often, but had never seen this door left open. Until then I had no idea what was on the other side. There was a long dimly lit hallway, with bright light emanating from a room at the end of it. I entered the dimly lit hallway tentatively; the priest was nowhere to be seen. Toward the end of the hallway, not in the bright room itself, but obscured from it, a plainly dressed woman stood, the woman I spoke about before, the woman who saved me.

Appearing out of nowhere... seeing me... she gesticulated wildly... in a panic... terrified ... soundless... but so loud in her silence that the silence reverberated in my head... pounding it. She had an electrified, transfixed look which seized her face as if possessed... haunted ... mouthing... miming:

RUN... RUN... RUN...

screaming it... soundlessly...

RUN... RUN... RUN...

Making an amplified pushing gesture... her hands and arms in league with her face... a silent movie actor overwhelmed by histrionics... exaggerated... a ritualistic play she was obliged to reenact... the air forcing... pushing me over... forcing me out... transfixed... an hour elapsed in thirty seconds... elongated or compressed... struck hard by her frenzy... I pivoted, as if propelled by an otherworldly force and tore out of the church. Nobody chasing after me. I ran faster than I had ever run. I ran like the wind until my lungs ached and my legs buckled.

I ran up the stairs to my grandmother's apartment, above the restaurant on the first floor, above the offices on the second floor, to the third floor and banged on the door and banged and banged and banged. No answer.

The Greek lady next door finally opened her door. Her family was the only other residential tenant in the building. She wasn't mad at the banging; the opposite. She smiled a sweet embarrassed smile; embarrassed to tell me that my grandmother had gone; wasn't home. She didn't know where she had gone or why or when she'd be back. Actually, she hadn't spoken to my grandmother at all. It is as if she knew what was going on but was afraid to explain, afraid I wouldn't understand or worse still that I would understand which would call for even further explanation. She invited me into her apartment until my grandmother returned. But I was skittish by now and would remain skittish, perhaps until the day I died. For some reason I trusted this woman, there was a goodness that seemed to emanate from her, just as evil seemed to ooze from the priest; I trusted her as much as I would trust anyone but I wouldn't enter her apartment.

I'm sorry for referring to this woman as the "Greek lady", but this was 1950. My vantage point at the time was much closer to the ground. It was an age of vicious, vengeful tribalism. Everyone was referred to by their ethnicity or religion. You were Irish, a Pole, an Italian or, god help us, a Jew or worse yet a Protestant. Even if no racial epithets were used, you were pegged, fixed and frozen in some dark pigeonhole.

And I heard everything; all the slights, all the pettiness and hate. It was as if I didn't exist. I was a secret agent. People spoke in front of me as if I were deaf and dumb, as if I were invisible and could understand nothing, so I heard everything. These were mostly rotten people and it didn't do me any good knowing it, or did it? It had the effect of alienating me from the very people, to whom I should have been ingratiating myself. But then wouldn't I have been just another dumb little Catholic boy sucking up to the priests and the adults who were their oblivious instruments. Didn't being a spy ultimately save me, save my soul. But how does a little boy explain his insubordination as an act of existential defiance, even to himself. To an absurd extent I was the only adult in the room. And I heard everything: how the two Roman Catholic priests at Saint John's were hopeless "alkies" who were sent away periodically to "dry out". But although the one always reeked of whiskey, the other, if a drunk, was more circumspect; this, my attempted abductor. But was there some other more confidential reason he was sent away and disappeared for long stretches? They paid visits to the Congregation of the Servants of the Paraclete, whose significance escaped me, a place which would become notorious years later for their relentless industry in re-disseminating pedophiles.

I sat down on a pile of old newspapers outside my grandmother's door. I waited, knowing that the Greek lady was inches away, right across the hall, and could hear everything; paid close attention to the comings and goings. I think she knew far more then she let on. I don't think she was strong enough to intercede if somebody tried to grab me, but, somehow, I believed she would try, or yell or scream even if she didn't succeed. Perhaps I fantasized the benevolence of these forces, mostly anonymous, with only a tenuous connection, an old housekeeper, an old Greek lady, arrayed against the evil that enveloped me, that was closing in on me. Did the hope of these meager forces coming to my rescue hearten me? They were all I had. I survived, if only just.

My mother finally showed up to pick me up. She asked me where my grandmother was. I said I didn't know.

She was more concerned about my grandmother than she was about me being abandoned there. "Are you sure she's not home?" and proceeded to bang on the door for five minutes. I told my mother what happened in as precise detail as I could muster, which seemed to have absolutely no effect on her. She didn't accuse me of lying but acted as if I were lying or imagining it.

My grandmother, when she returned, had no explanation whatsoever but donned a sheepish grin like the cat who just swallowed the canary. My grandmother had infinite dispensations with my mother. My mother worshiped her mother as only an old European could and she wasn't European. And even if I had disappeared there would have been no repercussions, not for my grandmother. "Kids disappear, it happens. You can't watch them every minute." My mother was always off "gallivanting", her brother's word. She couldn't afford to lose a convenient drop off for her kids; as far as the danger of kidnapping, she was willing to take the risk.

Sex might not have been the only motive for the priest; although rape would have proceeded the murder; kill two birds with one stone.

> "Why do you have so much and Georgie has none?"

My grandmother complained repeatedly. Did my grandmother whine this to the priest? Did they scheme together? With me out of the way there would be more for their Georgie. Little did she know how little I would get once my mother got finished looting it? She might have saved herself the trouble.

114

But I didn't disappear and details of my attempted abduction by a priest didn't impress my mother. The thought of going to the police never even occurred to her. Even if she had incontrovertible proof that every word I spoke was factually accurate, she still wouldn't have gone to the police. She never confronted the priest about the incident; never even talked to him. She wouldn't have dared. She was afraid of these priests as a little girl might be afraid.

"He didn't do anything to you, did he?"

This was more by the way of a statement, an assertion, a defense.

"Nothing happened. Nothing happened."

She was emphatic. She became especially dismissive when I explained that this was the same man I had seen so often at my grandmother's. And if she had gone to the police, what would the point have been? An Irish Catholic priest in an Irish Catholic town and an Irish Catholic police department against the story of a four-year-old boy and who wasn't even Irish to boot. You've got to be kidding me. "It takes a village to abuse a child." These people were more than complicit; they were co-conspirators. "Good Germans" every one, who aided and abetted with every coin they scrimped and dumped into the collection basket and thereby paved their own way straight to hell. I doubt that the police would even bother to disturb the priest or file a report. If missing, would some devoted rogue detective continue to look for me for forty years until felled by dementia, the way they do in the movies? That's fiction and this was 1950. Would they find my body? What secrets remain concealed in that church? Will they ever dig up the basement?

. . . .

I hear that Saint John's is empty now, seventy years later, taken over by its loathed arch rival, Our Lady of Mount Carmel. Only a stark little back chapel is used for mass now, mostly for Hispanics; how ironically appropriate that they should truly inherit this Irish pile of rocks, that children once went hungry for. The main church locked-up like a mausoleum, hunks of plaster and stone falling. No more packed houses, no throngs to watch a deranged priest burn himself to death. The arch rival: Our Lady of Mount Carmel, the Italian church, its reluctant custodian, last man standing, last one in line, being bled dry by exorbitant maintenance. The discrimination against the Italians had been so outrageous that they were forced to open their own school only a mile away, next to their church. The Italian parents believed the stories their children brought home. My mother didn't.

. . . .

After my attempted abduction, whenever I would pass this priest in the street, he would glower at me or look through me like I was dirty air. There was a price to pay for disobeying a priest, especially if you refused to march to your own murder. He had no sense of embarrassment, not the slightest sense of guilt. This was a man consumed by his own sense of entitlement. He was chosen by god and would do whatever he god-damned pleased.

As dutiful Catholic children, we were expected to address all priests and nuns in a subservient, gleeful, sing-song:

"Good morning, Father"

or good afternoon as the case may be; "hello" wasn't good enough; too abrupt, too "rude"; not enough of a song and dance.

But this priest would patently ignore me, stare me down. After a while I got tired of singing out this greeting, unreciprocated, kowtowing like some idiot. So, instead I would walk past him as silent as he was. As a consequence, I would be dragged into the principal's office to be beaten by the principal herself; a rare distinction I was told. She usually left the beatings to her underling minion nuns. It was explained to me that my sin was so grievous, that only the highest authority could mete out the proper punishment.

"Once again... you failed to show proper respect to a priest."

Each time wielding the stick with emphasis, "priest" whack, "respect" whack, whack, whack.

"But sister, he never answers me back... never says good morning back. I can't even be sure he sees me."

"He? .... He?"

She flew into a rage. Whack. Whack.

"A priest must always be referred to as father. Father."

"And no back talk."

Whack, whack, whack. You weren't allowed to explain or defend yourself or in any way clarify the situation. This was "back talk", a grievous sin of impertinence and disrespect. I was branded as a "back talker", a calumny I carried with me. He's a "back talker" I would hear the nuns cackle to each other, as if I were the devil's own spawn. You were required to stand silently and accept your punishment as if mute. Whether you were guilty or not was really beside the point. And so, like a fool, I stood there for my beatings. And I would take my beatings with a grim conceit but never again would I sing hello to that goddamned stinking priest.

But eventually I got tired of my beatings and found another way. I don't think the priest could see too well, which gave me an existential consolation; that the monster who stalked me was half blind, like in a comic book where the alien beast succumbs to simple water. I learned a simple but profound lesson. I learned that the beast, no matter how powerful, could be outwitted. As soon as I spotted him, I would pivot instantly, never looking back and walk the other way, taking a circuitous route to wherever I had to go. This made me extremely vigilant, always surveilling the distance, always trying to distinguish faces; situational awareness, a quality I bear with me to this day. I am always on the look-out for monsters closing in on me. Dodging the priest became a kind of survival game, which made me late to school, often, and made me explore parts of the city I never meant to see. I learned to walk great distances until my legs ached and would remain a great walker to my last days. Sometimes, I would see him in unusual places, disguised in civilian dress and knew I could approach him with impunity as long as I knew enough to shut up and pretend I couldn't see him. To quote from another story about the same priest: "the dumpy squat obese little priest, who squeezed like grease from the Tubes in civilian dress, almost daily, disguised, with his boys trailing after him at a decorous distance."

. . . .

I learned from all this that I could never depend upon my family to protect me; that they would send me off to be victimized again and again and again. I would conclude later in life that the advice, the "guidance" I received from my family, devout Catholics every damned one of them, was not only erroneous but counterproductive and entirely destructive. They were wrong about everything, everything. Did these Catholics make a compact with the forces of evil to send off their sons to be sodomized by priests to gain a back door into "heaven"; Satan's heaven which might actually be better, for them? They couldn't have been that blind. They weren't that stupid. Were they self-deceived, refusing to acknowledge what was staring them straight in the face?

. . .

There is no doubt that all this poisoned my existence. I doubt that one boy in a thousand eventually came forward; this problem was endemic and infected the entire Catholic system. You didn't have to be physically raped to have your mind murdered and soul desecrated; brain death, the peculiarly Catholic disease; these people were all crazy.

. . .

Then there was Balman, the second-grade teacher; she with the sissy, priest in waiting, son. She made everyone raise their hand to reveal who the Irish were; there was a great shuffling of feet and marching and crying; the Irish in the front everyone else in the back. The only difference was, there were no trucks waiting in the street to haul us off. One little girl, crying uncontrollably, the whole time, tried to pass; but was singled out and publicly shamed because of her German last name; it turns out she was only half Irish which she couldn't prove; but she was given a free ride and allowed to sit in the middle, no man's land, presumably because her first name was Sharon but mostly because she wouldn't stop wailing.

Even Sister Margaret George, in the next grade up, was appalled when the only songs we could sing, the only ones we were taught, were Irish ditties which reeked of the barroom; beer, piss, sweat and pine oil, which clung to our flesh like a poisonous fungus. She would roll her eyes in exasperation when we insisted on belting out, with enthusiastic gusto: "When Irish Eyes Are Smiling" or "MacNamara's Band". By then we were beyond saving.

After incessant indoctrination, Balman posed the loaded question to us: "If you could be any nationality, what would it be"? Of course, the almost unanimous answer was: "Irish". I said almost unanimous. She was suspicious of the holdouts, the silences, so she commanded a show of hands. Some of the holdouts folded; only me and a gang of Italian boys, including John, who revered Al Capone, stood our ground and refused to wither under her febrile glare. She would think back on us; our names forever impressed in her minute malicious memory. And we few, would all stand obstinately, in silent solidarity when that whole god-forsaken hammered crew sang "MacNamara's Band." And "the drums they banged and the cymbals clanged and the horns they blazed away." I loved that stupid song.

. . . .

I once told a friend, later in life, that I know exactly how it feels to be a Jew in Nazi Germany. Being a Jew, she was deeply offended by this, telling me I was trivializing the horrendous plight of the Jews; that my situation couldn't even begin to compare. But in some sense my case was worse; I was isolated and abandoned; there was no solidarity; no genuine family; my sister, a "self-hating Jew", collaborated, becoming their mindless, enthusiastic creature; the rest of the family didn't seem to fully understand that these Irish were the Nazis and that they themselves were the Jews. We are told we must never forget; and I agree whole-heartedly, but what about the uncountable like me? What about my own private holocaust which I am doomed to drag around with me, even if that world no longer exists, exactly; and I use that term, holocaust, advisedly. How many others, just like me, had the jackboot jammed at the back of their head and their face squashed into the muck? If there are deniers it is because the idea is so preposterous and being so, especially embarrassing for the victims. And it may also seem entirely irrelevant today. Everybody loves the Irish, or so they say. There is no doubt that victims assume a greater guilt than the guilty perpetrators; guilty for their perceived weakness, their vulnerability, for "allowing" it, for succumbing to it. Why was there no payback, no Sicarios or Sicaris, if you please, (I am referring to Roman-Jewish Palestine not Medellin)? Certainly, the Slavs were tougher in every sense; especially adept at killing each other. A small band of Cossacks could have taken out the entire Irish Jersey City police department, stealthily, in one brief night. Why was there no "race" war? There are times when war is holy, redemptive, righteous; when a troop of glorious bastards would have been cleansing, purifying with the fire of retribution. Is it any excuse that these fools, my putative family, were duped by Georgie, who, for reasons they utterly misunderstood, was treated like the quintessential Nazi; so how could I, with blond hair and blue eyes and Aryan good looks be their Jew?

There is protection in a ghetto, self-imposed or not; what keeps you in keeps them out; fortification against the alien onslaught. Do we instead, throw our babies into a nest of rats; see if they can fight it out? Philip Roth's imbecilic criticizers bemoan that he was eternally stuck in the rut of his own never-ending Weequahic, the Jew's home or could it be his heaven, which he never shed, nor wished to, lugged around with him, sometimes stumbling over it, a fulsome shield, invincible. Philip Roth:

"Am I completely mistaken to think that living as well-born children in Renaissance Florence could not have held a candle to growing up within aromatic range of Tabachnik's pickle barrels?"

I envy him, that, whether he's being funny or not.

Certainly, the other kids in my class knew they were being abused while the Irish got a free pass. But there was no solidarity among the kids, no sense of cohesion. Their parents knew and listened to their children; hence the Italian exodus to a school a mile away. But I don't think the kids could see clearly that they were being singled out for persecution. My first-grade nun was truly psychotic; her preferred method of abuse was to sneak up behind you and hit you on the side of the head with her fist. I was hit so often and so hard that by the end of the day I was not fully conscious; and dizzy, cotton in my head. I had trouble keeping my balance; barely able to walk home. Sometimes it would take weeks for the cotton to clear. More than once the nun struck me so hard, she knocked me right out of my seat onto the floor. I think she might have damaged my brain which perhaps was her aim.

It is perhaps indecent to suggest that Slavs and Jews might take some lewd consolation from the fact that the Germans were, on-the-whole, at least, tall, good looking and intellectually accomplished. But the Irish? By what obscene perversion of fate could the Irish be allowed to persecute anyone. America. Oh, America. Land of the eponymous Dream, unleashed the filthy beast without meaning to. The Irish had one particular word for people of color and they loved that word, cherished and treasured it; sucked succor from it, letting it roll off their tongue incessantly as if there was lewd music in it; the devil's dance; and they hated the Jews with an even more particular ardor and the Protestants infinitely more. Who didn't they hate, except their own congenital tribe? What greater indignity or ignominy, than to be given the bum's rush out of a cheap, filthy saloon by the stumbling, drunken barkeep who looks suspiciously like W. C. Fields, only slovenly?

My dark skinned sister, (my mother's mother, sickened by her granddaughter's darker color, would have smothered her in her crib if given her leave, and never ceased to refer to her by the same epithet she reserved for people of color; a word which simply means black, or dark as in the song [Dark Eyes]; shivering violently in mock horror, as the word passed her lips, daring only a whisper) inexplicably, with cosmic irony, self-initiated herself into this paler than pale tribe; and like her adopted kin, who never signed the papers to let her in, joined in the chorus with the neophyte's suspect enthusiasm, noisily broadcasting her loathing of Jews and Italians, as if this would solidify her precarious standing within that pallored, pasty, inbred crew.

Years later my mother complained to me that Janie would only date Irish "freaks"; that Janie claims to hate the Jews and Italians, that she won't even date Slavic boys. I tried to clarify that they weren't all freaks; "were they"? "Oh yes they are, the one with the hare lip, the other with the club foot and the one with the lisp." "But didn't they repair the hare lip, surgically, I mean" "Well they didn't do a very good job, did they, now?" she countered. "What about the freak with the club foot?" she insisted. "I heard he had a knee that wouldn't support his weight, a "trick knee", he calls it." "Yeh, the trick is on him. That's the lie they circulate."

Janie did finally marry, the character from the movie, *Deliverance*, the backwoodsman at the garage with the "whale eye"; but I'm told he wasn't Irish, so I may be mistaken, although the resemblance is dead-on, and I have to defer to my own judgement; he must be Irish and hiding it. His cousin revealed, in confidence, that he's ashamed of being Irish and that he consistently lies about it. (The cousin, turned proud actor, played the hillbilly who the Burt Reynold's character killed.)

·········

I had one reader complain that the world I write about doesn't exist anymore; that I was unnecessarily dredging up a painful ancient history best forgotten; that I was whining; that most people wouldn't even understand what I was talking about and might even deny that the world I depict ever existed; that it was even remotely possible for one grossly inferior people to persecute, as best they could, multiple groups of far superior people. For God's sake, wake up. Remember the Germans and Jews. I don't believe that the Germans, for one minute, thought the Jews were actually inferior; it was the Jew's superiority that threatened them.

125

. . . .

At the age of eighty-one, in 1994, a few years before she died, apropos of absolutely nothing, my mother said to me, out of the blue, as if she were asking advice on the best brand of cheese and as if I were a fount of infinite knowledge; an encyclopedic guru supplanting the now dead Georgie; a pregnant pause:

"There's something I've been meaning to ask you... Were the priests homos?"

Sorry about the politically incorrect phrase. My mother was an out-of-step old woman and this is the way she spoke. The more jarring thing is that this bizarre insinuation, delivered with total matter-of-factness, came from a so-called devote Roman Catholic, (she had long ago forsaken her Greek Catholic Faith) who went to church every Sunday without fail her entire life. She asked the question only because she already knew the answer. What had she heard? What stories were circulating? Was the truth finally coming out? She had never taken what I said about the priests seriously. After a pause, I answered:

"Yes".

"All of them?"

she asked.

"I don't know about every single one all of them."

And then she said something that knocked me off my feet:

"I always thought so."

126

She "always thought so", "always thought so?" Is that why she sent her beautiful young boy off to them? And then she said something even more unsettling:

"Did they ever make a pass at you?"

"Pass", "pass?" What an inappropriately gentle term. Was she sliding inexorably into dementia?

I said:

"Yes".

She said:

"Why didn't you say something".

Was this self-induced amnesia to soothe an aching conscience?

And that was it. Not another word. "Say something?" This is the Twilight Zone. That was it. She wanted no elaboration and I didn't offer any.

I wanted to remind her, but I didn't.

I said something in 1950 when a psycho priest tried to abduct me.

I said something when a priest at Don Bosco Camp in 1956 slid his fingers nonchalantly down the inside of my bathing suit and said I was too "sexy", his word.

I "said" something when I unequivocally refused to go to Saint Peter's Prep any longer. When they refused to hear me, I travelled the bus they put me on, to the door of the school and then walked home, eight miles, every day, for a week, before they found me out.

I said something about Richard M. Barry, S.J., the butch sadist who forced all the boys to strip down naked, shower and lather up methodically, from top to toe, after every gym class, which he insisted on monitoring at close reach, practically inside the tightly crowded gang shower, getting the edges of his long loose hanging cassock dripping wet, drooling, devouring the just pubescent newbie boys with his mean lascivious wolf eyes, seething hate for what he craved.

I said something about the creepy office visits with the principal, Cornelius J. Carr, S.J., who was revealed, only after he was conveniently dead, to be a serial rapist of boys. My mother added insult to injury by sending Saint Peter's a $500 donation, for reasons I could never begin to fathom; a huge sum in 1958, along with forfeiting my prepaid tuition.

It reminds me of the scene from the movie *Spotlight*:

> "What did your mother do?"

> "What did my mother do? What did my mother do? She served them cookies."

After the donation I just gave up, figured this was the way the game was played and even I became brain-washed. I was ushered to my final doom, from which I never really recovered, to a Catholic College, not by coercion, but by abundant ecstatic praise which is more insidious. My uncle, my father's brother, called it the Catholic Harvard (Fordham University, which was ludicrous) and finally clasped me to his bosom like a true uncle in a way I found seductive, disarming but also subversive, destabilizing. We are more often despoiled by affection, especially by affection previously withheld for no apparent reason. Mike took no direct interest in me as a father figure, never once inviting me to his house; not until I was in glorious Fordham; but me and my sister stood him up, purposely; it was too late by sixteen years. However, Mike would carp about me endlessly from the sidelines, berating my mother. When I was given a "battery" of tests and skipped a year, in a new school, he had not one word of praise or commendation. He ridiculed it as the "Jew School"; a school in which I starred, until the demon priest and his minion nuns reached out and crushed me with their lies. The new school saved my life. I would not have survived three more years of the Irish school, the degradation, the humiliation, the belittlement.

Inexplicably, my uncle, Mike, worshipped the Jesuits; which should have alerted me. He would die before I graduated college, but not before I was subjected to the revelation that his  own son, Eddie, had been corrupted in the obscenest manner. My uncle was not a stupid man; is it even possible that he could not see? Was seeing me off to my doom some weird revenge against my own father, who bullied and beat him? He was famous for going off on benders, carousing with Jesuits, always game to pick-up the bar bill for these perpetual parasites. Did they go hunt down boys together? Was his own son offered up; to become the priests' collaborator, their prized birddog.

Years later, Eddie's mother, Margaret, my uncle's wife, started to elaborate, in detail, on why Eddie had "resigned" his Navy commission just two years before his twenty-year retirement eligibility. Assuming I knew far more than I actually did, she carried-on excitedly, breathlessly, about how people misunderstood entirely, that her son "took these boys under his wing, mentored them"; but she stopped dead in her tracks, midsentence, a little shaken, no doubt taken aback by my appalled look, the look of horror, of disbelief; could she be so blind; could she really not see, or see that I could see? Although I had heard nothing of his "boy's mentoring", as a Navy physician, I knew the deep background story, more than she imagined; here was someone, her only son, who structured his entire existence to quarry young men and boys. I found out, in my first year of college, that cousin Eddie, Doctor Eddie's life was an intricate racket; his nice guy routine a con to suck you in; never making waves, bending over backwards, never disagreeing, avoiding scrutiny; his life, a sham; volunteer doctor for the sport's teams; "sport's doctor", isn't that what he called himself; ready supply of boys is what it was; to play doctor with? He was part of it; one of them. They must employ some sort of spy network; scouts looking out for prime meat. When Eddie was president of the student body at Xavier, which made him General or Colonel, or some such rot, he preyed upon the younger boys with the collusion of the priests, offering his choice picks to them, softening them up for the kill; schooling, grooming, priming them; he was one of the elect, singled out for special privileges; their tight-lipped pimp; the priests were crazy for him... because of his prodigious physical attributes.

I am cursed with sharing an unusual last name with this Eddie. I came to shrink in revulsion from the grinning faces accosting me; coming up to me smirking like idiots, with a calculating sneer; wanting to know if I went in for the same things as Eddie, wanting to give me their number, wanting mine. I learned to cringe, congeal at that very particular infernal grin bearing down on me. When I told one of them Eddie was married, almost as a defense, a counter-argument, he nearly busted a gut: "You're not serious" and then "I thought he was going to become a priest. His priest buddies must be broken-hearted. I guess he made a deal. Maybe she likes to watch."

When Eddie's worshipful, dutiful, dopey sister thought her brother died prematurely, at 53, before the plague was on everybody's lips, she unstintingly, systematically shook down each and every member of the family, and everyone the family knew, sucking out every last cent that she could muster, her unrelenting entreaties, for a so-called "memorial fund", a testament to obscenity which ballooned to $2,000,000; most of this out of my grandfather's business which her father had cheated my grandmother out of with the help of a crooked lawyer.

It was only my cousin Joe, my father's brother's son, who had the balls to threaten to sue and got cooperation from no one; least of all, the fleeced. Helen and Steve Matter were unembarrassed freeloaders who occupied my grandmother's house, holding her a virtual prisoner, stuffing her full of vast amounts of cheap food like a tethered goose, until she couldn't move, hastening her death; Helen and Steve, spongers, paying no rent. Mike, my father's brother, ran my grandmother's business as his own piggybank, doling out a pittance to his own mother. He bided his time till the last minute, until she was senile at 83, swindling her out of the business and conspiring with his sister Helen to get her title to the house. This was like something out of Hitchcock. These people were unabashed thieves; and murderers, perhaps.

. . . .

My early college years were a period of incessant sexual harassment. This was the priest's playground; their hunting preserve and it was open season. I learned to never be alone with one of their priests.

. . . .

The old retired pope explained that rampant pederasty was a result of the loose morals of the sixties; this is complete idiocy; boy rape was a culture, long ingrained, which priests exploited to hand pick their successors, all of whom magically had a vocation and all were "sissies" like themselves. (I apologize for the politically incorrect word, but there is no other language to explain it; effeminate doesn't do it; there was nothing vaguely feminine about these boys; "natural eunuchs" doesn't do it either; even eunuchs were bolder than these misfits. But they weren't really misfits, were they? Through some bizarre historical anomaly, they fit perfectly; they would be perfect priests, lacking all masculine characteristics; and so, you accuse me of toxic masculinity; but according to these chosen ones who are devoid of it, all masculinity is toxic.) This was Darwinism turned up-side-down;

the societal ascendency of the least fit; that could never pass any ancient society's rigorous initiation into manhood and would have been relegated into non-personhood, neither male nor female with the privileges of neither. What pious Catholic mother didn't rejoice, that at long last her darling, little "sissy" boy would no longer be beaten and hounded by the other tougher boys; all he had to do was acquiesce, avow a vocation; just mouth the magic words or just nod yes. How many such boys were shunted into the priesthood out of their own desperation; once declared, they were out of bounds and safeguarded by the priests and nuns. They were the saddest victims of inbred societal constraints that allowed them no coherent alternatives. Today they would be able to, perhaps, transition and become happy little girls or proclaim their open gayness or transsexuality; but back then there were no such options. Without a single exception every boy who alleged a priestly vocation, in my neighborhood, was just such a natural castrata or gender neutral, transsexual or intersex or however you're allowed to describe it and stay politically correct.

. . . .

There were two exceptionally nasty "lay teachers" (that's what they called the non-nuns), O'Donnell and Balman, (already mentioned) at Saint John's, who far outstripped the treacherous sadism of the sisters. God had "blessed them" with their own "sissy" little sons who made them positively glow with gratification; they beamed over them, so jubilantly proud of their little priests in waiting, swooning over their own precious little sissies, who, puffing up, so proud, preening for their mommies. Were these boys born this way or were they systematically enfeebled, emasculated and crushed by their cow mothers, every-last-drop of testosterone squeezed out of their squashed testicles? But perhaps, deep, deep down at some visceral tribal level, even these cow mothers were secretly appalled, even nauseated by their pitiful little weaklings, boys in name only, who could never win the girl, and who, at some level knew, could at most hope to become the catamites of some sick old pedophile; if lucky, the bishop or maybe, at most, they could bag the cardinal. Perhaps that's the real reason they so hated and persecuted those tough, smart little boys who flirted with the little girls and were everything their little boys were not.

. . . .

So, I was sent off to the Irish grade school like a sacrificial lamb to ritualistic slaughter. And for six long years they would systematically flay my flesh and scourge my ego. Not entirely because of Georgie, but also because of my slow sister. I didn't quite put together that she was retarded. (Oh, I'm sorry, I have absolutely no idea what to properly call her; according to a 2003 survey by the BBC, "retarded" was voted the most offensive word relating to disability; and idiot, imbecile, and moron I suspect are even more frowned upon.) At the time, though, before mandatory political correctness set in, I could plainly see, my sister was "dumb as a post". Years later I would hear my mother scream into the phone at the nuns, safely at the other end:

"My daughter does not have an 85 IQ."

My mother made a large donation to the girl's Catholic High School, Saint Dominic's Academy and the nuns dutifully lost the test; or rather they let my sister take it home with her and agonize over the answers. Simple analogies were entirely beyond her ken. She couldn't grasp the concept. When I tried to help, she attacked me ferociously.

My sister, two years older and ahead of me in school, was a dyed in the wool, committed masochist. She ached for Saint John's like a jilted lover for the punk who beat her. She was besotted and wouldn't consider going to any other school. She craved to suffer, yearned to be despoiled; she hankered for the psychological whip to rip at her brain flesh. These kids despised her and taunted her and like any good masochist or victim of Stockholm syndrome, the more they mistreated her the more she wanted to be with them. Since they were convinced that they were better than she was, she internalized the contempt and hated herself. She would be goaded by self-disgust for the rest of her life; obsessions don't die easy.

. . . .

I didn't want to go to Saint Johns. I refused. I had gone to the public school which was fine. I had gone to kindergarten in the Greek Catholic School which was idyllic. But my sister, two years ahead had already started Saint John's and wouldn't transfer. The two schools were each about the same distance from our home but in opposite directions. My mother wasn't going to fight the heavy traffic in the morning, not for me.

I truly believe that our lives can be utterly ruined by one false move, our lives soured by one seemingly insignificant misstep; that one failure of courage, one failure to stand your ground or simply one bad or stupid decision, can sow the seeds of inevitable, catastrophic doom. And if at the age of six, I absolutely refused to go to Saint Johns, what would they have done; sent me off to reform school for the incorrigible; this was not an idle threat in 1951; could it possibly have been worse? Saint Johns was a pocket of unalloyed though prosaic evil, a metaphysical anomaly. The story itself sickens me with its petty tawdriness, its apparent massive insignificance; and reminds me of another writer's observation:

> "... of the terrible, the incomprehensible way one's most banal, incidental, even comical choices [or lack of choices] achieve the most disproportionate result."

It wasn't as if the other Catholics weren't fully cognizant of their own persecution by the Irish; especially the Irish church hierarchy. Most ethnicities had their own exclusive parishes. The Poles had Our Lady of Czestochowa; the Slovak, Czech, Lithuanian, Slovenian, the Italians all had their own; but the hierarchy remained Irish. The Ruthenians or Carpatho-Russians were so infuriated by this Irish maltreatment that as many as half of all of them formed their own "Russian Orthodox" parishes splitting from their Ukrainian Greek Catholic brothers and thus amplifying the, only perceived, ethnic differences between them; and, more importantly, driven to split from Rome itself. They abandoned the pope and their own ethnic identity just to get the Irish off their neck. Even Poles, not content with their own parishes, also broke with Rome because of the Irish bishops and formed their own separate Polish National Catholic Church, joined also by Slovaks and Lithuanians.

. . . .

But mostly, my mother acquiesced to silly Janey because the nuns had paved the way for Georgie. I complained bitterly of the beatings, the unceasing humiliations, the downright discrimination. But my mother refused to listen. How monstrous could they be?

> "Georgie did wonderfully... They loved Georgie so."

(My mother actually-spoke like this, in pretentious school teacherly lingo.)

It took me seventy years to figure out why: "they loved Georgie so".

I didn't have his advantages. I wasn't the bastard son of an Irish Roman Catholic priest.

Georgie turned out to be my Judas goat, conducting me to my own slow slaughter.

And thus, my mother and dopey little Janey succeeded in trashing my existence like it was a sick little joke.

Poor little Janey, equally the victim of my mother's stupidity; she was a child after all, devoted as she was to these monstrosities. She cherished them and abased herself in the process. She was their willing co-conspirator who gleefully, proudly wielded the Irish whip, clutching it as the nuns and priests cheered her on. She was their tool, their slave, their soulless, brainless zombie. Every year in college she marched in step, to her wreck and ruin, to utter perdition, sporting her iron collar, her mark of pride, the mark of the beast burned into her lost soul; down, down, down Fifth Avenue, in the Saint Patrick's Day parade, which only proves that indoctrination works, at least for idiots.

. . . .

In college I roomed across the hall from a guy who had gone to this very same Greek Catholic school I was denied, from kindergarten to eighth grade, ecstatically proclaiming that it was the best school he had ever gone to. He was Italian and claimed it was the happiest time in his life and that there was a waiting list to get in; that his father had to get up an hour early to drive him there. I suspected that he came from one of those enclaves of Orthodox Greeks trapped in Italy by history who felt a bond with the Orthodox Greek Catholics. The thing he could never understand, that he pestered me over and over and over about: Why didn't I avail myself of the sacred kingdom, enter through its golden gates. Why didn't I go to the school, the school he loved so much? He figured that if he asked me often enough, I would be able to formulate some rational explanation.

"But these were your people... the priests and the nuns... Your kinfolk... although they treated everyone the same... I loved those nuns and priests."

"Kinfolk", that's the word he used. What he didn't know was that my father had been a revered member of that community, a founder of their national ethnic center. And this college friend knew nothing of the alternate hell I had been imprisoned in. How could I possibly explain that my mean, dumb sister polluted my life and that they allowed her to do it. What sense did that make?

. . . .

But until the damned revelation, the unholy epiphany, the question always remained in my mind: why did my grandmother send her son off to the loathed Irish school, connected to a church she would never set a foot inside?

George, my grandmother's son, was embraced by the Irish nuns as if he were one of their own. He became their favorite boy; their pet, lavishing the most extravagant praise on him, making it impossible for him to integrate into any real world that didn't worship him. They gave him unassailable confidence, which served him well, no doubt of that. But they blew him so full of himself that he grew monstrous and learned to resent a world that didn't kneel at the feet of his own self-perceived preeminence. They arranged scholarships to Saint Michael's Catholic High School and Saint Peter's College.

I always marveled at how he managed to pull this off. Was he such a gifted con artist? He was smart but he wasn't that smart.

There was one particular nun, a kind of surrogate mother, who he would pick up and bring to his home for family occasions until her death. She would meet his children, who I was told, years later, resented her. Perhaps, she felt these children were unworthy of her glorious Georgie.

But Georgie paid a price, a terrible price. He had his prodigious brain stuffed and perpetually spoilt with the nun's and priest's pompous tripe. He lapped up their hatreds like a docile dog, especially their hatred of Jews. I never heard an anti-Semitic remark from his mother or his siblings but George would rant that the Jews only got what they deserved, from the Germans.

He insisted on the various illiterate Irish locutions: erl, berl, terlet and myriad others; a head-strong child, who at the very least knew how to speak English, I would insist on correcting him which earned me repeated beatings; after-all, I had television to teach me; who on television said "erl"? And this is the incalculable price Georgie paid for being the cynosure of inextinguishable idiots; he mimicked his mentors; even his own slighted siblings spoke English, while he, in deference, smugly adopted the patois of this reviled and rejected underclass for the mere fact that they worshipped him; so, he too sounded like he stumbled out of a bog. Georgie would announce loudly, whenever he rose to go to the bathroom: "I'm going to the terlet." I always found this perplexingly vulgar, the utterly unnecessary proclamation compounded by the mispronunciation. It was only later that I grasped my uncle's pathetic, cultural appropriation; watching Steve Allen, on his Late Show, who was himself Irish, mock his kinfolk for feeling it obligatory to declare explicitly that they "have to go to the terlet"; Allen found the custom peculiar and mortifying; worthy of derision and through his self-deprecating mimicry, made it sound hilarious. (George Carlin, also Irish much later, totally appropriated Steve Allen's routine without the courtesy of attribution.)

Where did Georgie get his intelligence? His mother was wily, shrewd, and cunning, if ignorant. Certainly not from the demon priest who dispensed ignorant, illiterate homilies, more accurately, harangues, sanctimoniously from the pulpit in his own bog argot; who existed for no other purpose than to have his ass licked. Was it the nurturing, from George's own mother, from the nuns; the infinite expectations, the meticulous cherishing?

. . . .

These Irish nuns were vicious and hated every ethnic group except for the Irish. They would brow beat and humiliate all-of these others among their pupils equally without distinction.

As a child I agonized, what was his secret? What made him so special, Georgie, this Slavic boy? Or was he Slavic? What did these nuns know that I didn't know, that I couldn't, for the life of me figure out, at least up until now and I'm supposed to be so goddamned smart? These are the life puzzles that we fail to

141

decipher at our peril. They <u>are</u> life and death. How could I miss it? He looked like a Jew, for God's sake. People said so. Georgie got more of my father's money than I did; but that was okay. He was family and if his father was a Jew; better still.

But even my mother was persuaded that Georgie was her father's son, her full brother, and told me so, many times, insisting too much, perhaps, about her special bond with him; so, there would be no mistake and I could act accordingly. I think she mistakenly believed that this familial obligation would work both ways; that George, like any good uncle would give me a helping hand when my time came; but this was the opposite of the truth; he seemed to be a reincarnation of his diabolic father, the priest, who crushed and humiliated me in every way he could conceive.

. . . .

There was one specific revelatory incident when I was 18 and half way through college and looking for summer employment. I had gotten my real estate license and was about to start working for a firm in New York City. My mother told me not to; that George would give me a much better job, as an executive, perhaps, a vice president, maybe, of George's own company: "that's the least he could do... he owes us that much. I financed it." What George made clear, but my mother refused to hear, was that George had made other plans for the 30 thousand my mother gave him. Self-infatuated psychopath that he was, he wagered it all, on Lockheed call options, certain in his enduring self-delusion that the stock would skyrocket, never even allowing himself to imagine that the stock would plummet, together with the Lockheed Electras, which promptly commenced dropping out of the sky like Canadian wild geese on opening day of hunting season. But it was not enough that he took my mother's money. He sucked out what little money his wife's family, her sisters and her mother, possessed on this crazy man's wild gamble. But what the hell did he care; the money wasn't his. (My mother had "lent" him $30,000 in 1960, but without a promissory note: which he paid back partially in dribbles; devalued 1980 and 90s dollars, only to further fund my mother's second husband's addiction to the track and cheap scotch whiskey, saloons; and Cadillacs) And so, I dutifully waited, by the phone, literally, almost, for over a week. But there was no call. I suggested to my mother that I call, but she rejected this suggestion, categorically, as totally inappropriate. I must wait; and wait I did for another week until the call finally came with the news that there was indeed a job for me, not as Executive Vice-President for the company my mother thought she funded, but a job for minimum wage in the stock room. The woman, of course, as I expected, was delusional.

· · · ·

This is the laughter of the Fiend who comes to sit at the edge of my bed, nudging me from my sleep with a broad grin plastered on his dead head to mock me in my final years; who would not let me die in ignorance and peace.

This is Rose Mary's Baby insinuated into my existence to steal my earthly inheritance, beat and terrorize me and slice open my veins to stand by vigilantly, gloatingly, to stare at the life blood draining out of me over a life time.

Why did this particular despicable priest single me out for especial persecution and more than any other human being make my life a living hell when I was most vulnerable? And I didn't figure it out. I didn't piece it together. I didn't come close. It was staring me straight in the face; all the pieces there. I inhabited the space so effectively, disguised as a child; but not disguised to myself. Me, the prescient little boy, the spy who heard everything; the unspeaking watchman who must have heard this, who definitely did, but couldn't make sense of it.

The puzzle's key had to be bestowed upon me on a salver, my own head on my own platter, to mock my stupidity; a gift I didn't ask for, a truth I didn't need to know. Not now, when it's too late, when there's not a damned thing I can do about it. The devastating moment of:

"Aha, that's it, that's what I missed."

The instant of existential derision. The world is absurd enough, without this. This isn't mere meaninglessness. This is a world in which evil reigns and Satan is king and exercises his will while laughing hilariously.

I think we love a well-crafted detective story, high level pulp, because of this; the final revelation when everything becomes perfectly transparent, when all the pieces fall into place as if by magnetic attraction.

> "Yes, yes, I see now what I missed. It was there right in front of me. How could I not have seen?"

We reread the book only to see what dunces we had been. But with life, we cannot re-read the book, we have no such luxury.

But this isn't even good fiction, but rather life, as gothic horror tale; my worst torturer having injected his foul seed into my family before I was born. You can't lock the doors; there is no place to hide; the beast is in the kitchen and sits at the head of the table and cooks inedible stew.

. . . .

My mother's mother was an immigrant who came to America as a child; who spoke imperfect English. Uneducated, she travelled in a closed tight circle of her own ethnic group. The neighborhoods she lived in were mixed, Slavic and Jewish, often speaking the same Eastern European languages. Or was she wilier than I took her for?

An Irish priest was a powerful man who could pave the way for his own son, who would also be hers. She would hitch along for the giddy ride. But this priest never did come through, never met his paternal obligation in any real sense, financially. He easily could have skimmed the collection plate; many did.

Many people, especially aggrieved ex-Catholics believe priests such as these are merely conmen and exploiters and that's convenient; it explains everything, but nothing. Black and white, stark good and stark evil usually makes for weak literature and bad "truth". The world is subtle, shaded, mysterious and profound. It is too simple to say this man was pure evil, the devil at work, case closed.

But, this man believed. He believed. I remember his hands trembling as he raised the communion chalice high above his head during mass. This man truly believed that he was performing a miracle, transubstantiating the bread and wine into the actual body and blood of Christ in his own hands. He believed that he himself was chosen by God. He wasn't one of these priests who raped boys with impunity and then trotted off to his chosen confessor, a man like himself, every week to make his easy peace with God. So, you say he was deluded, self-intoxicated and maybe stark raving mad. That explains nothing; and the fact that he did believe made him infinitely more dangerous. Perhaps it provided him with an easy dispensation to have sex with as many young boys as his stamina could suffer. A good flimflam man believes in his own blather and this priest was utterly persuasive. He managed to convince an entire church, a congregation; of credulous fools, you say? Easy pickings.

The man was haunted, wracked by his own guilt and conscientiously set the stage for a burnt offering, of himself, sending himself, he supposed, to heaven or hell, before an entire congregation of devout worshippers. He was a showman, no doubt about it. Would he have made history? Has any priest ever immolated himself during mass in front of a packed house? Was it some lost medieval custom, better forgotten? Why does nothing of his act show up on Google? The Jersey Journal has been digitized. Has the record been expunged? Did it even reach the papers, then? The Church rewrote history at its whim.

. . . .

Were the nuns Georgie's surrogate mothers, a stand-in for the priest, their emblematic husband, right next to Jesus Christ himself? But it took my father's money to lift my mother's family out of poverty. Georgie always promised to make his mother rich, to buy her a big house and fancy cars. Did she single out powerful men to get her with child? She was a Darwinist in a fundamental sense. To be a priest's wife was a mark of privilege in the villages she came from as a child; this, however, was the mark of the beast. In the villages the married priests were genuine shepherds of their flock. I remember the married Greek Catholic priests, warm and friendly, addressed by their parishioners by their first name: Father Joe, not Father Joseph mind you. What young maiden wouldn't hanker after a single young unmarried priest? The pastor of our church, (the Byzantine Catholic), was a real muzhik, a mensch, a real man with a houseful of children; not a swishing capon like the Roman Catholic priests.

My grandmother's experience with her demented priest must have been more than culture shock; this was another universe, alternate reality in a black mirror, a Bizzaro comic book anti-hero oozing and trickling to life. If a priest in her village had gotten a woman with child, especially a single priest, he would have helped with the support of the child, clandestinely.

My grandmother hadn't bargained on a psychopath with his alien ideals of sick celibacy. He must have come to loath her sexuality and to loath himself and especially to loath the beautiful young boys who always tempted him. It was the uncontainable yearning that lured him to slaughter; my own botched slaughter.

What did she think? So, what if the priest liked young boys better than he liked her. It's not like she had to live with him; that she had to witness it or procure for him. (Or was my set-up a procurement for sacrifice.) She was a practical woman. What man didn't have his peccadillos? Besides, he had a perfect cover. He was a Roman Catholic priest, untouchable, unassailable, perfectly safe.

. . . .

*[I am sad to report that Roman Catholic Latin rite celibacy has thoroughly corrupted, like a flesh devouring microbe, the Byzantine rite Catholic Church, in the last seventy years; under pressure from the celibates its priests no longer marry. In 1978 I attended a Byzantine mass performed by a priest who was flamboyantly, unembarrassedly, sissy. He was also certifiably crazy; offering the mass up to his, not so recently deceased mother; he intoned her full name, repeating it ten times during the service; sticking it in at every artificial pause; he no doubt believed in magic. During the sermon he also claimed to have been robbed the previous Sunday, carrying the church collections*

*from the church to the rectory and that the police refused to do anything about it. By the disjointed and contradictory way he told the story he convinced me that he himself had stolen the money. He pleaded that the "the biggest and strongest men surround him" and form a cordon as he walked from the church to the rectory. From what I could tell there were no "big strong men" in the audience, only very old decrepit men and women and children.]*

. . . .

George's son, my cousin, submitted his DNA to 23andMe and for some unknown reason opened the results for all eyes to see. Although "predicted" to be my first cousin, the shared DNA was so low at 7.65%, that he was in fact my second cousin or more accurately my half cousin, meaning that we had different grandfathers; also, his ethnicity, the proportions, were all wrong; 18% Eastern European as opposed to my 80%. Like me he had zero percent Ashkenazi Jewish. Blood will out and haplogroups don't lie. The R-Z16521 haplogroup of his father, through his grandfather, a recent mutation, is exclusively South Irish. The internet is ruthless and bombards us with information that we are ill-equipped to do business with.

Certainly, his "cousins", connected to his Irish grandfather, must be pouring in. It's only a matter of time before he connects with a cousin who tells him:

> "Ah, yes, there was this great uncle... my grandfather's brother, or was it his cousin... who was a priest at Saint John's Church in Jersey

City. He loved the little boys, he did. But his name hasn't come out on any of those godforsaken lists... Thank God... so few of them have. My father let out that he's mostly famous for catching himself on fire during high mass... while giving out communion. I hear he was a grand sight to behold with his cape flowing behind him caught by the wind from the window which he purposely kept open... pirouetting like a dancer... light on his feet he was, and a very fine dancer in his day, and his cape catching on the blazing votive candles... every one of them lit purposely... and him holding the communion chalice high above his head to keep the flames away. Some say he was trying to kill himself... to go out in a blaze of glory, in front of the whole congregation no less... holding the chalice high above his head like some crazy pagan priest trying to self-immolate... all shrouded in flames... he would have succeeded too if the busybody ushers hadn't spoiled the show... knocking him off his feet with a disrespectful tackle... rolling him on the ground like an old rug to put the fire out... spilling the wafers all over the place. I hear he never forgave them, nor did they ever usher again... not in his church. Busy mouths say he reeked of gasoline that day... which to give him the benefit of the doubt, was often used as a cleaning fluid... back then. He loved to keep his vestments clean. He loved his whiskey, though... none other than Bushmill's Single Malt would touch his lips."

I remember the story and remember catching the priest's theatrical performance, a mass earlier, the dry run before the conflagration, a taste of the inferno, and thinking to myself that that son-of-a-bitch is going to catch himself on fire. The nuns explained to us children that the actual body and blood of Christ scooted out of the wafers the instant before and only the un-transubstantiationated, plain bread and wine struck the floor. This is the way God works his miracles, they expostulated with a straight face. The question is why didn't he hand off the chalice to one of the ushers? Ah, the nuns discussed this too. The obvious answer is: because they weren't priests and were forbidden to touch the holy grail filled with "consecrated hosts" with their unclean, unpriestly hands; and besides it would have ruined the show; which was ruined by the ushers anyway. It must be confessed that none of the parishioners dared lay hands upon the holy priest and were frozen in their seats by the spectacle. The ushers, perhaps privy to his doings, which in their own minds unsanctified him, had no such compunctions. I only wish that the ushers were duly awed and left the priest untouched, to his own devising; they would dance the jig and feed the flames to celebrate in heaven on such a day.

. . . .

The haplogroup R-Z16521 is so recent a mutation, so rare and distinctive that they've connected it to specific names and families: R-Z16521, Michael Sullivan 1825- Feb 3, 1883; William Bartlett, b. 1784. Leon C. Fleming 1914-2006. Also, O'Sullivan, McGill, Stovall, Teague, Moody, Anderson, McCarthy, and Keith; all R-

Z16521 and Irish every one and welcoming each other to the "tribe", the very word they use on their websites; an obese, grinning fool, food smeared on his soiled shirt, opening his blubbery arms.

But little Georgie probably didn't know the secret either; nor did he ever figure it out. It's not something you told a boy back then, that your father's a priest, especially this particularly despicable priest. Although I'm not sure he knew how truly despicable this particular priest was. It might even have been considered sinful, certainly disgraceful to be the son of a so-called celibate priest. And so, he was sustained in his continuing fantasy that the nuns nurtured him for his genius only. Perhaps if he had known the real reason it would have tempered his runaway ego.

George was intensely proud of his Slavic roots; he spoke the language; a master of the Cossack dances, one expected to catch him, in a flash, catapulting himself onto his steppe horse at full gallop. Unlike his brothers; and his sister's first marriage, he married out of his tribe, which broke his mother's heart, she said. But that proves nothing, for "the Irish girl" he married was charming and pretty and far better than he deserved. I would go so far as to say she created him, made him human; she even taught him how to speak English; no more terlet. I think she even persuaded him to bathe more often, once a week, even. Prior he smelled like a rank animal.

The big question is, where on earth did my grandmother chance upon this Irishman in the year of 1928?

It is a characteristic of the human mind to seek patterns, to find order, where there is none; hence religions, complex philosophies and conspiracy theories; and especially, paranoia. We yearn for order and answers; even if those answers do nothing more than churn the chaos.

I pray that some lost Irish longshoreman or marooned seaman, beguiled by my grandmother's beauty, her long blond hair and green eyes, sought shelter from the storm and wooed her by his looks alone and the sound of his music. I pray, most of all, that it is not this lewd, loathsome priest. But I fear that it is.

# Orphans

Never underestimate the power of a photograph. There was one photograph of my father that I was always drawn to; that magical amalgam of silver residue fixed to paper became the most substantial evidence I possessed that he was once flesh and walked on this earth. It attested to more than just the physical existence of this one man. It was evidence of a departed state, before the fall, before the catastrophe, before I was born. Even when I was a small boy, I would sneak the album out and analyze that picture. It haunted, mesmerized me. I would study it as if it had some secret, some clue hidden somewhere in it and that if I looked long enough and hard all would be made clear to me.

It was not for my father alone that I would pore over that image. There was a beautiful woman in it, a princess in a magical kingdom, young and slender, with shoulder length dark brown hair, a modest print dress and only a hint of makeup, as if makeup would mar her unaffected beauty. My mother told me that this was her picture but I never once believed it, not for a second, since only a few years had passed since then and nobody changes that completely. I was forever looking for a resemblance but could find none. I think I longed for the beautiful woman, my real mother, as much as I did for my father. I secretly believed that this woman who masqueraded as my mother was in fact an impostor who had devoured my real mother and father, as a witch in a fairy tale might. The pretender was obese, with short frizzy hair, a permanent wave gone terribly wrong, bleached blond which she insisted was natural, whose makeup was caked on in thick layers which scared me as a child, as a horrifying clown might.

The photograph was not without its foreboding. It was populated by these alien children, "who ruined it", the woman who called herself my mother said. She called them the orphans, the morons, the wild kids who:

"…broke your father's heart and tore him apart".

One must be extraordinarily careful when speaking to young children. I took "tore him apart" literally and had dreams of bloody butchery. She despised them. But she had her point. The children didn't match the picture; they did spoil it. Here was the great man posing with his beautiful young bride with a baby in her arms in front of his great white house, which seemed to give off light, to glow on the summit of that hill. It was a jarring juxtaposition, Town and Country meets The Bowery Boys. Why did he allow them on his property? Another man would have let the dogs loose and run them off.

I had this incongruous image of him scouring the city slums, collecting the homeless filthy street urchins into his immaculate limousine, or coaxing them with bowls of food to come down from the trees or from out of the woods. They looked like they might turn on him in an instant; like feral kids whom he had displaced in assembling his estate and took misplaced pity upon. Underneath they looked dirty, hungry, stupid and mean, but scrubbed with a brush and brown soap and camouflaged in donated clothes that didn't fit, just for this occasion, a Sunday presentation put on to flimflam prospective adoptive parents by the orphanage matron, a cunning nun. My mother had no idea what in hell I was talking about.

Later still, I had gotten the idea that the photograph was really a sham, a setup, that this was all a charade, that the great man only seemed to be in command, but was the prisoner of these orphans, who refused to leave after their day in the sun, at the rich man's house, that they had taken it over and now the white house on the hill belonged to them.

The photograph revealed beautiful young landscaping with an intricate series of stone walls terracing the ground as it rose up the hill. My father had killed himself building these walls and planting these young trees, working himself to death or so my mother said. It turns out he did very little of the physical work himself. However, since he was in constant command, he created this illusion that he himself brought it into being by an act of sheer will, which one suspected must be incredibly strenuous. But this was a worn-out tune. The common thread was that he was culpable in his own demise. She never stopped blaming him for it. He was the love of her life and for that reason she hated him for dying.

Even more, she hated him for these children. And they were his children as I would only discover many years later. Not the disparate offspring of his late-night philandering, but every one of them his, from his beloved first wife, Elizabeth, and it is for this, especially, that my mother so detested them, evidence in flesh and blood staring out at her, proof that he had not loved only her.

She also hated his great white house on the hill, the summer house, the country house, because he had not built it especially for her. As far as my mother was concerned it was the first wife's house, Elizabeth's. My father had designed the house himself, failing to consult my mother, who didn't yet exist in any true sense. Every man before he dies should design and build his own house, a culmination of his dreams, a legacy of sorts.

As a little boy I begged to see my father's estate, with the great house from the photograph I loved so much. But there was always an excuse. It's unsafe, it's falling down, structurally unsound, should be condemned, out in the middle of nowhere, impossible to get to. She let that house rot to pay my father back for God knows what. She selected the tenants, the kind that would guarantee to transform it into a slum in the least possible time.

Finally, we made our trek to the earth's edge to behold this house, twenty miles west of the George Washington Bridge, no man's land. We parked at the foot of the long driveway like burglars casing the neighborhood or like down-trodden evicted peasants approaching the former master's mansion with averted eyes, incapacitated with fear and trembling. Even with my father buried in the ground his house exerted its power. She was afraid to come nearer to it, as if the remains of his magic emanated from it. So, we stood there like cast-out children ogling the house on the hill, still aglow but with dirty peeling paint. I half expected the orphans, dirty and naked again, to attack with rocks and sharpened sticks from behind the overgrown shrubbery. I asked why we didn't just knock at the door and ask to inspect the property. After all, it did belong to us. My mother, aghast, was especially taken aback by the "us", that I should include myself in its possession. She never really believed that she was its owner, that it ever belonged to her in any real sense. Deep down she was still the frightened, cowering girl from the wrong neighborhood, (the sassiness was a facade) and this was the master's house. But she got her revenge but good as the proletarians so often do.

I would learn that the beautiful lady in the photograph was, after all, not in any genuine sense my mother. The lady was a fiction, a creation of my father's overwrought imagination, held together only by his will, a brief, bright flicker, ephemeral, just as the house was wholly his conception and would crumble simultaneous to his decomposition. He was like Tito who held a country together by the sheer force of his personality. With his passing all hell broke loose. He was a director on a movie set, an impresario, plucking his ingénue out of the rubble she subsisted in, kicking, screaming and making her a star without her volition.

> "Your father never allowed me to be myself. He wanted to make me over in his own perfect image of what a woman should be. I was always starving. He said that if I got fatter by one pound, he would divorce me."

I have this picture in my mind of my mother with a big piece of black chocolate layer cake clutched in her chubby fist, taking huge bites, with the crumbs falling like dark dirty snowflakes, covering my father's face as he lay dead in his casket. The binge began as my father grew cold and would proceed unabated, according to the photographic evidence.

"Your father made me take off my make-up before he would take me out in public."

This story grew with retelling until my father is strong arming her, rubbing her face raw to remove the make-up with a rough wash cloth and brown soap. She liked to deck herself out like a painted lady, which to her was the height of fashion. She regarded her taste as impeccable as most people without taste do.

My father spent money like an old-moneyed, Anglo-Saxon Protestant. He put it into his beautiful white house on the hill, with its exquisite ceramic tiles and marble and hand rubbed hard wood moldings of cherry and mahogany and walnut. He treasured fine antique furniture and amassed a collection of antique oriental rugs, which he purchased at auction, during the depression of the thirties, from those same old-moneyed families, ruined, but whose style he admired so much. He spent a "king's ransom" on landscaping the gardens encompassing his house. He had his contractors scouring the tree lined moneyed avenues for the finest examples of stained-glass windows, which by then were considered old-fashioned. He actually bought old front doors, right on the spot, in exchange for a brand-new front door, snug and weather tight, installed at an unbeatable cut rate price; a free-wheeling capitalist ready to make a deal.

Well-dressed, he believed in a classic wardrobe. He had custom tailored suits that never seemed to wear out. And he had expectations that his wife would dress accordingly, that she'd be satisfied with a "respectable Republican cloth coat". He didn't believe in ostentatious displays of wealth. You had to hide what you had behind the high walls of your estate, for propriety's sake. The way my father parted with his money galled his second wife. She tallied up every tree, every flowering bush translating them into the fur coats and lavish hats which he cruelly denied her.

> "Can't you plant small trees and bushes, eventually they'll grow big."

> "Yes, when I'm dead and six feet under."

But she saved most of her vituperation for his antique Persian rugs.

> "They're filthy. How can you live in other people's dirt?"

Used to hand-me-downs, she treasured everything brand spanking new. Of course, he had all of the carpets cleaned upon taking possession, but cleaned meticulously, by hand, by a picked specialist in Persian rugs. After the interment she had the prizes of his collection really cleaned, a second time, thoroughly, and all of the gorgeous colors, natural dies, ran together, producing a uniform hue of muddy pink. And when the fringe, the continuation of the essential warp threads, wouldn't come white enough she had it cut off, amputated, the rug gutted, the handiwork of a clumsy eviscerator and a new dead fringe tacked on, sewn on in its place, of ridiculous white fluffy cotton. She had his antique furniture stripped down to blank wood, the patina of two hundred years eliminated by a refinisher from the phone book who eradicated the "grimy film" and then she abandoned it all with the great house to the cherry-picked tenant.

Most of all, more than anything my father wanted his children to be accomplished, to be educated. He yearned for doctors and lawyers and scholars and statesmen. And this is where he went terribly wrong. This, more than anything, is what crushed him. His first two sons were intelligent, and he loved them. He would do anything for them. He would never dream of striking them; why? There was no need. But, my God, the rest, they were like demon seed, and he at a loss of what to do. They wouldn't learn and he couldn't teach them, nobody could. He beat them, he threatened them, he terrorized them, but it was they who broke him, into pieces. I don't think he ever faced up to the realization that these children just might lack the native ability. He thought they were spiting him. And eventually, when nothing he did worked, they wound up doing just that, spiting him.

My mother once claimed that the only reason my father married her was to have his own private teacher for his children. And I think in the beginning she actually did try, tried very hard, briefly, back when she existed as that brief flicker, just long enough to be photographed. Back when my father was alive everybody loved his beautiful young bride, even her stepchildren. They said they were proud that their father had married such a beautiful young woman. But, however hard she tried, her efforts were doomed. She kept going to their school, and talking to their teachers at a time when such parental intervention was not encouraged and barely tolerated. She had been a public-school teacher before she married my father and she was hoping that this would help her to intervene on behalf of his children. But I guess she was making too much of a nuisance of herself and in her conferences with the teachers and the principal she seemed to be blaming the school for their problems. I don't think it ever occurred to her that the children of her husband, no matter how she felt, could be anything less than full of promise. She asked for yet another conference with the principal, and the man had simply had enough, or maybe he was just exasperated and he lashed out in a manner that would be unthinkable today. It was a speech that my mother would repeat word for word hundreds of times. It was a cruel speech at a time when IQ scores were kept secret. It was cruel in that it wounded my mother's feelings toward my father, perhaps irreparably. How could he produce such progeny? She resented them when she presumed that they had great potential, that they were of superior stock; now in her own mind she had every reason to hate them even more as imposters, interlopers.

The principal raised his voice as if he were chastising a child. Madam, (in her memory people were always calling her Madam whenever they were reprimanding or admonishing or giving her a speech):

> "These children are doing as well as can be expected.
>
> "They are all, every one of them, borderline morons."

Or did he use the term mentally retarded? In 1943 could he still get away with "moron" or is this my mother editorializing?

> "The school and its teachers can in no way be held responsible for their want of academic proficiency."

And then the principal did something which seems especially cruel. With great moment, he put on his reading glasses and began reciting from a paper that he had held in his hand like a weapon or a trump. And it seems that he was getting his revenge for all-of the times my mother had dared to bother the busy school authorities with her silly intrusions. This would be the last time. She would never dare to show her face again. He began in his best dramatic voice, as if proclaiming from a stage. He read each of the names of my father's younger sons and his one school age daughter. He read the full name, first, middle, and last and then the IQ number. My mother began to quietly sob as he slowly pronounced the judgment. The numbers would be seared in her memory. It was as if he was reading a roster of the dead. She told different versions of different stories at different times but she always got the numbers right. I think she fancied herself a raconteur.

Of course, this was a lie of omission, for dramatic effect, or to make his point. He left out the two oldest boys with the very high IQs. But, they were never the subject of any discussion. Both had recently graduated and gone to college. Their grades had been excellent. And he left out Stephen, fourth oldest, his IQ high but his grades deplorable. (I think it is important to note that school administrators were much more brutal in their assessment of intelligence; "borderline mentally retarded" referred to the eighties). It is the supremist of ironies that my mother's cherished first born was her very own little near idiot; but when the schools threw it in her face she refused to stand down for her own blood. I remember her screaming at the nuns: "My daughter does not have an 85 IQ."; they were even suggesting a special school. With the help of a hefty "donation", the nuns, dishonest to their core, managed to revise the test results and loose her SATs which divulged a combined math and verbal of 622.

I was never able to discover whether my mother divulged this information about my father's children to my father, whether she even dared to. Or whether she saved it, savored it, delivered it like an obscene coup-de-grace at the moment he was down, at his weakest, at his most vulnerable or when he was in high dudgeon, or ranting at some incompetency or perceived idiocy.

It isn't that he couldn't see what was obvious to any fool. Gerard, the one with infectious charm and movie star good looks was never addressed by his given name but invariably as: Dummy, Idiot, Fool, Moron; a sure way to nurture your offspring. It was Gerry who confessed when drunk that the happiest day of his life was the day his father dropped dead. "You don't know how lucky you are. He would have ruined you the way he ruined us."

Like the old Protestants he so admired, my father aspired to establish a dynasty. How do you launch a dynasty with idiots? It threatened everything he lived and worked for. He wanted to give his sons everything that meant anything to him, money, power, position, education. He was willing to sacrifice everything for them. He was a Darwinian who despised socialists and here he was flooding the world with inferior goods. It's the last thing he meant to do. He was also convinced that he could transform his wife, that the world was perfectible, yet he couldn't educate his own children.

. . . .

My mother was like one of those atrocious tropical flowers that feed on putrefaction. She only needed the compost of the dead man's loot to really swell into a monstrous bloom. The heavier she got the more she spent on garish clothes to adorn her increased girth. It never occurred to her that if she only lost weight and scrubbed off her thick clown face, she'd look more beautiful in rags. She shopped every day the stores were open. She'd wear the clothes once or twice and hand them down to her poor friends who returned the compliment with hate.

Her fur coats could depopulate *The Central Park Zoo*. There were foxes and minks and lynxes and ermines and stone martens and beavers, a veritable menagerie strung up dead in the closet on wooden hangers. I learned how a wardrobe could drag an exchequer to its knees; and hats, crazy, bizarre hats, a hat for every occasion. I remember a bird of paradise that seemed still alive perching there on her stupid head, as if she didn't have sense enough to shush it away.

But most of all I remember the sable. For the sable coat she sacrificed a twenty-four-family apartment house, among the properties my father left exclusively in her name. One of her friends almost cried:

> "How could you do it Annie? How could you sell an apartment house to buy a fur coat?"

> "Olga, when I walk into a room with that coat on, I feel like a million dollars. That apartment house never made me feel like a million dollars."

The sable wouldn't last. The pelts were defective, rotten, chemically treated, improperly bleached or something; the skins started splitting. The furrier was a crook, out of business. That million-dollar feeling existed exclusively inside my mother's vacant head. It certainly didn't elevate anyone's estimate of her, quite the contrary; it only confirmed in their minds what she was. They said so, in front of me. A child's perspective is unique because people speak too freely. They're like spies; treated as if they can't hear, or they're so stupid they can't understand, or if they repeat what they hear nobody will believe them; mute witnesses, as if invisible. Or did they purposely speak this way in front of me. And if I repeated it to my mother?

"He's only a boy, Annie. He misunderstood... he imagined it. We weren't talking about you. How could he think such things? What terrible thoughts he has about you. How could he repeat such words? We were talking about that female down the street, the one who lives above the saloon."

Laughing all the while up their sleeve. This was better than saying it straight to her face, instead, increasing its venom by channeling it through the voice of her own child.

My mother was too taken up with her own bounteousness to ever suspect. She looked upon herself as a generous benefactor. She handed things away without charity, with the demeanor of the grand dame dispersing her largess. And everyone had to pay a price, a grave price, a ritual humiliation. Different people perfected their genuflection to differing degrees, some guaranteed to extract the maximum cash with the minimum obeisance, but always obeisance.

Her brother Steve had his act down pat like an old Vaudevillian, a kind of shuffling lackey routine, a "step and fetch it" that would move my mother to tears with his hang dog demeanor, averted eyes glued to the floor, puppy dog devotion jumping to catch her every word and hanging on it, even repeating it, shaking his head up and down. He showed up every two weeks for his hand-out, which amounted to doubling his take home pay; but there was a price to pay. He never got it without the obligatory kowtow. He was a born bootlick, a genuine saint my mother proclaimed him, her eyes welling at the very thought of his devotion.

It was Stevie who would stupidly spill the beans, stopping his act cold turkey, when his sister latched onto her anchor, her second mate ("the decrepit old piece of sewer sludge") who she was obliged to keep, in a manner to which he had never been accustomed. It was this second mate who served as the conclusive vengeance against the first husband; who dared to die without her permission; she would fix him good with her own slow self-annihilation, her abasement, degradation, humiliation; lashing herself to this markedly old, an ugly man, a Fred Mertz clone, but not so pretty, with loose limp drooping turkey waddle and bulging gut, washerwoman hips; encumbered also, with his even more repulsive daughters. No matter what you said about her first husband's children, they were all comely in their own way, handsome even, some especially so, and genuine geniuses next to this number two, who if he knew how to read, kept it secret. She plundered her inherited assets with a vengeful determination, and threw in my own held-in-trust patrimony as a bonus, an icing on the sugar cake, bestowing it upon the Ass-headed Bottom, besotted; so that this bum, who never pushed anything but a used-up rust bucket could possess a brand-new shiny Cadillac driven straight off the showroom in a yearly ceremonial until his lingering death from dementia; he didn't have far to travel. After it was much too late to matter much, I had assumed the position of reigning guru supplanting her brother Georgie; and she asked me as she became accustomed to do, as if I now knew all the answers; as if I too, were the walking talking Encyclopedia Britannica:

"Was Bill evil?"

"Yes"

"I always thought so." She answered.

Did she think so when he forbade her to see any of her many Jewish friends; when he wouldn't allow any of them to attend "his" wedding and certainly not allow them inside "his house"; when he invariably referred to Jewish males regardless of their age as "Jew Boys" and Jewish woman as "Jewesses" with a hiss. A man of such profound ignorance that he pontificated at the dinner table that it was perfectly "normal" for a straight male to be "serviced" by a homosexual male: that is, to become the beneficiary of oral sex. All-of his friends without exception accepted this as gospel, so he insisted. This is not as bizarre as it sounds; the same dogma is enunciated with custodial authority by the Jon Voight character in Ray Donovan: telling his grandson that it's perfectly alright to let your friends blow you, "just don't take it up the ass"; words of wisdom from a grandfather. But then this, my mother's second spouse, had many dear homosexual friends, all of whom he seemed to revere; his "best man" at his first wedding was just such a flamboyant homosexual male, ostentatiously out in the open long before it was respectable. (This same best man was notorious for lavishly entertaining the homosexual priests from Saint Peter's Prep, just down the street from him in Jersey City.)

. . . .

By the time my mother's brother Stevie turned-up for his habitual remuneration it would be much too late, her purse having been capably ransacked by the sticky fingers of her sermonizing spouse and his siren call to the track; his perpetual round of cheap saloons. Stevie, a family man who worked two jobs and shied away from the bottle and wouldn't be caught dead inside a bar, took one look at this semi-employed wage-earner with a powerful thirst for the drink and a weakness for slow ponies, and knew enough to reassess the lay of the land and figure the jig was up. There would be no more cash stuffed brown envelopes sealed with scotch tape. The well was being sucked dry much more systematically, closer to the source.

# Stephen

It was through my cousin Joe that I had my first run-in with Stephen, who had the same father that I did, which father was a proud and devoted graduate of the Bing Crosby School of Parenting. Joe had a score to settle with Stephen and he wanted my help in leveling the field. Joe was a bundle of righteous grievances which seemed to fester and multiply as the years went by. However, with Stephen there might just be sufficient reason, just cause.

Years later I would come to realize that although Stephen reputedly was highly intelligent there were major portions of his brain that did not function properly, or didn't function at all. Stephen was a thief, but a stupid, clumsy thief, who did far more to harm himself than he did to the people he stole from. He didn't break into strangers' houses. Rather, he stole when the opportunity presented itself. So, he stole mostly from people he knew, people who might have trusted him once, but would never trust him again. Stephen, if you left him alone in your house, would rifle through the drawers and take only a few choice items of the most value. Being disorganized himself, it never occurred to Stephen that other people were organized and knew exactly where everything was and would immediately notice something of value missing and since their houses had not been broken into would conclude correctly who the thief was. But then he would forget he stole the item, or not comfortable with the idea of himself as a thief would fabricate some scenario in his own head to explain possession of the stolen item. I think after these repeated mental acrobatics he actually came to believe that these ill-gotten goods belonged rightfully to him. This compulsion to grasp every penny that came within his touch was tangled up in his megalomania, a frugality or rather abstemious stinginess that would lead him to leave, upon his long-awaited death, all his earthly goods, his fastidiously, methodically hoarded treasure, his house included, not to family or "friends" or wife, even, but out of visceral spite, to a nest of voracious pedophiles, whose church he worshipped at, who he fantasized clutched the back-door keys to his concocted paradise, which would prove to be his hell and that of the priests, in happy league together.

So, it was one day, years after the visit with Joe, Stephen was ineptly snapping pictures with an expensive camera he had no clue about. This was, it itself, suspicious, because Stephen had no personal possessions of genuine material value. He had no clothes, no books, no records, nothing. He was beggarly, monk-like in his tightfistedness to himself and others. The niggling little that he purchased was always of poor quality. Even the food he ate, which he preferred to consume in prodigious quantity, was third-rate. Suspicious. I had an identical camera vanish from my car trunk during a former stop at the derelict house, now Stephen's flop. Inventing a fib so Stephen could save his face, I asked him how he liked the camera and whether he was finished with it. Stephen shot back a crafty laugh:

"What bull shit is this? What are you trying to pull?"

He went on about buying it in New York, the hard bargain he drove and even the details of what the salesman said. He couldn't shut up. "What did you pay?" He came up with a price a third of wholesale. However, I had engraved my initials, a kind of minuscule logo in an inconspicuous spot with one of those electric engravers. With the evidence in his face, (which he argued was a scratch), he insisted that I left it at his house:

> "You should keep better track of your stuff; I have one exactly like it... you must've walked off with my camera... mine was in much better shape... you probably pulled a switch... If you're going to get nasty about it."

He didn't give it up without a struggle. The next time I saw Stephen, years later, was more by chance. I was passing by the great wreak of a house and made a turn without thinking, as if on automatic pilot; or guided by a ghost. I guess I was just curious to see if the house was still standing. I didn't expect to see Stephen scouting the perimeter like a vindictive evicted tenant looking to torch the place or an inept burglar casing it. He recognized me, "oh shit", as I slowly drove past, jolted, since we had seen each other at most twice before. No making a graceful getaway, as hard as I tried. He acted as if I were his long-lost brother. He dragged me into the house so I could meet his new "bride". I would have expected to see a young pretty thing but I was forewarned. A woman who looked like his mother, a mother who had given birth late in life, embraced me warmly, as if I actually were Stephen's brother. She didn't seem to grasp that we barely knew each other, that we had been raised separately in two distinct households, that the resentment for the second family by the first was so strong that the two families didn't acknowledge each other's existence. It seemed rude to say:

> "No, no, you don't understand, I'm not really his brother brother."

Stephen actually seemed to be going along with the gag, without volition. I don't think he ever explained the family context to his "bride", had never gone into the intricacies of the resentments and might have been embarrassed by the fact that his family was so broken. And so, I played along too.

My mother's second husband, the sewer sludge, had described Natasha as the ugliest woman he had ever seen, which was very unkind and could not possibly have been true, (this from a man, no looker himself, who had two daughters who were qualified to enter just such a competition and who usually knew better then to cast aspersions too broadly lest they regroup to militate against him). She had an extraterrestrial look, other than human.

She had been a nun, a dark secret that she revealed only to her most confidential friends. She had been compelled to quit the order under curious circumstances, conveyed conspiratorially in hushed tones:

"One of the older nuns, reputed by all the other nuns to be a saint, Sister Margaret Alice, called me into her cubicle so that we might pray together. I was so honored."

The older nun recited the prayer in a low drone and took Natasha by the hand and pushing her gently by the shoulders, guided her to kneel at her feet, as she sat in the big easy chair all the while continuing to pray, as if this were all part of some prescribed ritual that must be exactly repeated. She took Natasha's head in both her hands and guided her head into her lap, with great authority and confidence as if this was a critical sacrament performed with a ritualistic regularity, all the while continuing to moan with a drone the long monotonous prayer which the dear old saint knew by heart. Natasha bolted from the room in a panic straight to the Mother Superior. The Mother Superior listened with infinite patience as if she understood everything and she smiled and wagged her head up and down:

"I understand. I understand everything. We all love Sister Margaret Alice. You were dreaming, my child. This is quite to be expected from the young novices who aren't able yet to distinguish dreams from reality, and who love Sister Margaret Alice so much, that they long, in their confused imaginations, for some closer contact."

Natasha stood her ground, could barely speak:

"This was no hallucination."

The Mother Superior's attitude switched in a wink. She turned angry and impatient:

> "I have no time for this nonsense."

Natasha would be given time to think about it. If she persisted in repeating these vicious lies then:

> "We will have no choice but to conclude that we were all mistaken in believing that you had a vocation."

Having a vocation meant that you were chosen by God for the religious life. Only God could give you a vocation. Since it was unlikely that God would change his mind about who he had chosen, anyone the nuns wanted to drum out could never have had a vocation in the first place. It was more than a mistake it was a sin, a sin of pride. Catholic school children were always taught that there was no greater sin of pride than to think you had a vocation when you really didn't have one. The nuns and priests were especially skillful in recognizing the positive indications of a vocation in their charges. Many a young girl came running home ecstatic with the news:

> "Sister Margaret Mary says that she sees signs of a vocation in me."

Only to be told weeks later after failing some minor ordeal.

> "Obviously I was totally mistaken in believing you might have a vocation. It was sinful of you to believe that you were so chosen."

Obedience and devotion to those who have already recognized that they had been chosen by God was a sure sign that you too had been chosen. I think Natasha was happy to leave the veil without being drummed out of the Catholic Church absolutely. Her history in the nunnery seemed to have no affect whatever on Natasha's complete devotion to her Catholic faith. She never connected the two.

Stephen owed his life to this woman, Natasha, who was fond of reminding him of just that fact in moments of public ridicule she gloried in subjecting him to:

> "If not for me you would have lost your Daddy's precious house and that would have been the end of you. No more Stephen... Poof."

Although he had gotten the house for a pittance together with a substantial sum of money, he had mortgaged it and lost it all on some ridiculous business he'd gotten into, a business about which he knew absolutely nothing. He filled his basement, which he had emptied of his father's glass, with obsolete machine tools purchased at auction which required a small crane to deliver. But he never upgraded his electric service to power them. This was a residential zone and a three-phase service would have alerted the inspectors and the town that he was running a factory out of his basement. So, they just sat there rusting, unused and mocking him. The bank was about to foreclose when Natasha came up, like a sugar daddy, with the full ten grand to pay off the mortgage note, in return for a marriage certificate and her name on the deed. (She wasn't Russian, in spite of the name, but born in Italy to a communist father with a fixation on things Russian.)

When I got inside the house, I saw what I thought was an apparition at first, this huge woman, she must have weighed three hundred pounds, draped in a moo moo skirting the floor. She moved so fast for an old, large, fat woman that I thought she might be on some sort of a wheeled contraption. Whenever she came near, Stephen would nimbly step aside like a matador two-stepping with a bull to avoid being gored head on. At first, I thought the woman was blind. But it was only Stephen that she was blind to. I suspect she might have been aiming at him. She was deaf to him too and would speak over him as if he weren't speaking at all.

I was introduced to the woman with great ceremony as if we were both personages of great importance. She took my hand in her two rough peasant hands and shook enthusiastically with exaggerated vitality and spoke a bizarre lingo rapid fire. Natasha spoke to her in this same outlandish tongue and I was able to learn that this, in fact, was Natasha's mother, who now inhabited the house as proclaimed landlord. They both spoke with the exaggerated animation of silent screen actors. Natasha would translate, but it was like one of those Japanese monster movies with English subtitles where there seemed to be no correlation between the translation and what was said on the screen. Natasha said that her mother liked very much that I was tall and had blond hair and thought I was very handsome, like a movie star. And then Natasha said Stephen's name and the old woman repeated it, grimaced and spit, then shook her head forcefully back and forth.

Natasha said that her mother would not believe I was Stephen's brother, that this was not possible. She was angry and thought we were trying to make fun of her. She was not a woman to be trifled with. I made reference to the language they were speaking and Natasha said with complete equanimity and a perfectly straight face:

"Do you speak Italian, Tommy?"

(Nobody called me Tommy except my closest school day friends. This was a usurpation but that's okay.) She was implying that this was an incredible feat, to know this lost language spoken only on the far side of the moon. I had been to Italy. I knew what Italian sounded like. This was not Italian, although there were a few Italian words thrown in here and there as a gag. This was gibberish. I surmised that the old woman had lost the ability to speak any coherent language because of senility or madness and that Natasha rather than embarrass herself and her mother simply faked it and played along imitating her mother's voluble nonsense. After all her mother had never spoken English. It was Italian she had lost the power to speak and who would know the difference? Natasha, knowing her mother many years, was able to guess most of her mother's needs and if she guessed wrong who would her mother complain to and how would she complain? On some fundamental level they understood each other perfectly.

During the visit Natasha would repeatedly interrupt herself to ferry food to her mother in what appeared to be a perpetual process. I counted four melted cheese sandwiches, each with four slices of yellow cheese and soaked in butter. These were her snacks after a gigantic dinner. Natasha would raise her eyes to heaven, in awe:

> "God bless her, what an appctitc, and at her age."

She implied that eating was some extremely difficult feat, performed at peril to life and limb and her mother, a magician, uniquely able to pull it off. Once before, I had heard my mother exuberantly praise gluttony in the selfsame lyrics, after her brother had devoured fourteen large ears of sweet corn, as he sat there catching his breath, satiated, stuffed to bursting at last, with tiny bits of corn all over his face, even in his hair,

> "God bless you, Stevie, what an appetite."

......

Without the benefit of this future experience, I moved onward with Joe toward the blasted house, which had glowed so magically, once, in the photographs of my youth. Stephen had finagled the house seven years before as a fractional portion of his share of his patrimony. He stole it by paying off an appraiser to value it at one fifth its replacement cost. He swindled my mother, who was easy pickings, and I guess he swindled me, ten years old at the time. Back then I didn't know he existed. But the swindle suited my mother's purpose perfectly, who hated the house, Elizabeth's house, the despised first wife and the appraisal proved perfectly what she had been saying all along, that the house was worthless, the house my father adorned with exquisite detailing while she suffered without fur coats. As for the other children, they allowed themselves to be rooked, anything to pry the house out from the possible clutches of the detested second wife.

The house had been in Stephen's hands for seven years now, just long enough to finish the ruin the tenant had begun. The lawn had been worn bare by the traffic of running naked feet, a horde of children, dark skinned, who seemed to be coming out of the trees, playing a vicious version of hide-and-go-seek amongst the fallen tree carcasses and withered bushes. I half expected the wild kids that haunted me as a child to be made substantial and pelt us with dirt and feces, screaming obscenities and begging for blood. At first, I assumed they were Stephen's children. But Stephen was childless and would remain so, always. Stephen had cut the house into apartments, into a tenement really, rented the rooms to the downtrodden, people worse off than he was. He cut it apart himself, with make-shift partitions. His materials were rummaged from the dump or salvage yards, from houses that were being demolished, pink toilets and worn-out bath tubs, rusted metal kitchen cabinets, repainted, junk that wasn't worth the trouble of hauling off much less installing. He was a real real estate mogul just like his dad. Although I doubt that he ever called his father "dad". I'd half forgotten that Stephen was one of those wild kids in the photograph that stole my childhood imagination. Although not a "borderline moron", he belonged entirely to them, one of them. The two oldest, brightest boys, one reputed to be a "genius", dead now, from suicide, were absent from that picture, rightfully so; they didn't belong. And so, I stood at the foot of the great white house, as if it too were insubstantial and would vaporize with an explosive poof precisely at the moment I approached.

Joe and I couldn't get all the way up the driveway. It was blocked by a felled tree, a once magnificent big blue spruce which seems to have been cut down ineptly with an ax purposely to block the way and keep the nosey neighbors at bay. We abandoned the car at the barricade and took the long trek up the winding drive on foot. As we got nearer, we could hear what sounded like the periodic shattering of glass. Was the house being systematically wreaked by trespassers? The crashing was ominous. Finally, we could make out what appeared to be a scaffold fifty feet in front of the house, gerry-rigged of scrap wood. It was crooked and appeared to wobble hazardously as a lone, short, fat man, huffing mightily mounted make-shift stairs to a platform without railing about twelve feet off the ground. Was I about to witness an impending execution? Who was this man going to hang; something or someone? Himself? I was waiting for the hangman's noose but it never materialized. The fat man, from a distance, seemed to be a clown lost from his circus, struggling with something he held with great difficulty in front of him, then the noise, the noise we had been hearing, the sound of crashing glass.

Although Stephen perpetually had a ready, congenial smile, there was a forced nervous quality to it. His eyes would dart from side to side and though continuing to smile there was terror in his aspect as if he half expected someone or something to jump out from its hiding place and pounce on him at any moment. This time his smile was more nervous than usual, as if he had been caught in an obscene act, forbidden, ritual slaughter, and blood still dripping from his hands. His hands were cut and he was dressed funny.

I didn't know then that he usually dressed funny. He had on shorts that were salvaged from  worn shiny dress pants from an old suit that were cut off above the knee, held up by a worn leather belt with an extra notch clumsily punched into it off center,  black nylon Suppose support stockings that came up just below the knee, old leather dress shoes that had once been highly polished to camouflage the wear; a relatively clean, white, Fruit of the Loom style tee shirt, a size too small, accentuating his bulging fat; his dark hair slathered down with Brylcream, stickum or Vitalis, neither for sale anymore. He had on big eyeglasses with thick dark plastic rims. He was a sight to behold. If you told him he was dressed funny he'd think you were messing with him and wouldn't believe a word of it. He seemed to lack all critical ability, incapable of seeing himself as others might see him, entirely closed off, no antennae out. I've known stupid people, dumb as shit who seemed to know what was going on around them at all times. He was always talking, never listening. And he didn't modulate his behavior or conversation according to the person or situation, a true democrat and that is crazy.

At first, I thought that he was about to bolt, turn tail and run like a rabbit and that we would have to chase the fat man through the woods until he ran out of steam and gave up like in a demented children's game. Instead, he shook my hand, warily, and pulled his own hand back prematurely, as if he suspected I wouldn't let go, that this was a trap, worked out in advance between Joe and me. He knew why Joe had come. Joe had been pestering him by phone for a year now and Stephen would promptly hang up; that was before the phone company cut everybody off permanently. It had to do with a boat and promised pay for work.

But Stephen had in mind to turn the tables and impress us into service in this preposterous ritual of mindless demolition. I didn't know then, that this was subsistence money lying at our feet. There was a heap of broken colored glass at least four feet high with strips of lead accentuating the ruin. We caught Stephen red handed hurling a beautiful panel depicting a forest scene and a knight in armor and a magnificent coat-of-arms, which we could just make out in the rubble.  He bragged of having "mined" a ton of lead, and was just about ready to make his "run to the scrap yard". He was proud of his "killing". He talked funny too; with no gift for language. I think if he hadn't been so isolated in his own head someone might have told him that he could get more from an antique dealer, that there were people who specialized in this. He might not have believed them. He believed what he needed to believe.  It damaged Stephen's ego to take advice, which partially accounted for his steely ignorance. He wasn't the first one to break up stained glass for its lead content. Stained glass had been out of fashion. I had seen it as a child, the barbaric act of exquisite stained glass crashing against the concrete sidewalks, as if Vandals had been loosed; but that was years before, in the early fifties, and this was 1962. When I objected and suggested that the glass was valuable, he got nasty, as if I had accused him of being a fool, of knowing something he didn't know. The basement had been cluttered with it and he needed the space so that he could carve out a home for himself and rent out the rest of the upstairs. My father had collected stained glass, systematically arranged on wooden racks, in neat catalogued rows, filling the cavernous basement.

"What was he going to do, open a museum?"

My mother mocked behind his back to her floozy, boozy girlfriends.

The year before Stephen had invited Joe to the lake (a short walk away from the house, a resort in a bygone age, sucking in its last, desperate gasps) the summer after Joe's father died when Joe was sixteen. Joe, elated, somehow got the silly notion he was going on vacation. The minute he arrived Stephen set him to hard labor mixing concrete and mortar and piling up rubble stone walls with the promise of pay. This was more like boot camp without the three squares. Joe came with a kayak, (which he had borrowed) cushioned with a threadbare quilt strapped precariously with clothesline to the roof of his mother's dilapidated old Buick, which knocked like a band of castanets, as it labored up the long, weed clogged drive. Joe suffered under the misapprehension that he'd get to paddle in the lake. I think he purposely left the kayak at the lake thinking he'd be coming back.

He was hoping but he was never invited again and that was the real, though, secret, offence.

Bottom line, Stephen sold the kayak and refused to pay Joe for his work. Joe expected me to help persuade Stephen of the error of his ways. The astounding thing is that Stephen was not in the least apologetic but quite the opposite.

Joe:

> "I want my boat back.  Where is it?  What did you do with it?"

For a minute I actually thought he was going to search the place.

Stephen:

> "The boat was a piece of crap.  It was taking up valuable... rentable... storage space.  I should charge you."

Joe:

> "Valuable storage space?  You got nothing but shit in that basement."

Stephen:

> "I threw it out... I thought you didn't want it. You know... you should take better care of your stuff. You're very careless."

Joe:

> "How could you get rid of the boat?  I mean, how could you do that? It didn't even belong to me.

I'm going to have to pay my friend Tommy who I borrowed it from."

Stephen:

"I don't owe you a damn thing.  You ate me out of house and home... I was going to send you a bill for all the food you ate.

Joe:

"I broke my ass all summer working for you."

Stephen:

"I took you to Randall's Island... the amusement park... spent a fortune on you.  You did shoddy work... shoddy work... and besides you goofed off most of the time."

And on and on in an avalanche of contradictory self-justification.

"I'm not gonna give you beans."

Stephen screamed.

(Joe saved up until he finally did pay his friend Tommy for the kayak. The opposite of Stephen, Joe had a particular skill in nurturing friendships over a lifetime. Tommy died young which broke Joe's heart.)

And then, out of the blue, apropos of nothing, Stephen had a proposition, that we treat him to dinner out. I got this impression that a burger joint and a beer would have been heaven, that he hadn't had a decent meal in some time. Although fat he had a starving look. So, when dinner on us seemed like a no go, he dejectedly delved into his empty refrigerator and plucked out a head of cabbage, like a rabbit out of a hat. Beaming radiantly, he carved the rotten portions neatly out, and fried the remainder up in saved bacon fat from underneath the sink with the misplaced panache of a gourmet chef in a four-star restaurant. He had been on permanent KP as an army draftee and fancied himself a cook. Stephen had flashes of wit and good cheer. (Strangely enough Stephen could be good company). I suspected that he had been subsisting on this fare for some time, that he had sacrificed the kayak reluctantly to buy cabbages and onions, an insurance policy against starvation. However, from the look of it he might have scrounged the food from the garbage dumpster in back of the local A&P before the dogs could drive him off. From the looks of him he put up one hell of a fight; he was all banged up. It seems peculiar, the possibility of starving to death when he could knock on any neighbor's door, neighbors who had known his father. If nothing else there was pride left in him.

Many years later, I lost my mind and took Natasha and Stephen to a half-way decent restaurant. Everything was ala carte, entrées mostly under fifty dollars, this back in 1988. I didn't drink at the time so two people could share an appetizer, have two of the best entrees and get away paying a total of  under $130 with tip; considering the quality, not so bad. Be careful taking someone out of their natural environment; it's cruel and upsetting for everyone and condescending. What I knew but seemed to have forgotten was that Stephen and Natasha were huge fans of cheap all-you-can-eat buffets, where waddlers lined up to fatten up on gargantuan quantities of chow unfit for human consumption. The two of them would jubilantly pile their table high with soups and salads and various inedible sides, heaps of entrée upon entrée, and plenteous desserts all of which made you nauseous just witnessing it. And what would any reasonable person expect, cruelly ripped from their comfort zone; they did their best to replicate where they felt most at home: "Jack's All-You-Can-Eat Emporium." They started with drinks which I refrained from, perhaps inadvisedly:

> "What are you a teetotaler or something? Are you one of those Protestants? There's nothing wrong with having a drink once in a while. It's good for you."

They both ordered appetizers. I attempted to share an order of oysters Rockefeller with my girlfriend:

> "What are you cheap or something? Let her have her own."

Which they insisted on ordering for her, which she left mostly uneaten. And so, the nightmare went on all evening. They ordered soups and salads and various side dishes. I attempted to take charge; it was supposed to be my show after all. But there was no reining in Natasha and Stephen. So, me and my girlfriend waited, waited and watched amazedly as they gorged unembarrassedly. I tried to explain that the entrees were quite generous but to absolutely no avail. And then they ordered dessert for everyone; but here I stood my ground; going to the waiter privately and cancelling my own order. Then came the obligatory coffee.

The waiter rolled his eyes when delivering the check, over $600; $700 with tip. Being a regular customer, I'm convinced I wasn't charged for everything. This was by no means an expensive restaurant, 'till now.

. . . .

In a cloud of blue smoke, he appeared, once, all hopeful smiles, tentatively tapping while peeking through the glass, in anticipation, through the front door of his grandmother's house. It was a long haul from the lake, in the days before the Interstate, blowing the last of his dresser change on gas, stomach growling viciously to the time of the staccato misfiring of the trusty old Chevy, billowing blue smoke in his wake. She barred the door with her substantial bulk.

> "She left me standing in the street and calling me a bum, a bum... her own grandson."

> "Don't you have a home...? Don't you have a home...? Don't you have a home?"

He would quote her down the years to come. Why did that phrase so capture him, stick in his craw? Why did he repeat it so many times? Because he didn't have a home, not since he was thirteen, the day his father dropped, "prematurely dead", stricken, as the obituaries used to so poetically lament, "in his prime", of heart failure or was it failure of the heart? With the death of that one man, he would be homeless until the day he died, in spite of the mere technicality that he legally held title to the house his father built, the dream house (the closest thing to Eden he would ever come near), the summer house, the lake house, and he could never part with it.

He never showed his face at his grandmother's house again. He materialized at her wake. He showed up at all the funerals, which he seemed to love, invited or not. (The only reading he warmed to were the death notices.) They were the real heart of his social existence. Death gave a context to his consciousness. He bloomed in that sickly flower stink imperfectly masking the scent of formaldehyde and putrefaction. I still see him beaming, mindlessly; seemingly oblivious to the corpse just inches from his feet, just within reach; having a grand old time of it.

# Jon Breedlove Panders

My devout Roman Catholic dimwit sister actually married one of these priest's catamites; hubby, possessed by a "whale eye"; corpulently thick, ugly, androgynous, anemic; pasty alcoholic; a "homo", as my mother ignorantly and tactlessly pigeonholed them all, but missed him. This is the hand of God working his wicked way: cosmic justice; black magic.

Janey played out in real life the lead in *Light in the Piazza* without Mimieux's beauty; pathetically ingratiating herself into this family that was so stupid and talked such drivel that they didn't notice her handicap. Any minute I expected them to start pelting her with chocolate; would she ever fight back? She fit right in; possessed of a simple-minded devotion to the Madonna, the Virgin Mary Immaculate Mother of God, which insinuated her, if not at their table, at least into a secure place in a near corner.

There is an accepted subculture of homosexuality among Catholic schoolboys and their beloved priests. The pretended shock of the faithful to unveiled priest boy-rape is a perfected, practiced act, honed over centuries, a masquerade to shield their enabling complicity from the greater uninitiated non-Catholic public who weren't in on it. This was an ingrained culture, like a secret society of cannibals, close knit, tradition bound, formal dinner every evening. They had been doing it for so long they took it entirely for granted and didn't think twice about it. Shame? Does a native cannibal feel shame? This is his cultural heritage that must be protected at all costs. Remorse? They adored the taste of human flesh, its incomparable lusciousness and the good hunt for it; they gloried in it and simply pitied or dismissed those who didn't. It was a prime reason for their being.

Jon Breedlove Panders, that was his actual name; you can't make crap like this up; falling down drunk, waxing ecstatic about his wonderful, idyllic schoolboy days and his cherished Father Herbert W. Rogers, S.J.; he of the beret and purple opera cape, pied piper trailed by dutiful goslings, entourage of gunsels, dedicated, more than willing catamites. Rogers, compassionate, magnanimous man of Christ, never laughed at Pander's teensy little child's dickie like the girls did; they had their limits; Rogers could close his eyes and imagine a six-year-old; he was in heaven. This priest was his savior, confessor, dispenser of easy absolution exchanged for a quick blowjob for the priest; no doubt sorely missing being fucked in the ass (please excuse the coarse language but euphemism demolishes the truth, makes the poison palatable and reduces us to domesticated imbecility; the language is important here; the good father didn't "molest" an endless number of young boys, he "fucked them in the ass" or better still, inserted his penis into their anus, if you prefer ridiculous delicacy; for God's sake; and if my crudeness offends you take it up with Rogers; or better yet take it up with the pope) by the little holy man; tears in his eyes; Panders proclaimed this godly man a saint; which priest would join in league with the notorious Cuntsler, tireless champion of terrorists, saboteurs and wreckers, in 1973, that diabolic year, to hound the university for "full recognition" of the University Homosexual Club, of which this priest was the proud and active faculty chairman, tasting tirelessly of its subjects; which Club back in those heady days vigorously lobbied for the ineffable glories of pederasty; having been granted "the right to open discussion and a place to meet on University grounds" which wasn't near enough for the pint-sized priest, who none-the-less couldn't help crowing in defeat how they "achieved their immediate objectives" and further bellowed: "If you allow any minority group to be discriminated against, you're in for trouble"; who propagated his contagion, diseased and loitering to the ripe and rotting age of 95, in 2007, tended by his brethren at inordinate expense and deposited with Jesuit esteems, requiems and halleluiahs, in hallowed ground, (laid in the dirt by Farenga Bros. Inc., Directors, who, if they knew, would have saved a buck and heaved his cadaver into an open cesspit) with a paid obituary in *The New York Times*.

These priests didn't have the decency to commit their crimes quietly or in private. There seems to have been this nauseating need in them to advertise, to flaunt, to shove it in your face and laugh or giggle. Rogers loved young boys, unembarrassedly; would plant these young, dainty, sweet little androgynies on his mantle, so to speak, in front of the classroom facing him; so aboundingly, burstingly, delighted with his catches; glowering, swooning over them; eyes glued, positively melting, like he couldn't stand to be away from them. His captive audience, complicit; Catholic school boys, inured, oblivious, brain-dead, hadn't a conscious clue. (Catholic school-boys are uniquely immoral,

194

committing the most outrageous sins, only to run weekly to their chosen confessor, to emerge from the confessional as pure as the driven snow, wiped clean, reinvigorated to "sin" again.)    Rogers, outrageous, would strut around with these young trophy boys like they were showgirls hanging on his arm or hard won child brides, prizes secured through protracted, hard negotiation with the fathers, late into the night over cheap blended Scotch whiskey proffered by the priest over tap water ice provided by the father, the nominal host and a bottomless bowl of bar nuts, little broken peanuts, purchased in bulk in big used brown paper bags stapled shut, the daily leavings from the local gin joint down the street; which always saved a backroom for the priests, right next to the stinking can.

# Panders, Senior

I am reminded of my sister's father-in-law, a man almost entirely devoid of admirable attributes: fat, lazy, mean when drunk and often drunk; inexplicably arrogant for an entirely ignorant man, wedded obscenely to his Roman Catholic Church. He missed his calling. He was loved completely by a charming woman who worshipped the ground he walked on, even until her early death. She was unduly impressed by his degree from one of those parochial colleges of indoctrination which inexplicably allowed him to teach in a public high school, proving how sick this society is with its profligate accreditation standards, failing to separate Church from State.

I remember travelling through three hours of rush hour traffic, arriving depleted, to be at her wake, to share my grief; what right had I to grieve so much? And choosing my words, crafting them ever so carefully in my mind as I sat bumper to bumper, to try to console him, which I thought would be useless in any event; (words mock and taunt us because we fancy they would outface death). I found him instead, beaming ecstatically like an idiot who had found the master's whiskey. I don't think I ever wanted to beat a man so much in my life, to his senses. Here he was all puffed up and full of himself, the life of the party, strutting like a peacock; a man who was loved by a woman. He didn't even have the decency to properly mourn for her: to grieve, to rend his garments, to tear out his hair, to run howling through the streets. He was intoxicated by priest rot, empty stupid words uttered by barren desiccated spiritual eunuchs who never loved or were loved by a woman, incapable of loving anything but themselves or pretty young boys in their fevered imaginations.

> "She's up in heaven now... watching over us... praying for us."

So sayeth the Idiot with euphoric grin and eyes rolled heavenward.

Rage, rage against the dying of the light. Do not go gently. Do not go gently. This is no good night.

# Saints Out of Charlatans

Thomas Bucknell, from his archives, untitled, unnumbered:

> The Roman Catholic Church is habituated to making saints out of charlatans. There is something blasphemous in presuming to write God's book of stars. There was one particular mountebank who had all the presence of a demonic carnival barker, with his mad monk's eyes, but without the sexual prowess of the authentically charismatic Russian, at least not with the ladies. He nauseated a solid minority of the faithful reigning as he did on the early days of TV, neck and neck with Uncle Miltie.
>
> Later on, past his prime, he exuded what passed for oily charm on the television talk shows, appearing on Johnny Carson to tell the uplifting Hallmark tale of one of the staunchest of the Roman Catholic faithful, a desiccated leper, eaten out limbs, crawling on his belly to catch up with the holy man as he traversed the jungle quick of foot; to partake from the fakir's very hands, into his diseased stubs, hungrily, the genuine body and blood of Christ. Carson, in disbelieving horror as much as shock, with a journeyman's professional, practiced poker face wondered, almost out loud, what mad-house this creep, steeped in his own brand of dementia, slithered out of.

The priest with the mad monk eyes fell upon hard times; ostracized; a falling out with the all-powerful archbishop of New York, who he had best not fuck with; ostensibly about powdered milk money but really a jealous rivalry over matters of the heart.

# Hemingway

Hemingway's wet fecund prose is succinct, laconic; its legacy was done-in by the cut-rate copycats latching on, unfatted leeches flaking off unrequited, bloodless, like dead dry skin, desiccated, mold infected.

Hemingway's prose was distilled poetry, especially immune to obvious mimics; epigones with razor teeth devoured by acclaiming him, drowning him, choiring an avalanche of Halleluiahs; unacknowledged idiot progeny with unnerving caricaturistic similitude, stomping up to the bottom of his castle keep, squinting up, slobbering to claim their patrimony, which will teach you to fuck with the native girls who only look pretty, notwithstanding their tight young pussies pulsating; but squeak and speak gibberish.

The Hemingway sentence perished from too many inept descendants. It will be resurrected by a nameless savior, god-sent, who never heard of him. His worst imitators sound like deponents seated, handcuffed, before a court stenographer. Or are his characters dictating a telegram? To whom? Certainly not to each other.

Fine writers don't deliver a message they cast a spell. Most of them haven't a clue as to how they do it. What Hemingway does is more difficult than it seems. Pare down your prose and you run the risk of self-evisceration, seppuku, a painful procedure, especially when done properly. Remove what you think is excess baggage and it turns out to be a vital unheard-of organ the purpose of which will be discovered by some obscure unlicensed physician twenty years from now who flunked out of a Caribbean medical school. If you want to convey simple information or write an operating manual or a how-to book read Strunk and White or whoever; none of these ever wrote poetry nor do they have any idea what poetry is; great prose is poetry. Hemingway wrote poetry, so did Fitzgerald in a different way. Take out all the excess words and you run the risk of taking out the mortar that holds the bricks together. Expand your vocabulary; expand the language, rival Shakespeare. Shakespeare used 31,534 different words; 14,376 words appeared only once. It is estimated that he knew 35,000 more words that he didn't use; would that he had. As far as big words, the bigger the better; and never, never use a thesaurus except to remember what you knew; you must own the word; it must live within you. Searching for the right word is like searching for an exotic beast thought to be extinct in a tropical rainforest only to realize it belongs to you; sports your collar. There are not half enough words in the English language to express the mind of man, pathetically small as it is.

And if you're so arrogant as to think the proletariat is stupid, write to them in crayon on big poster boards carried by homeless men decked out in dirty clown suits, jumping around and pointing to it, like the updated sandwich board men, by the side of the highway doing an erratic d t's dance to get you to get your taxes done.

But never forget that Hemingway's style is a perfected act; it is a stylized naturalism, if I can call it that. It is craft but with all the screws showing for effect and the pieces hewn smooth with a razor-sharp ax.

It is like the method actors that try so hard to be real that they bust a gut. Who in the world acts like this? Who manages to exist teetering on this edge of hysteria? Brando is just as mannered as any stage ham, as mannered as Olivier. With the early Brando we may forget that he is acting for a moment; he pulls us into his whirlpool so we can drown with him but we always pull back, come to our wits, in time to see the stage he's on. With Olivier we never forget the stage; we hear the machinery creak which drowns out the speech. Olivier was persona-non-grata in old Hollywood; the moguls hated him; knew he couldn't act, at least not movie act, which is all they cared about. Olivier himself tells the story of one of the Jewish moguls coming down to the set on a regular basis to berate and belittle him publicly and loudly in front of the other actors; for his lack of acting talent. He tells the story to prove what idiots and vulgarians the moguls were. But these men had superb instincts, far better than his. He only proves how right they were. Olivier quotes another critic, and he had countless, who said that he finally revealed his "true self" in *Spartacus*; his chameleon camouflage finally peeled off; but his camouflage consisted of flashing lights. Both Dustin Hoffman and Raul Julia had the discernment to loathe Olivier's "acting". Kael, crazy and contrarian, as usual, just worshiped him. He ruined Shakespeare. Olivier is the embodiment of poshlost; resuscitated by late night talk show hosts who wallowed in bad taste and foisted it upon us.

The Academy gave Olivier the Oscar for the most hilarious over the top caricature to hit the big screen. Was this an inside joke? "Mister Wheelock … Mister Wheelock". The whole movie was a hoot. Even Gregory Peck, not famous for his comedic touch, was hilarious.

Never, ever quote your critics, even to prove what fools they are.

Steve McQueen, who I admire, far more than Olivier, quotes one of his early reviewers who compared his looks to that of a Botticellian angel crossed with a chimpanzee. He thought it was funny, or so he said. Since I esteem McQueen, I wish he hadn't said it.

The American public craves self-deprecation; they want their elected gods to wallow in it: "shucks, twere't nuthin". Reagan had it down to a science, concocting his persona from a mishmash of old B-movies. Sometimes he forgot what was real, if he ever knew. He practically toed the ground, shyly looking down when he spoke. He took a page from the book of Charles de Gaulle who never would have made it in America. But that McQueen image sticks, indelibly.

. . . .

This Hemingway, of which we speak, was the same Hemingway, the magician, who scoffed at Fitzgerald: like a tough little boy sneering at a delicate but talented sissy little boy, and Hemingway never once came close to forgetting that where he came from the Irish were scum. Hemingway wrote as if he were part of the club, which never let Fitzgerald in and never would. We like to forget how much of a bigot he was and how he and his first wife, Elizabeth Hadley Richardson, could joke hilariously about going to "Wopland".

# Newspeak Nazis

The Christian majority has no monopoly on mind control; there are newspeak nazis of every denomination. (And there are those who would give me infinite grief for using the word "Nazi" in this context.)

The following exchange was personally witnessed at Hunter City College, City University of New York in its graduate program in the year 1969.

A student holding forth made the catastrophic miscalculation of using the politically charged and racially insensitive term, "Old Testament", which led to a withering barrage of venom from the professor (John Hollander, a preternaturally ugly man, which ugliness cannot be voiced or acknowledged today or in any way alluded to; even to avert your eyes would be tantamount to mocking lepers, paraplegics or the war disfigured; the unspeakably ugly are a protected group in line for reparations; this Hollander, fifth rate poet, proclaimed best friend of that other similarly afflicted beast, the swaggering, bragging serial rapist of underage undergraduates (Bloom); who scribbled so excessively, compulsively, that his fatuities alone stuff an entire volume; and though I applaud his dogged, if juvenile defense of what he affectedly, brazenly calls the "canon"; his picks are so problematical that he is his own worst enemy, and mine; by his silly selections, undermining his squabble).

Hollander:

205

"The use of the term 'Old Testament' is offensive to a great many students in this class... I assure you it is not their Old Testament. The proper name is the 'Hebrew Bible'... I insist that in the future... in this classroom... you refer to it properly. Otherwise, you will be asked to leave."

The student was dumbfounded, speechless, almost:

"Are you reinventing the language now? 'Proper name'? Whose proper name? What you're doing is... subversive. The language is loaded. Every time I open my mouth, use language, whatever language that might be, I buy into a whole system of prejudices that I don't necessarily accept. If we redefine the language every time we speak, communication becomes impossible.

"'Define your terms', the most 'jesuitical' of shouted tactics to devastate your opponent by knocking the language out from under him... Now, are men with clubs and crucifixes in long black dresses going to lay in wait for me? ... (It is to be noted that he pronounced jesuitical with the s pronounced as zju, a shibboleth which revealed that he had more than passing knowledge of this reviled order. Even the dictionaries get it wrong.)

"Are you going to rewrite the dictionaries? This is 1969 not 1984... not yet, not yet. I can guarantee you that to most Christians it is most decidedly the 'Old Testament'. In case you haven't noticed they've appropriated it as their own. You might want to pretend that

Christianity doesn't exist but every time you write the date 1969 you testify to its existence... to its ascendancy. I'm sure you'd like to change that too... to hell with the chaos it creates.

'My grandfather was a proud Jew and a defiant atheist and he despised the Christians but he would have detested someone like you. You have your impregnable position of power; your irrevocable tenure and you use that authority like a club to pummel all those you imagine to have offended you. You Professor, and I use that appellation advisedly, are a pompous ass."

This was his moment of triumph; or was it? What the other students couldn't see is that his eyes brimmed full. He calmly collected his things to the infinite perturbation of the professor and ceremoniously walked out never to be seen again, not in this professor's classroom or any others in this school at least. These professors formed a tight clique; you offended them at your peril. I know for a fact that he never got his tuition back and he looked like he could have used it. This event was more cataclysmic than anyone could have understood; the end of an intended career, a life path altered irrevocably; the lost wasted savings of a struggling divorced mother who had few options. Why couldn't he keep his fucking mouth shut? Couldn't he learn to just play the game, a little bit and eat shit and smile like all the rest of us.

(There was no proof that his grandfather was in fact a Jew; but under the circumstances it sounded too good to be untrue; it was a family rumor or rather a rumor he heard from others about the family; the family denied it. He chose to believe it and would nod or shrug in mock reluctance when questioned about it.)

But there was more to it; there always is. He found this teacher excruciatingly mind-numbing; the other teachers merely unendurable. Sitting still and listening to them was punishment enough. He found most of the books he was required to read worthless and not worth finishing; and finished them only as an exercise of a steeled will. As obedient students we are expected to listen mutely in our seats to fools prattle on about less than nothing. And this the other fools regard as positive; so much so that they have named the inability to tolerate fools as a disease.

All the progress of humankind has resulted from just such deficient beings, who refuse to sit; who refuse to take notes; who write instead of read; who create; instead of consume the swill served up to them in dented dirty metal prison bowls as if it were manna from the gods. Being well-read is vastly over-rated by the soi-disant literati; the canon can be used as a bludgeon to pound us with. The vast majority of books are not worth reading and they adulterate, contaminate any style a writer might strive to develop. But it is not only an original writing style that might be ruined, there is the danger that the brain itself might be clogged with nonsense not worth refuting. "Reading, after a certain age, diverts the mind too much from its creative pursuits. Any man who reads too much and uses his own brain too little falls into lazy habits of thinking." Albert Einstein.

I have a dream that I'll see this student's smiling face, alive and well, once again, on the front page of the literary supplement to the New York Times for winning the Nobel Prize; an unfamiliar author whose books, unknown, went unread in America; famous in Europe, living in France.

# Bill Cosby and Predator Priests

From the files of Thomas Bucknell, uncatalogued, undated. It should be noted that Bucknell died in 2003 before the Cosby controversy broke open; although Cosby's antics were well known, infamous in the industry. I have no possible explanation for its contents.

> Bill Cosby got away with raping white women and black women too, because he told his white audience exactly what they wanted to hear, that Black people were responsible for their own problems. Cosby was untouchable. It could only be a black comedian who finally had had enough of Cosby's self-serving bullshit.

> Cosby is like the Roman Catholic priests. They were allowed to rape as many boys as they liked as long as they recited the right magic words at the end of any confession, no matter how vile. How many monsters did these priests send back into the world on a weekly basis with a wiped clean conscience? These are psychopaths skipped loose; these the friendly fiends cleansed of all their sins, enabled, refreshed, empowered to go forth into the world and ruin more souls. If this is not blasphemy, presuming to forgive in the name of God Himself, what is? This was their currency, medium of exchange, which aggrandized them, the jingling, shiny silver in their empty pocket.

There is nothing more amoral than the Catholic schoolboy who trots off to his priest every week and comes out of the coffin-like box reborn, rejuvenated, reinvigorated.

"Deinde, ego te absolvo a peccatis tuis in nomine Patris, et Filii, et Spiritus Sancti. Amen."

Ego te absolvo, I absolve you; I, I, I, ego, ego, ego; who the fuck are you to absolve anybody? Say the magic words; the duck comes down; the slate washed spotless no matter how heinous the crimes or how often committed; like cracking open the prison gates of hell; go forth, with a slap on the back; come back next week, same time same place and bring a little tidbit for the good father, something to share with him, so that we may pray together for your eternal soul:

"What did you do with her liver, my son?"

Pouring the slops back on the deck, the innocent slip into the sea and drown. A true angel of the Lord would sit in the confessional in disguise with a 45 magnum in his lap, and God's thunder clap in his pocket:

"You did what with her, my son?"

BOOM, BOOM, BOOM; blown to hell. We need Charles Bronson with wings in the confessional, undercover.

Shortly before he was hanged by Poland for war crimes, Rudolph Höess, former commandant of Auschwitz returned to the bosom of Holy Mother

Church, like a wayward son, to the Roman Catholic Church of his youth, having once when young perceived in himself a vocation, a special selection, touched by the hand of God to become one of His priests. On April 10, 1947, he received the sacrament of penance and was granted absolution by Władysław Lohn, S.J., provincial of the Polish Province of the Society of Jesus. On the next day this same Jesuit priest gave him the actual body and blood of Christ into his mouth, the most sacred sacrament of his church, Holy Communion. In five short days Höess would slough off his mortal coil with the help of a Polish rope, and so long as he didn't have impure thoughts or masturbate, in the meantime, the glory of the kingdom of heaven would be his for eternity.

Cosby's proclaimed indictment of black women's slack morals and non-existent parenting skills fed right into the hidebound beliefs of the grateful whites who flocked like supplicants to form long lines to kiss his dirty ass; they loved it; ate it up, like dogs eating their own vomit; he got two prolonged standing ovations in Melbourne Florida... after the revelations; of all places, Melbourne, beloved hold-out bastion of the Ku Klux Klan, proud murder capital for the Christmas 1951 slaughter of civil rights workers Harry T. & Harriett V. Moore who organized the first Brevard County Branch of the NAACP; a bomb blew away them and their house and their fine dust settled on all Brevard, a permanent, indelible curse; a great hurricane will come and wash it all away, Please God; fittingly famous for its crooked judges; they named a "Justice Center" after them in mockery; no doubt the good old boys shared a keg and a raucous drunken laugh over that one.

"'Five, six children, same woman, eight, 10 different husbands or whatever... ... Pretty soon you're going to have to have DNA cards so you can tell who you're making love to. You don't know who this is; might be your grandmother.'"

# Letter from the Catholic Harvard

November 2, 1962

Dear Father,

You have to save me. I just can't stand it any longer. I've made such a terrible mistake.

I'm sorry I didn't tell you sooner but I just couldn't. I know how you feel about the "stinking Papists". I just didn't see that I had any other options.

Aunt Sally called it the Catholic Harvard, which was ridiculous and was willing to foot the entire bill including a preposterously generous weekly stipend and I just didn't think I could turn her down. I've saved almost all of the allowance money. I've saved it for you, Dad. How is the new job? I'm so proud of you.

I sometimes feel I've died and gone to hell. This place is a looney-bin with the inmates as trusties.

You wouldn't believe the stuff they talk about: the shroud of Turin, the sighting of the Lady by some uneducated peasant girls in a dump and when they're going to reveal the predictions she made to them. They go on about whether Mary Magdalene was really a prostitute. They talk about the Trinity, the Immaculate Conception, the virgin birth, that the Eucharist becomes the actual, the actual body and blood of Christ and that even a mass murderer who tortures and rapes little children could go to heaven if he was really, truly sorry, and made a good confession thereby proving God's infinite mercy; but an innocent child that wasn't baptized couldn't get in, neither could anyone who died before the atoning death of Jesus, neither could John the Baptist, because he wasn't baptized, not by Jesus anyway and that's the only way that counts. They take this stuff deadly serious. I thought at first that it was an elaborate put on, some-sort-of-a lame initiation. They consider this nonsense intense intellectual conversation. Those who can make you believe absurdities can make you commit atrocities. Anybody who believes crap like this is capable of anything, any crime.

And it's not like they are all stupid. That's the frightening part; they're not. It's like some essential part of their brain has been removed, all critical capacity burned out with sulfuric acid poured into precise holes drilled into their skulls. Either that or they're born slaves or they have somehow been reengineered into thralldom. These are all geeks who have formed a tight clique; a union of girly boys dribbling spit, panting like beaten bitches in heat, sucking up to the wolfish sissy priests; Catholic school boys jostling in line to lick the asshole of these ersatz holy men. I was told that the admission standards are somewhat exclusive. But they are looking for a particular type; then there's the self-selection. Who else would want to come here but the kind that are here? The term Catholic University is an oxymoron. To call a Papist a Catholic is an absurdity, buying into their big lie; there is absolutely nothing "catholic" about the so-called Roman Catholic Church; it's like surrendering the field before the battle has even begun. It just proves that by corrupting the language we corrupt our souls and surrender even the possibility of conveying reality.

And they all have bad skin. And they're all fat, not necessarily overweight but fat, soft, even the athletes; like they lack muscle tone, hardness; they all look sick, like they do filthy things, gorge on putrid, maggot infested meat. They dress badly and eat like pigs and speak in these heavy low-class accents, not English, really.

And they're self-important, self-intoxicated, even. The fact that they don't know how to eat, don't know how to dress, don't know how to speak, are ill-educated doesn't bother them in the very least. They're too pig-headed to hang their bloated pig heads in shame. They're Catholic: God's chosen ones, with their own exclusive back door into heaven.

There's a careful selection process at work here. It's like wheat gone rotten that's been sifted and resifted again and again until all the iron is out, all the grit, all the germ with nothing left but a fine worthless white dust devoid of nutritional value puffed into an insubstantial breeze to eventually vanish into nothingness.

And this school is a mecca, pulling as if by magic magnetism, the homosexual Catholic high school boys, their numbers legion, from far and wide, who form a coterie here, a protected class, the coveted, cosseted, coddled darlings of the priests. The priests indulge them, spoon-feed them their peculiar, inbred pap, which these boys are uniquely receptive to. And, their numbers are inordinate, all out of proportion, or maybe they just seem so, so unembarrassed, glorying in their special, blatant, provocative eminence. They make gross, lewd passes with impunity and immunity, a license, or rather dispensation, which would be preposterous, and likely perilous, in any normal non-Catholic school.

There was is one particular initiate, or inductee, John Soldo, who is an especial favorite, the honey of these Jesuits; their mouths water when he opens his, discharging his drivel with ineffectual gush. John Soldo is engaged in a personal scrutiny of the idiosyncratic mannerisms of Truman Capote and takes them as his own; although he never quite gets them right, which is usually the case with impersonation, which becomes caricature. John Soldo is a vicious bitch and doesn't take rejection well; he doesn't take it at all, and exacts his own peculiar revenge. He's not in the closet, either; there is no need for it; it's his milieu; he's in his glory; he positively revels, exults, wallows in his in-your-face homosexuality, with the priests cheering him on, he, their devoted acolyte.

But the Jesuits don't fix their attentions exclusively on these, their cherished, chosen ones; they cast a wider net. I learned very early-on never to be alone with one of these priests. But it's like all the students and their parents are in on it. It's like this is the way the game is played and if you don't know the rules you'll be locked out. I haven't seen an overt nod and wink but it's there, just beneath the surface or a quick nod when you're not looking. This is their club. They are all collaborators, just as guilty, guiltier than the prime perpetrators. Let them have it. Let them have each other. They deserve it. Let them send their sons off to be buggered, send them off like lambs to ritual slaughter for an empty pocket full of change.

Evil in high places is an incubator of evil; it infects and spreads the pestilence like a medieval plague house. The predator priests run rampant unembarrassed by their boy-rape. And if the minds they infect are locked shut, it does not inoculate them against the infection; these voluntary internees are incapable of any sense of smell, they carry the infection with them like shit on their shoes spreading it as they go about the world. And what do they become: fifth rank attorneys thieving and padding their rates, prosecutors mercilessly entrapping the merely avaricious, college professors as dumb as a post thoroughly demoralizing their charges by the impenetrable depth of their stupidity?

Also, I found out that cousin Eddie, Doctor Eddie is a big imposter. His really nice guy routine is a racket to suck you in. By never making any waves, by bending over backwards, never disagreeing, he's avoided scrutiny. His whole life is a fraud, volunteer doctor for all the sport's teams, the CYO, Boy Scouts; team doctor isn't that what he called himself; ready supply of boys is what it is; to play doctor with. He's part of it; one of them. They must have some sort of spy network, scouts looking out for prime meat. I've had two of these come up to me grinning like idiots, wanting to know if I went in for the same things as Eddie, wanting to give me their number, wanting mine. When I told one of them Eddie was married, he almost busted a gut and said: "You're not serious" and then "I thought he was going to become a priest. His priest buddies must be broken hearted. I guess he made a deal. Maybe she likes to watch." I guess his wife is in on it too. I made the mistake of telling this to Eddie when he came up to see me. He wanted to make sure the shackles were good and tight. Maybe he thought it was time to make his move. I ruined it for him, rained on his parade. I don't know what possessed me to tell him, to stick it in his face like that; it was a wicked, reckless thing to do. Maybe I was trying to get back at him. I got sick when this all happened, sick in the pit of my stomach. I had to vomit. You have to remember that with my mother and Aunt Margaret, Eddie was on a pedestal, a paragon of virtue and hard work, to be admired and imitated; no, someone to emulate. The earth had shifted off its axis, which is ridiculous; I'm embarrassed to say that, embarrassed that I made myself vulnerable, that I'm not made of tougher stuff. These people are worse than murderers; they are devourers of souls; they eat you up. I know I haven't been in war, that I haven't been hunted down in the streets like an animal or tortured on a rack. But this is in some ways worse, more nightmarish. This is the demons in disguise as saints. Where do you turn? Who do you tell? Satan had more dignity, was a Prince of the realm compared to these lowlife pigs.

I don't know if Uncle Mike knows, whether he's in on it. But how could he not know? From what I was able to learn, when Eddie was president of the student body at Regis, which made him General, or whatever stupid name they called it, he preyed upon the younger boys with the collusion of the priests, offering his choice picks to them, softening them up for the kill;

schooling, grooming, priming them; he was one of the elect, singled out for special privileges, their private pimp; the priests were crazy for him... because of his huge physical attributes, that's what they say. I'm sorry to talk like this; it's very embarrassing. But I'm desperate. I can't take it anymore. Now it all comes together, makes peculiar crazy sense.

Everything is topsy-turvy, upside down, helter-skelter; I'm stuck down the rabbit hole. The Irish who are the lowest of the low everywhere else reign like tin pot despots here; the sons of pipe-laying contractors, ambulance chasing lawyers and crooked politicians, lording it over the Italians and Poles who they treat like their inferiors, calling them Wops, Guineas and Polacks; the Germans stand on the side laughing. But they all hate each other; the Poles, Italians and Germans think the Irish are scum. I have to get out of here. This is a crazy house.

Please come and get me. I'm afraid they'll try to stop me, call the police if I try to leave by myself. They know the police; they're all "devout" Catholics; they keep the priests well stocked, pick-up boys in off the street for them, for "counseling and mentorship". In the future I will run like hell if I even hear the word mentor or protégé.

Please, I've learned my lesson. I've had enough. This is it. I am so sorry that I didn't listen to you. I was so wrong.

I love you and think about you often.

Your Devoted Son,

# Nicolas

# John Dean?

However, one must always remember John Dean, whose colossal, pitch perfect memory before a live audience, under oath, in front of Congress, was all an elaborate figment of his overwrought boy's imagination, as the Nixon tapes, later, definitively reveal. Was he lying, did he misremember, was he self-deceived, half-way into early onset dementia? Did he crave the attention like poison sweets, or did he like to be seen as a man with a steel trap memory, super mensch, or all of these? Was he manipulated without his knowledge? Was his Halloween Kewpie doll, Kansas homecoming queen from hell, ever in attendance consort, really a high-end hooker picked and groomed by higher ups, the grownups, to playact his real-life wife? But didn't he win that case? Was her creepy vigil meant to help or hurt? Was she his handler, his dominatrix, his watcher? Was her proximity essential? Did she transfuse him with hidden bloody tubes underneath her skirt? Would he instantly fold if the puppet master's puppet master failed to materialize or never came back from lunch? Would he crumple to the floor; wind up in the janitor's rag pile? Could Dean even hope to get a real girl on his own?

# Do Not Get Down Off Your Horse

Roth describes Bellow through a fictionalized stand-in as emotionally surrounded by a moat so oceanic that you could not even see the great turreted and buttressed thing it had been dug to protect. Good for Bellow and his engineering skills but especially for his herculean general contracting knack; he got good help. There is something to be said for mystery and self-protection, licensed carry. This is why Bellow earned the Prize.

Where the hell is it written that we're required to bare our souls; that we must present ourselves psychically naked to enable intimacy? This requirement is modern psycho-babble, equating self-revelation with the ability to love. Sharing secrets is something little girl-friends do, so they can undress, play, and cry together. How decadently bizarre that even men now are required to make public declarations of their intimate secrets. Next comes public ritual castration with everyone smiling and stomping their feet rhythmically in syncopation.

"I want to get to know the real you". Fuck the real me. Fuck the idea of the real me. Fuck the idea that the question of the real me makes any sense; that there can even be a "real" me.

Do you want a vulnerable basket case or a fully functioning ego, a knight on a huge war horse with gigantic hooves, with both man and animal in full armor decorated by a master engraver?

What's all this gibberish about being ourselves, authenticity? To hell with being ourselves; most of us are no damn good. We should be better than ourselves; recreate ourselves in a more perfect image. Hitler was sincere; said what he meant and acted upon it. God save us from sincere people. Give me a humble hypocrite or phony any day.

And as far as knowing each other, revealing the real me; this is a game we play, a futile game, a child's game to waste our time, and while our life away. No human being can truly understand another human being. Someone said that's why we invented God: A Being capable of understanding us. This turns the catechism upside-down. Why did we make God?

> "To know us, to understand us, to love us in this world and quite possibly in the next, if it exists, or if He exists."

Do not get down off your horse. I repeat: do not get down off your horse. What? To play in the mud with the other children, smear mud on each other. Do not take off your armor even when you sit down to eat; eat standing; better still, eat while in the saddle. They didn't build moats for nothing. It is an apt image. Make my walls of granite, high and thick with impenetrable battlements. I'll call Bellow for an architect with the right gifts.

# One Very Old Woman

One very old woman, at the periphery of the Ambassador's clan, was a gold mine and sat for a total of 36 hours of taped conversations. She was extremely lucid and convincing and seemed to be possessed of total recall, describing Gatsby in the minutest detail as an absolutely charming man who the women were crazy for. She hinted but only hinted that she had been "intimate" with him. She was in many ways pre-Jazz Age and quite conservative in an almost coquettish way, which sounds absurd for a woman of her age. While chattering she seemed to go back in time and re-inhabit the experience, to bring it all back. She despised the Ambassador who she said, attempted to "violate" her. She suspected, from what she knew, that his sons and daughters acted as his pimps, procurers, whether knowingly, she didn't know. They would bring their friends home who the big man would proposition and if that failed, he would rape them. But what she loathed the Ambassador for most of all was:

> "...foisting his incompetent crippled son, his debauched, debased, degenerate progeny... the emanation of his poisoned loins to foul an unsuspecting, gullible nation... spraying his toxic ejaculate on the ecstatic populi squealing like giggly girls for more, more. This was his greatest criminal act, the consummation of his evil, the ultimate megalomania. The rest was peanuts, a lark, boyish pranks.... this was far worse than his murders, his extortions and all the noxious remainder.

"Don't get me wrong... I liked this second son... he managed to pull it off, in spite of himself... miracle of marketing... and mass hypnosis. I just couldn't stand his high pitched whiney nasally voice... pretentions of Harvard."

Which she imitated to great effect, amusing herself exceedingly, laughing immoderately. Her late first husband had been to Harvard and:

"I can assure you sonny-boy did not have a Harvard accent... it's phony, an affectation... a fraud... a failure to realize the desired affect... a peculiar amalgam, like mercury and silver but mistaken for silver through corrupt dental industry propaganda."

She always loved "Dick Nixon" as she called him and his:

"...beautiful deep base baritone with a perfect stage actor accent".

"Sonny-boy was a lousy speaker with his anachronistic, bombastic, 'stump-grinder' style.

I think she used the wrong expression here but she seemed perfectly happy with it and I dared not correct her.

"Sonny-boy. I think it was Lyndon who called him that."

She liked Lyndon, a "seducer", that's what she called him, not a rapist like that "pig" Joe.

"A honey-dewed hillbilly who knew how to lay it on thick."

That he came from the Texas hill-country, and not Appalachia, was irrelevant.

"Everyone and I mean everyone... all the men of power, thought sonny-boy was a putz."

She was showing-off, using a jarring word for effect, not part of her everyday vocabulary.

"The General [Eisenhower], I think it was, who called him little boy blue or something like that.

"The General, everyone loved the General. He was so energetic and powerful when he started. They infiltrated his inner staff... You know that... The ones that should have protected him betrayed him... after his heart attacks... his strokes. He spoke beautifully during his first campaign... during the war. Watch those films... they're out there.

There was absolutely no need to give those incessant, interminable press conferences... that convoluted, fractured prose... like a dog chasing his tale but unable to find it, but trying, oh so hard, non-the-less. They sent him out there to make a fool of himself, to seem old, worn-out and confused. This was no accident, no, no... this was all part of the plan... the strategy... the bastards... they sent him out there to humiliate him... to die publicly. He could have given one very carefully rehearsed, carefully scripted speech, once a month and no one would have been the wiser. He would have preserved his former glory. And that god-damned golf with its old man stink and rich man's decadence. Whose idea was that? He would have been better off cavorting with high class prostitutes in the White House basement bowling alley... I don't think Truman's bowling alley was in the basement though... was it...? Couldn't they find a more private pastime? Even then people didn't hate him... they just felt sorry for him. They were exhausted and befuddled just staring at him falling apart on that infernal TV screen. That medium eviscerated him. Sonny-boy was the lazy son-of-a-bitch... What did some writer not on the take call his work ethic... 'Seigneurial'... that was it... decadent nouveau riche... that's more like it.

"They all thought the country was going to hell in a hand basket with baby blue and his rickety hands at the helm. That's what Lyndon called him... a 'rickety cripple'. They all had names for him... none of them good... It was Lyndon who swore that he was turning into a 'nigra':

> '... that was no suntan... that was hyper-pigmentation... that's what they call it... from his Addison's. Soon enough you won't be able to tell him from his nigra lackies, if he lingers long enough. He'd be a limp-dick sally if he wasn't all juiced with his cortisone and steroids... and speed and god knows what else. What do

you think he hangs onto that Doctor Feelgood quack for.

You know, I have to confess... I didn't vote for Roosevelt... my first husband loathed him... but whatever you say about him... he was no cripple. That monument or statue, the memorial where they have him bound in a wheelchair is an absolute disgrace to the man. I knew people who swore... swore that they saw him walk... walk right up the capitol steps... the entire flight... double time... quick on his feet. They believed he could walk and by god he did walk. If the connivance of the press could make Roosevelt walk how much easier to change lead into gold, water into wine and the rickety cripple into a great orator.

"He should have excused himself from powwows with big men. They despised him, bullied and overpowered him. They sensed his weakness like dogs smelling fear ... he reeked his incompetence. It leaked out of his pores like putrid sebum, which stuck to everyone's shoes and soiled the floor. He shrunk and shriveled in their presence. He should never have met with Khrushchev in Vienna or wherever. Khrushchev famously dismissed sonny-boy... brushed him off as a lightweight, someone to push around just for fun. I'm surprised Khrushchev didn't induce... that's the word, induce him to dance for him... pull down his pants and make him do the hula-hula. He was no great shakes."

She explained in detail that Khrushchev's men, writing years later, lamented that they were actually embarrassed for the United States, saddened that it had fallen to such depths. She had her secretary search for the passages in her library but could come up with only two. The part where they pitied us and lamented our sad inglorious fate, the humiliation of a once great nation, demeaned and degraded, lorded over by a weak-kneed Lilliputian, a self-infatuated weakling, I found self-serving.

> "Sonny-boy should have sent in the real men to speak to the real men... they knew the language. The Russians never would have made their move if General Eisenhower had been in charge... The clumsy, inadvertent... arsonist... bumbling... fumbling matches ... sonny-boy set the fire... then... only, just, managed to put it out, grabbing extravagant credit... no doubt willing to murder every last one of us to show the Russkis that he was no pussy... that they got him wrong, that he knew how to play chicken with the big boys.
>
> We must remember... he had a Rendezvous with Death... also a wicked need to drag us along to keep him company on his way down to midnight in some flaming town. That he was willing to risk, even court the death of his withered, sick, decrepit own corpus could not be classed as courage... more like self-slaughter masquerading as valor... taking out his own rotting garbage."

She spit out these words with a sharp, visceral fluency dripping with purified contempt. She sounded like Norman Mailer... who hungered for an Ezra Pound as his editor. She laughed. There was a joke here somewhere, more than one but I'm not sure which ones she thought were the funniest.

She insisted:

> "Sonny-boy should have been a nightclub comic... a stand-up... Vaudeville or the Borscht Belt... No, No... more like the seedy Holiday Inn at the edge of town bypassed by the Interstate... one of those top bananas with the trick pants... delivering one-liners. He was hugely entertaining... he missed his calling... I just loved his 'routine'... so well-rehearsed... the press, his lapdogs, panting orgasmically for their bone, barking like trained seals, bought and paid for by the big man... delivering the setups on cue for sonny-boy to knock down. It was all an hilarious show, a circus for his credulous 'constichency'."

She loved this mispronunciation and repeated it and laughed again.

She had heard one rumor that they had rehearsals with the reporters who sonny-boy was scripted to recognize, which would devolve into orgies catered by old man Joe; but the orgy part she did not believe; her imagination could not take her there. I assured her he had in fact gone to Harvard but she discarded this as hype.

"The Ambassador bought the degree, rigged his transcript? He hung out there for a few years... yes... he was seen... Yes, I grant you that... You'd be amazed at what enough money will buy. He had ghosts write the book. But I can't understand... why he talked so funny, that whiney, high pitched, ridiculous voice with the preposterous cadence: thumpety, thumpety, thump, thump, thump. Imitation must not be as easy as it seems. It must take a magician or a great actor.

"I know for a fact that voice coaches had trooped in and out, battalions of them... but all to absolutely no avail... he was hopeless... this man was no quick study. I read that he practiced his one pathetic Berliner phrase for days on end. It was all so contrived... it didn't gel... very careful ... too careful. Who is this man? Some said he had a tin ear for languages... more like a tin head. 'Lay-oss'. Who in hell talks like this? He couldn't even learn to pronounce the name of the country he was destroying. This accent, a poison stew of low-class Boston Irish Catholiceeze tacked on to a reluctant, resistant Harvard Brahman fighting back tooth and nail and winning hands down. Old Man Joe promoted his ne'er-do-well son the way he would a nubile young female into a Hollywood star. But the incipient star had potential at least... Jack, entirely lacking, had none.

"In some cases, it is easier to manipulate the perceiver than the one being perceived? It was easier to change the perception of his speaking ability than the ability itself, which was immutable. He was hopeless, beyond improvement?"

But when I tried to follow-up, after speaking with the people she sent me to, in confidence, the sons and daughters of those who could and did verify her "testimony", but only second hand. When I came back, I was told by a servant, but more a secretary-jailer, who intercepted her phone calls, that the lady was suffering from dementia and had probably gotten her information from publications she had studied (she was a "voracious" reader) and had "internalized these sources, creating false memories" or that these facts were "planted" in her by her first husband who was a "powerful mesmerizing presence," who "loathed the Ambassador" and was a "staunch Republican". But after a dogged search I could find no publications with such exact, particular accounts as she gave. She named names, places and dates. Her keepers assured me that she had not been "cogent" for at least a decade; they explained that she had "moments of clarity" which was "deceptive" and could "lasso you in" and "disappeared without warning". But a friend who she referred me to for corroboration assured me she was as sharp as a tack; she had been caught writing a book; the manuscript was confiscated; she was a virtual prisoner in her own house. Suitcases full of money changed hands; the same forces were still at work with different names. The Ambassador had, after everything, succeeded in raping her, belatedly, in old age; reaching through his myriad progeny, his desiccated hand from out of his stinking grave to strangle her.

# Jackie Gleason

I had an uncle, a man I had great affection for, who did a dead-on imitation of Jackie Gleason, an imitation which was his life. He spoke like Gleason; he was Jackie Gleason. He ate too much; he drank too much; he was a raconteur; he was immensely lovable and he was smart and funny. Now the question is: was he like that prior to his absorbed consciousness of Gleason or was Gleason himself tying in to a whole set of values and mannerisms that preexisted, out there, in the social ether and did they both tap in to common roots? There was something quintessentially Irish about Gleason. My uncle was christened Michael but called himself Mickey, a very Irish moniker. When tanked-up he titled himself an Old Russian, which was closer to the truth, technically; certainly, he had the muzhik about him. He was Leonid Brezhnev, Richard Daley, Arthur Kroc; but most of all, most certainly, he was purposefully and admiringly Jackie Gleason, the one and only; he owned every single one of his records. No, there is no doubt about it; he reinvented himself modeled against a person that he never met, that very well may not have existed, did not, in fact, exist; a creation of the performer, the image he projected; Gleason himself was never so sweet in real life, and this artificial sweetness no doubt sweetened the man my uncle might otherwise have been, that he absorbed only via an insubstantial, glittering display of flickering artificial light from a cathode ray vacuum tube. Why not Clark Gable or Cary Grant? Out of his league. In Gleason, along with the immeasurable common man charm, he could indulge the other person he himself had been, a legitimization of his gross fallibility, an easy dispensation for his most conspicuous lapses: alcoholic, gluttonous and a bit of the buffoon but a genuine character as real as rain. It granted him absolution to descend when uncontrollably, miserably drunk into Ralph Kramden, a vulgar, crude, ignorant blowhard.

But who is to say the best man is not the man of the tube; that the TV persona was not thc real Jackie Gleason; his best foot forward, the man most acceptable, the man he wished and hoped to be on his best day in the best possible world?

Was my uncle real? Was this an imitation of an imitation, an act based upon an act, a submergence of identity into some nebulous mass culture or were his sources rather an ever-expanding birthplace and birthright, of far richer possibility of self-realization, of deeper wells magnified and multiplied, supplying a fertile cornucopia to critically and carefully choose from? There is a mass culture that enriches and enlarges us and a mass culture that degrades and demeans us. The all-pervading modern media, the great corrupter and destroyer, of societal values, also facilitates a process of class simulation and emulation; and lets us impersonate giants who blow themselves up in our faces.

# Peterson

I knew a fellow who repeated a story that was genuinely touching. His name was Peterson and he spoke of his Norwegian mother with an almost holy reverence.

Peterson:

> "I remember every Saturday night Mama would sit down at the kitchen table and count out the money Papa had brought home in his pay envelope.
>
> "She would carefully count out various stacks.
>
> "'First of all, for the landlord' Mama would say, separating out the money.
>
> "'Second, for the grocer.' And yet another pile.
>
> "'For John's shoes.' That was my older brother, John.
>
> And we would all watch in fear as the original pile got smaller and smaller.
>
> At last Papa would ask: 'Is that all?'
>
> And Mama would nod and finally we could breathe easy.
>
> Mama would look up and smile at each of us in turn. 'It is good,' she'd say. 'We have enough'".

Peterson never tired of telling this story, endless times, like a ritual incantation, a founding, sustaining myth, varying only slightly each time. Tears would well up in his eyes and I was always moved, somewhat. It always sounded unsettlingly familiar, like I had heard it before somewhere, in a dream maybe; that it was unoriginal, a borrowed suit that doesn't fit right, big in the shoulders, too long in the sleeves; it rang false. One time when Peterson was performing his ceremonial with particular animation, his drinking buddy Joe, a prototypical Irishman, is standing in the background out of view of Peterson, making mugs, extravagant faces and an exaggerated jerk-off motion, howling in pantomime. I didn't have the heart to break up Peterson's accustomed routine, which seemed to mean a lot to him. But the next time I saw Joe I asked:

"What the hell was that all about?"

Joe:

"I'm tired a hearing that crock a shit. I heard it a thousand times. His mother wasn't Norwegian... his father was... so he says... or thinks. His mother was a drunken Irish whore who never paid a goddamn bill in her fucking life... stole every cent the poor old man brought home... snuck out and got drunk on it... that's why the father took off when Bob was a kid... went out one night when he found her drunk in her own vomit... whacked out on the floor and never came home again. And what's this Mama and Papa shit? Every other time it's 'my old man' or 'my old lady'.

Peterson was very proud of his Norwegian roots, of the father who wasn't there and never tired of telling people, who for some reason refused to believe he was Norwegian. He looked just like the Russian general who traded insults and toasted with Patton in the movie or maybe the actor who played the general. Everyone called him a Polack, friendly-like; strangers always speaking Polish to him like a compatriot, a brother. He even learned a few Polish words so he could fake it and be friendly back. But he hated the Poles and hated even more being taken for one:

"No, I'm Norwegian... really."

"Yeah... sure. I'm a fucking Eskimo. Who you tryin' to kid... kid?"

It is only later that I came to realize that the story he repeated so often was lifted almost verbatim from a tear-jerking movie I had watched as a kid; the heart-warming schmaltz: *I Remember Mama*. This was curious because Peterson was a tough guy who would fight anybody, no matter how big, who looked funny at him in any bar. I think if anybody told Peterson he was parroting back a movie script and quoted it back to him he would be dumbstruck, wouldn't know what to think, might unravel right there and lose his grip; this was part of the fantasy that allowed him to exist, the sustaining myth. What do you say or do when your exact double walks into the room and claims to be you?

Peterson was intelligent and very funny, missed his calling as a stage comedian, aced the Fire Captain's test, first in his precinct, an alcoholic who got falling down drunk in a bar every night of his life, but prided himself excessively for showing up every morning for work without fail. He was always running into fires, rescuing people. They gave him his own firehouse; made him Chief but took it away almost instantly when they caught him in the act, in flagrante delicto, getting a blowjob from some bimbo in his captain's car while "on duty" outside his firehouse; he was turned in by his own men who called him a "self-hating Negro", to his face, which totally stumped him. To his last day at his own House he had absolutely no idea what they were talking about and that's the saddest part of it.

# Paul Tripp

I had a friend who seemed especially broken up about a death one day. There were tears welling in his eyes. He was a man of fifty-seven not accustomed to tears. The year was 2002.

I remember asking:

"Was he a relative?"

Friend:

> "No... until today I didn't even know his name. But it's opened up a flood of memories, like an iron gate rusted shut finally breaking open off the hinges.

> "I saw his obituary in the New York Times and recognized the photograph.

> "His name... I discovered was Paul Tripp. He was ninety-one.

> "This sounds incredibly stupid but if it weren't for this man, whose name I didn't know a week ago, I don't think I would be alive today. He introduced me to the human race and made me part of it... want to be part of it. He had this television show whose name I had forgotten until the death notice: Mr. I. Magination."

This friend, more forthcoming than he usually was, remarkably so in a frightening way, described an incredibly bleak childhood in which his mother and her brothers took turns terrorizing and slapping him around. His sister, who he never remembers having a conversation with, didn't even know she was alive, inured, comatose, the unthinking slave of the adults but equally their victim. The nuns and priests were vicious, sadistic. If he could have run away, he would have, at four or five, anything to get away, but there was nowhere to run to.

The early days of television in the late forties and early fifties were an astonishing time, he explained as if speaking about an ancient history he had lived through:

> "My mother, a vicious, stupid woman who everyone regarded as kind and generous and who I would always regard as clinically insane, purchased the magic box in 1949, manufactured by Dumont, for the astronomical sum of $900, the only rational purchase she ever made in her entire life. The small apartment we lived in had a market rent of $50 a month in an apartment house which had been owned by her dead husband, my father, a man of some wealth. Before his death the family had associated with doctors, lawyers and self-made entrepreneurs but after my father's passing, she slid inexorably back to a level which accepted her, which she felt more comfortable with, from which she had risen, but much, much deeper down now to a kind of human sewer sludge of assorted low life who preyed upon her, extracting from her the ever-depleting remnants of her husband's hard sweated wealth. She eventually married an old

decrepit piece of the sewer sludge and gave him all the first husband's money so she could pretend to everybody that the sewer sludge had his own money; trying to prove that he may have been sewer sludge but at least he was sewer sludge with money. She became a drunk, joining the sewer sludge in getting wasted every single night; she had finally found her soulmate, descended to her perfect gutter level; happy as a pig in shit; the delivery boys weren't safe with her; forever fingering her rosary, addicted to novenas which she travelled to, and hooked on suspect priests.

"My father's children by a previous wife, who had died first, were taken by their grandmother. My mother warned me about these numerous half siblings as if they were demon spawn who would kill me if given the chance, break my neck or even torture me. They were all idiots, she said, rattling off their low IQs, name and number, which she was privy to. I attributed this to her spiteful resentment of the dead first wife and discounted it accordingly. But when I sought them out later in life with open arms full of naïve smiling hope for extending my family, having been isolated and 'protected' from them by my crazy mother during my vulnerable years, I found to my absolute astonishment that she was right and she was right about almost nothing else. And not only about them being idiots; they would have killed me, no doubt about it; her prescient paranoia saved my life; she saved my life. I would have gone out an upper story window or drowned in a lake, a tragic accident. If my father had lived I, most certainly, would have died, painfully. I was too smart for my own good, which one of them warned me. Who the hell did I think I was? Be careful what you wish for. Be careful about wanting to rewrite history, of wanting to alter what you think is a cruel fate. And what did these fiends tell me about him, my father, this progenitor polluting the world with his foul semen, letting loose a brood of hateful degenerate morons? I dreamed in a fevered dream that my mother poisoned my father, to save me, her only son, from his host of evil progeny: a strange dream considering her latter perfect union with the piece of sewer sludge. I had never met people who dripped such thick venom; the hatred was palpable, intense and unambiguous; these were people who would hunt down and kill anyone they perceived as putting on airs which was anyone at all superior to themselves. I could feel it like the beast's scorching breath, sulfuric acid burning through my back.

. . . . .

"The apartment house we lived in was an island whose inhabitants clung precariously to a striving lower middle class, trying desperately not to become contaminated by the sub-human scum which always threatened to overwhelm us from the adjacent, encroaching buildings and intruding mean streets. I always especially despised the writers and media hounds, the flacks, the schlockmeisters of schmaltz who romanticized and fictionalized this despicable social stratum... an inept, maladroit way of attacking the decadent rich sideways but in the process disarming and emasculating those of us who fought so mightily... so desperately hard for our very lives, our existences, to rise out of this sloshing cesspool with its vicious undertow. Even the so-called realistic writers romanticize this stratum creating a more palatable world entirely of their own creation. They don't misremember, they lived in the fantasy... they survived through the fantasy. Money has absolutely nothing to do with any of it. Give this trash, this detritus, money and they become trash with money... infinitely more dangerous.

"And so the genie's in the glass bottle; the magic box opened up the world to me, revealed to me that there were humans who walked the planet earth, putting their best foot forward no doubt, kind and intelligent... that I was not alone, that there were others like me or rather like what I might come to be, not just the monsters who held me captive in their lunacy... and if not for this miracle, this medium, this perfect confluence of time and technology, would have gobbled me up, sliced thin on stale moldy bread or reduced me to a crippled automaton. Early television saved my life or brought me to life.

"'Mr. I. Magination', I just read, was directed by Yul Brynner, another maestro ... it ran weekly on CBS TV from 1949 to 1952... the benevolent

Pied Piper, Paul Tripp, the engineer in striped overalls at the helm of a toy railroad train, surrounded by young children... which passed through a magic tunnel to the land of imagination... he would tell stories from history and literature... Rip Van Winkle, the life of P. T. Barnum. Later, he performed magic tricks with the leading illusionists of the day.

"This was the unexpected captivating intrusion of what passed for high culture. The very high price of the tube insured its exclusivity, the niche market of wealthy urbanized patrons ... I was lucky to live right across from Manhattan... the signal emanating straight from the Empire State Building might as well have been a supernatural beam from a bundle of sacred stardust... live telecasts of Shakespeare and music from Carnegie Hall.

"'Studio One', 'Kraft Television Theater', 'Philco Playhouse', 'Playhouse Ninety'. They grabbed the best actors from the Broadway legitimate theater.

"We have grown accustomed to actors with marbles in their mouths mumbling inaudibly in high-pitched nasally whines. But I will never forget the hallucinatory voices of Ed Herlihy and Ralph Bellamy. We seem to have forgotten what a potent and persuasive, perfectly tuned instrument the human speaking voice can be."

I wondered if his grief hadn't overtaken his common sense; he had suffered catastrophic financial reverses recently, destroyed by an only son who he loved more than anything, who for irrational or sub-rational reasons plotted against his father and thereby himself, destroyed a substantial fortune which only he was heir to; having once been a rich man, now ruined, at least in his own mind; or if he wasn't having some kind of a complete breakdown, a psychological collapse, having nothing at all to do with, but precipitated by, the death of a man whose name he had long ago forgotten or never knew and whom he had never once met.

I reminded him very gingerly of the boob tube's, (my purposeful expression), "I Love Lucy", "Uncle Miltie" and "Howdy Doody". A little taken aback he simply insisted unconvincingly that he didn't like or watch those shows. He seemed to have blocked them out. They didn't fit his picture, his holy picture, the icon on the wall of his once magnificent house, boarded up and abandoned now, crumbling into clouds of choking dust. And Herlihy, while, granted, had a magnificent, compelling instrument, exploited it to hawk fake cheese. Alexander Scourby similarly blessed recorded the entire Bible for the blind without pay.

# Robert

But I, also, could be a total shit. Was it ongoing traumatic stress syndrome? Or is that an excuse? Had the nuns and priests beaten and humiliated me so badly that they irreparably wounded my brain? They certainly skewed my capacity for self-interested rational judgement. Was I set on an inevitable path of continual self-sabotage?

When I was twelve years old, I abandoned, betrayed, really, my best friend; and Robert was my best friend and perhaps the best friend I would ever have. He survived Saint John's better than I could; he was accommodating; and so good natured, which good nature seemed to inure him to the Irish nun's intended despoliation and depredation. He was the smartest kid in my class; oh, that isn't true. He was the only intelligent kid in my class; maybe, the whole school. And he was devoted; and worked, I mean worked, really hard at our friendship; and I was not an easy friend to have. I wasn't worthy of his friendship. My half-idiot sister made merciless fun of Robert, behind his back. Robert was just a little over-weight; a little clumsy, maybe; a little socially inexpert; but he was my friend, god-damn-it, my best friend; maybe the best friend I would ever have. We make friends at twelve years old that can never be equaled when we become adults; that stay with us, one way or another, sustain us or haunt us, for the rest of our lives. And I abandoned him, when he needed me the most. What? Because he wasn't "cool" enough? My idiot sister called him a "geek"; although I'm not sure she used that particular epithet, nor was it in universal use at the time, but that's what she meant; and maybe he was, a little; isolated as he was, entirely, by his intelligence. But he didn't seem to care what the idiots thought; he cared what I thought. And what did I care what my sister thought; who hated me and I returned the favor. She hated Robert, but only because he was my devoted friend; no other reason. But my sister didn't exist in any true sense; she was so dumb she never suspected she was alive. She was in no sense a sentient being; she was a mindless automaton, a corrupted creature, a perfect manifestation of the nuns and priests, who she lived for; and she gloried in their persecution of me.

And, I guess, I was a "geek" too, in spite of my punk façade. Robert and I read the Encyclopedia Britannica, together; can you even imagine that? I read him whole stories by Edgar Allen Poe, over the phone no less, early on Saturday morning; we got up early for the event. His was the only intelligent conversation I had ever had with anyone my own age. And why didn't I treasure this? Why didn't I grapple him to my soul with hoops of steel? Because I was no better than the idiots I so detested; and which idiots Robert knew enough to ignore.

But Robert was "game" and utterly fearless in some strange way. He was the only one who would step into the ring and box me at the CYO; screaming at the top of his lungs, grimacing, charging me like some deranged wild man. He wouldn't box anyone else; so, it was just the two of us, while everyone else stood aside and watched, frightened by the show. He always lost, but he didn't give a hoot. I think he boxed me, only because he was my friend, to make me happy, so we would have that in common, a brotherly bond forged in feigned "combat"; because after he left, there was no one else for me to box. They were all terrified, of me, because the two of us had put on such an extravagant good show, like a television wrestling match. Robert thought I was pacing myself, holding him up, but I wasn't; not by a long shot.

And then there was Prince, my magic collie dog, who I raised from a pup, who wouldn't wag his tale when he saw me, but wag his entire rear end, so enthusiastically, so violently, that he would knock himself off his feet. And he was Robert's dog, too. We both loved that dog; we bonded over that collie dog; my dog Prince. But this was back in the day, 1957, when male dogs weren't automatically castrated, so Prince, testicles intact, had a wild streak and an itch to roam. He would slip his leash and run ahead of me, turn and wait and expect me to chase after him, which I did for a mile or two; I knew how to play his game; but I finally, stupidly, gave up and trotted off home to get my books and head off for school; which school for me was a total waste of time. I should have chased after Prince, to the end of time. I half expected him to be waiting for me, obediently, by the door, when I returned home at lunch time; but I think he ran too far and lost his way and I lost my way, too. I lost my magic dog that year and I threw Robert away.

(I don't particularly believe in heaven; but I hear that the pope has opined, squatting on his golden throne, that dogs, now, can go to heaven; of course, of this I never had any doubt. If there is a heaven, Prince will be waiting for me, patiently by the door. Or in a replay of the past, which, I suspect, must be possible in heaven, I will have had the good sense to chase after him. But I also know that the pope, arrogantly presumptuous, hasn't got a prayer of a chance of getting into heaven, nor have his priests and nuns.)

Robert's parents were rich and they had class; but they had no money. They lived in what was known then as a "cold water flat", meaning that the only heat source was in the kitchen; the rent was $35 a month; and the housekeeping was immaculate. His mother was beautiful and slender and reminded me more than anything of my imaginary mother, the creation of my father's imagination; in that photograph, child in arms, that haunted my waking dreams. I envied him his parents and wondered what incredible heights I could have climbed with parents such as these. Wasn't it Freud who said that with a mother's love like this, who will stop a man from conquering the whole world? But it wasn't quite enough for Robert; even a mother's love can't save you from a nest of vipers; and Saint Peter's Prep was a nest of vipers. There is nothing more evil than Catholic school boys, who do whatever they damned please, over and over, and run to their confessor priest to wipe their slate clean, on a weekly basis, to reinvigorate themselves for ever more sadistic onslaughts. And then there were the predator priests, and the sadist, Mulvihill, who was his homeroom teacher. I had gone there, briefly, to Saint Peters and for the first time in my life I stood my ground, immovably, my feet set in concrete. I told about the creepy office visit with the principal, Cornelius J. Carr, S.J., who was revealed, only after he was conveniently dead, to be a serial rapist of boys. I told about Richard M. Barry, S.J., the butch sadist who forced all the boys to strip down naked, shower and lather up methodically, from top to toe, after every gym class, which he insisted on monitoring at close reach, practically inside the tightly crowded gang shower, getting the edges of his long loose hanging cassock dripping wet, drooling, devouring the just pubescent newbie boys with his mean lascivious wolf eyes, seething hate for what he craved; who was lavishly entertained by  Martin Tarby, Bill's "best man", who serviced him;  so  flamboyantly,  ostentatiously, outrageously gay, long before it was "acceptable" to be that way;  the same "best man" who's door was always open to the homosexual priests from Saint Peter's Prep, just down the street.

These Catholics are every bit as credulous as Manson's gullible girls; but crazier. They ship their top sons off to be fucked by priests; they vie, they jostle for the distinction, the accolade, the honor; they queue up and subject those sons to tedious admission tests; they coo and swoon so self-satisfied over their selected ones; and every last one of them will rot an eternity in hell with blood forever dripping from their complicit fingers. They are demented Abrahams lamenting only that they lacked more sons to dispatch to ritualistic butchery.

I, unequivocally, refused to go to Saint Peter's Prep, any longer. When they refused to hear me, I travelled the bus they put me on, to the door of the school and then walked home, eight miles, every day, for a week, before they found me out.

Even the few details I was only able to learn about Robert took me 62 years, a lifetime. If you have a Slavic name, unless you are privy to the spelling, it is impossible to trace on Google. The pronunciation of Slavic names is usually anglicized and bears little resemblance to original spelling, or pronunciation. To this day I still don't know what kind of crisis, what trauma enveloped Robert. I only know that he reached out to me, desperately; and wanted no more than for me to be his friend, to talk to him, to be with him in his time of pain and he was in deep pain; I could feel that. Even his mother called me; and then his mother called my mother, could I please help? I was his friend, his best friend.

Robert's good nature blinded him, so he could not see what was there, for everyone to see, who allowed themselves to see. He, originally, had been thrilled to be going to Saint Peter's. Was it the need in me to distance myself, from all associations, however peripheral; to pretend that Saint Peter's never happened; that it didn't exist; to start fresh? Was it the contamination, my wanting to be rid of the stench, the infernal reek which clung to me, enough to rip the skin from my flesh, to cleanse myself, forever, of the ineradicable stain of Saint Peter's Prep?

The guilt, the regret, enveloped me 12 years later when I ran into Robert's parents in Schultz's Supply, a home improvement center in Bayonne, just over the line. I recognized them immediately and they recognized me. They glowered at me with such a concentrated look of intense hate that I didn't dare speak to them; and they wouldn't take their eyes off me. They looked at me like I had murdered their beloved son. What-in-god's-name had happened to Robert? Had he killed himself? Was he institutionalized? Over the years I searched various permutations of the spelling of his last name; all that turned up was a very famous Polish actor, who crowded out page after endless page on Google, who didn't look at all like Robert. Finally, when the year books for Saint Peter's Prep came online, I found Robert as a freshman in the 1960 edition class photo, with the sadist Mulvihill out front, staring down the camera; (what makes garbage like Mulvihill so self-possessed?) I had been only a single letter off in the spelling of Robert's name; that and the Polish actor's voluminous entry pushed him aside and hid him from me.

I discovered that Robert had, in fact, survived, (as, miraculously, I guess, I did too); he graduated from Cornell Medical School and specialized in diagnostic radiology, practicing for some time in upstate New York, now living in South Carolina. He has a second wife named Constance and a daughter named Katya. Some photographs popped up on Google in an Eastern European setting in which he looks quite formidable, if it is him; it looks like Robert but it can't be him; the man is too young by 25 years. Robert and I had never spoken of our shared Slavic heritage, but he seems finally to have discovered his, as I have mine. Katya, what a wonderful, enchanting name. His younger brother Thomas, who was always tagging along with us, is never connected with Robert on Google, strangely; and is an esteemed orthopedic surgeon and professor, much more famous than his older brother.

So, the nuns succeeded and the demon priest reached out and completed. I was the walking wounded; suicidal, bleeding, self-sabotaged. I killed off my only true brother; and for no good reason. Who knows what summits we would have reached safeguarding each other? Indomitable, facing off the world together. Brothers.

# Wolf

## In a Forty-Second Street Cellar

In the middle of the summer of 1922 Gatsby drove in with his persistent trespasser, Carramel, to the City, booming traffic and the deafening blare of horns. In a Forty-Second Street cellar full of smoke, heat and din, pushed uselessly around by wobbly ceiling fans seeming to work their way loose by stirring the thick air, creating the illusion of ventilation, they met for lunch. Batting away the haze of the suffocating cigarette smoke burning his eyes, squinting away the brilliance of noon outside, yielding to blindness in the comparatively black interior, his eyes sensed shadows shifting in the distance and the figure of what might have been a man began to enlarge and clarify itself, rising out of the smoke, assuming a familiar countenance.

Gatsby:

'Mr. Carramel, this is my friend Mr. Wolf.'

Carramel had been pestering Gatsby for a "head-to-head" with Mr. Wolf, hoping to gain a "connection", a stock deal to "line his pockets". Gatsby excused himself after a hurried lunch leaving the table for an "urgent telephone call". Gatsby didn't want to hear any of this. He wanted deniability. He wanted to be able to deny that he had ever had this meeting with Mr. Carramel.

Gatsby:

"Enjoy your coffee... I'll be right back... gentlemen."

Lazarus Wolf was a large, powerful man with the deep bass voice, the trained, picked voice of a radio man announcing the morning news or a stage actor who had toured the provinces in the high heat of summer. He played King Lear when he was young. He looked like Lee J. Cobb when Cobb played in the movie "Anna and the King", but leaner and hungrier and without the make-up. If you did a movie Cobb might do him justice, combined with a Chaim Topol or a Walter Mathau, but fit enough to run the hundred-yard dash or go the distance, ten rounds in the ring. Wolf fought professionally in his youth. Sam Jaffe, as he portrayed Erwin "Doc" Riedenschneider in *The Asphalt Jungle* would be a good third choice. Jerry Orbach would be very good.

Wolf would indulge himself in a very slight Yiddish-German lilt and Yiddish locutions, self-consciously, to amuse himself, like he was play acting. This was a highly educated man, graduated from City College and NYU law school. He spoke in a strange mix of rich ironic street slang interspersed with a seeding from his prodigious vocabulary which he was unafraid to broadcast liberally. He had no tolerance for ignorance. This was back in the day when they gave elocution lessons in the public schools and students labored, hunched over long vocabulary lists in the public library; when even the city school teachers, proper spinsters, spoke in unembarrassed Mid-Atlantic accents and cracked your knuckles with an oak ruler if you didn't imitate them correctly.

Wolf's Flunky:

> "Mr. Wolf, I'm sorry... half the time I don't know what you're talking about. I don't know these big words."

Wolf gave him a book. From that day on all his flunkies studied vocabulary like dutiful schoolboys.

Wolf sometimes spoke quickly with a machine gun rapidity, rattling non-stop, which some took for browbeating, which it definitely was, not giving them time to breathe much less to think; that it was purposely hard to follow, to trip them up; their guilty conscience filling in the missed words and as a result saying the wrong thing; what Wolf wanted to hear.

Wolf did not relish this meeting with Nick, feeling put upon, looking for trouble. I don't think he fully understood the implied quid pro quo, payment for services to be rendered but rendered more to Gatsby than to Wolf. They were unequal partners and Wolf didn't like the risk, hanging himself out like this, to dry, for an unknown quantity, for a foreign loose cannon rolling around the deck of his own personal ship.

Wolf extended his broad, flat hand like a weapon, for examination, with not very well-concealed contempt.

Wolf:

> "I understand you're a college man."

Nick:

> "Yes, New Haven."

Wolf:

> "Yeh... I went to New Haven too... never liked the fucking place.

> "Me and Mr. Gatsby opened a play there... it bombed. We took it to New York anyway... ran 480 performances there... just goes to show you New Haven don't count for shit."

Nick:

> "Yes... Jay told me you invest together in shows. But New Haven..."

Wolf, insulted, purposefully interrupting, stepping on Nick's lines, every chance he got, squashing them like quick little bugs trying to run out from under a rug:

> "I never invested in a fucking 'show' in my entire life. You mean that musical shit. I would die a slow painful death first. They make me sick... in the pit of my stomach sick... so I want to throw-up... vomit all over the place. I get sick just thinking about it. I invest only in serious drama... promising young writers or the classical theater... Chekhov.... Ibsen... Shakespeare."

Abruptly, as if coming to his senses, waking from a momentary lapse of consciousness, realizing what was said:

> "Who is this 'Jay' character you're talking about?"

Nick, hesitating, beginning to realize he has said something wrong:

"Jay Gatsby."

Wolf:

"You mean Mr. Gatsby... James to his very... very close friends.

"This nickname shit always rubbed me the wrong way... got under my skin.

"This Bubba, Chuck... Curley... Billy Joe, BooBoo, Doolittle, Billy Bob, Billy Rae, JohnBoy, Cooter, Clyde, Clitus, Woody, Mooney. It's for retarded hillbillies... or is that a redundancy... retarded hillbillies.

"Jay...? You call him this? You have his permission?

"He told you to call him this?

Nick:

"No... but Delsey sometimes called him...."

Wolf:

"'Delsey'! What the... that's a fucking cow's name for chrissake.

"These crazy rich sons-a-bitches are as bad as the inbred slack-jawed cracker yokels, their Anglo-Saxon brethren, with their asinine monikers already. Cookie, Cece, Paige, Piper, Peachy, Pippa, Polly, Posie, Buffy, Bunny, Bitsy,

Booboo, Bambi, Heide, Happy, Sneezy, Kiki, Dede, Mimi, Missy, Muffy, Mindy, Maisie, Daisy, Sissy, Tibby, Topsy, Turvey. What an abomination... enough to make me want to toss my lunch. These people deserve to be separated from their money... cavorting like buffoons... they lack dignity, all sense of propriety. They give money a bad name."

Nick:

"Well... you see... her grandfather had a farm... a kind of gentleman's farm... where she spent the summer... as a child... over a thousand of the most beautiful acres and she had this favorite cow... the prettiest cow you ever did see... like out of an advertisement for milk at the A&P... and she loved this cow more than anything on earth...

Wolf, raising his voice:

"Stop... enough... enough already about the cow. I don't want to hear anything about any cows... goats or pigs either for that matter.

"Are we talking about this same twat he fucked down in Louisville... who's setting up the...?

Nick:

"Yes... but... but. (long, frightened pause) Don't you mean Charleston?"

Wolf:

"What the fuck... again you're at it. Does it really matter Mr. Carramel? Think about it. Who fucking cares where she comes from? This Annabel... or whatever.

"Are you a girl Mr. Carramel?

Nick:

"What...?

Wolf:

"I said... are you a girl?

Nick:

"What...?

Wolf:

"You say 'what' one more fucking time and I will blow your fucking brains out... I guaruntee. (the run and tee accentuated like a Cajun.)

"Are you a girl, Mr. Carramel?

Nick:

"No... but... but..."

Wolf:

"First the 'whats' now the 'buts'. You are trying my patience, mightily. Maybe we should have you examined... by a doctor, maybe, a proctologist psychiatrist... to get your head out from up your ass.

"There are three men in this restaurant watching us very closely... three more belong to Mr. Gatsby but they're busy watching him. I want you to look around at them. They are not as inconspicuous as they would like to believe... actually they stick out like a sore thumb... it's really comical when you think about it... they've got big heaters bulging out of their pockets... they might as well stick a sign around their neck... but that's okay... it's the deterrence factor. Like big dogs they scare people... just to look at them. What particular persons that don't last never figure out is that there is always a fourth man... that even the three others don't know about... he's tougher, quicker and smarter than the other three put together... you'd never be able to pick him out... and it is this fourth man that always saves the day. The three men, in fact, very often serve only as a distraction... like a decoy. Don't ever tell them I said that... it would hurt their feelings.

But you see... right now they all see that I am getting agitated and as a result they are getting very agitated... they don't like when I get agitated. It is their job to see that I don't get agitated.

"If you continue in this vein... I will give them a sign... two of them... it will only take two... will drag you out of here so I can personally shoot you in the nearest alley. I will shoot you in the head twice until your brains come out... so there is no mistake. If you resist, they will shoot you down right on the spot... right here... in front of all these people. Then they will leave town... for the West Coast... I have interests on the West Coast. They will be gone for years until the whole thing blows over... it will blow over... it always does. But they will most likely decide to stay on the West Coast... it's nice out there... the weather... the ocean... palm trees... that's if you like palm trees... I, myself can take them or leave them... these men will sink roots... it's inevitable. I will miss them a great deal... good men are hard to find... but I will manage.

"Now... once again... one more time... so there's no question... are you a girl Mr. Carramel and is Mr. Gatsby fucking you?"

Nick:

"No... no... absolutely not."

Wolf:

"So... if you're not a girl and not being fucked by Mr. Gatsby then please do not call him Jay... not ever... not in my presence, or anywhere I might hear about it from someone else. People are always carrying tales to me... like they're doing me some sort of big favor, like I want nothing better than to hear.

"If a little twat wants to call him Jay that's a personal matter between the twat and Mr. Gatsby... twats do and say very silly things... it can't be helped. Mr. Gatsby understands this... one could say he's an expert on twats. There are certain dispensations that accrue to the station... being a recognized twat, that is. Do we understand each other, Mr. Carramel?"

Nick, shaking visibly, not knowing what to say:

"Yes.

Wolf:

"Say it one more time so there's no misunderstanding. Say: 'Yes I understand'".

Nick:

"Yes, I understand."

Changing the subject clumsily in something of a panic, never knowing when to shut up, digging himself deeper:

"Mr. Gatsby tells me you're a man of culture, that you're a patron of the arts... sit on the board of the Metr..."

Wolf, interupting:

"What? Man of culture? What does the hell does that mean? 'Man of culture.' Everybody wants to pigeon-hole everybody else, put 'em in a box... so they can make simple sense of something that's not so simple.

For instance... here, in this country, the detective mystery book is looked down on as not literature. But a writer who writes of loftier subjects, of 'social significance' even if he's a stinking writer is taken seriously. This is the 'parvenu's insecurity', if I can borrow that fancy phrase.

"But the man who can take the humble murder mystery and turn it into art... this is a magician... this is the man I respect, that I can sit down and talk to. Who was it that called the fictional private detective: the new mythic hero, investigating a cultural response to universal unconscious fantasy and plunging into it without understanding society's narcissistic fixations? Boy... what a crock-a-shit. Do these bums even listen to themselves? But he's on to something... No? These writers also got murder out of the vicar's stupid rose garden and gave it back to people who are really good at it... murderers.

But it may take a real wizard to write shit one day and literature the next and not to carry the stink of the shit into the area where he lives. What serious writer dares to stray to write popular fiction in the optimistic hope of coming back by underground tunnels and devious ways into the light again, dripping with darkness? Mostly they dig down, accidently break into sewers and drown from the darkness or are asphyxiated by sewer gas.

As far as what is literature...? I know it when I see it. As for what it is, this I leave to the fat fucks... like Edmund Wilson who has the distinction in his own self-described 'serious literature' of making fornication as dull as a railway timetable... so dull that you would want no part of it... this is not an easy trick... take my word for it.

"I got side-tracked... I was off on a tangent... the tangents always get me. Getting back to the subject at hand... what the fuck do you know about culture?

Nick:

"No... I just...

Wolf, interrupting, more calmly now, getting control of himself:

"'No... I just...' You know you're a very annoying person... very annoying... What are we going to do with you? You don't learn. You don't listen.

"Whenever I hear the term culture... careful, so nobody notices, I chamber a round in my old Luger... from the war... a souvenir... pried from the cold, stiff fingers of a dead Heinie... his handsome face and blond hair pressed down in the mud... like he was nothing... and I finger it like a talisman... and laugh loud to myself.

"People who prattle on about culture are hard to stomach and don't know their ass from their elbow. These are the crumb bums that ruin it, walking around with their noses high in the air like the ground stinks... the ground does stink, sometimes... especially with people pissing on it... but not always. They have the attitude that

I'm better than you because I appreciate real art. Fuck 'em... that's what I say.

"You see these cuff buttons...? Take a good close look... Do you know what they are?"

Nick, leaning hesitantly in to look, but not too close, afraid it was a trap, afraid he would have his head bitten off:

"Molars?"

Wolf:

"Molars? Molars... yes... very good... (like Nick had just passed an important quiz and won a contest), human molars ... molars pulled from a screaming man without any anesthesia. I used to practice dentistry. I like to keep my hand in... my finger in the pie, so to speak... to keep in practice... so I don't lose the touch.

"I dream that overnight people won't want to buy pearls anymore (Nick at this point knew nothing of Wolf's pearl business) ... that they'll come to their senses... that they'll regard them as silly or they'll only buy them in little cheap cloth bags for pennies like glass marbles. I worry about such things. I have a nest egg of course... what man in my position does not... but a man must keep gainfully employed... for his peace of mind and to keep himself sharp... to keep his edge. You never know... if everything goes to shit, I have something to fall back on... a cushion... to catch me if I fall... my dentistry... my safety net... my first profession.

"I worked hard to be a good dentist... my parents scrimped and saved to send me to school. I wanted to be a writer but my father told me this is not a career for a real man... this is a hobby... something to do on the side. When you make a living as a dentist... when you're comfortable... independent... then you can write all you like. But until then... you can write on Sundays... evenings... on vacation... during lunchtime... early in the morning instead of reading the newspaper. This way you can write literature... by your own standards without having to please anyone but yourself. Chekhov was a medical doctor first... the greatest writer there ever was besides Shakespeare. It is Anton Chekhov, not Dostoevsky or Tolstoy who is the greatest of the Russian writers... the grandson of a freed serf, son of a ruined owner of a humble general store... Chekhov supported his family from the age of sixteen and put himself through medical school... started writing junk... pulp... made good money at it... but once he graduated to literature, he never turned to writing garbage again. And the garbage didn't suck his soul out. He could probably jump from one to the other without compromising his integrity; like it was a game... and he was on top of it. He was independent... his own man. He liked to live well... yes... I grant you... but not a slave to the dollar or the ruble... never having to demean and disgrace himself... to grovel in front of rich men... always able to hold his head high. I know there was that rich publisher, Savorin or whatever... the money bags. But he seems to have held his own.

"It is possible to write trash without selling your soul especially if it pays well... but it ain't easy... it ain't easy... Maybe it beats teaching writing in Podunk U. But you have to keep your wits about you... leave plenty of time to write the good stuff... be able to change gears and you need a big nest egg so you never feel forced to write the shit. It's too easy to drown in it.

"My uncle... my father's brother... who I never liked very much... told me I should be a college teacher... a professor of literature and language... as training to be a writer... if that's really what I wanted to be. I told him this was no good... that they were not 'analogous' fields as he said but instead were mutually exclusive ... had nothing whatever to do with each other. The college world of literature is a totally different industry like meat packing or car tires... only they don't make anything... not anything that you can use. The papers they churn out on fiction have nothing to do at all with writing fiction... they're not only useless they're probably harmful to a writer. It's a recycling business, a boondoggle to keep otherwise intelligent people uselessly employed and taking money for it... trying to capture precious chemicals from smoke. I can say categorically that if you want to be a great writer or even a decent one stay the hell out of the universities...

they wouldn't know great literature if it came up and bit them in the ass.

"Good writing is the highest form of human endeavor with the exception of the love for another human being. I have promised myself to write one good book before I die. And if I fail... so be it... at least I will have given it my best shot. What more can you ask of a man? Good writing is magic... you stare into a sheet, blank white, slice open an artery, figuratively, and bleed into the bottomless inkwell until there is nothing left to give and you become rapturous... probably from loss of blood.

"Life is funny that way... it pays to think ahead... to be prepared for any eventuality. I was especially good at difficult extractions... they would call me in for special, tricky cases... impacted wisdom teeth. I was a master at extracting impacted, infected wisdom teeth. It's not as easy as it looks. It's a matter of technique.

"This screaming man called me by a nickname... he owed me money too... very sad... a debauched gambler... a disgusting, immoral person... robbed food out of his children's mouths to play the ponies... to bet on the future... stole from the present to give everything to wager on a future that is problematic at best.

I think deep down all of these gambling degenerates want to lose or don't care one way or another. They ache for the fix... the high... that adrenalin jolt... like electrocution... they hunger for that brush with death... no... they want to dance the tango with a homicidal insane lady who wants only to eat them up or teach them crazy dance steps... hang on to her like a bucking bronco while she's working to sink her teeth into their flesh... lie in the mud with the hooves coming down on their head... wallow in their ruin. I got carried away. I don't know what comes over me.

"You live in the past... you live in the future... the here and now is what counts... the only real world... the present instant... the past is no good when we want to dwell in it... it robs us... we squander our time reliving all of our mistakes or fantasize about some magic moment that never was... we give up our lives for a dream of what we think happened... the future full of anxiety and anticipation... both rob us of the now... strangle us... stifle us... smother us in its soft down bed.

"Grab tight hold... the here and now and live... live for God's sake...

"The past can never be recovered but truly it can never be escaped. We carry it with us forever like a sack on our back; it makes us who we are. Without memory we have no identity.... We carry it with us forever; it makes us who we are.

"I don't know. No... No... this only sounds good but I don't know if it's true. We are not the prisoners of our history... mostly but not absolutely.

"Besides, memory is just another fiction which we create.

"I got lost on a side track. Sometimes I think too loud to myself.

"Another thing... another thing is you have to pay attention... pay close attention! Most people sleep fitfully through life like drowsing through a movie... a picture they never heard of... to be startled awake by people stepping on their toes getting out of the aisle. It's too late, when they finally realize it's over. They discover how little a light the sputtering, trembling glimmer of consciousness is and have no real clue as to what exactly the movie was about. They try to divine meaning from the closing credits while people are pushing and poking against them telling them the movie is over and they're holding up the line. You can't hide and stay for another showing... the ushers are uniformed alike... they look like doormen... or those stupid looking toy soldiers on display at Kensington Palace with those high furry hats and they keep close watch wielding old-fashioned batons... not those with the rubber cushions on both ends. Don't mistake it for the fancy stick either, that's passed from runner to runner in a relay race... make no mistake it's a cudgel or truncheon and it's deadly. You only get one ticket... that's it. They don't let you stay for another showing. Thems the rules. It's a real shame though... the second time around you'd maybe learn to stay awake and might actually discover what the movie was about. Life is like money... both act like spilt quicksilver in a nest of cracks. Try to chase after that.

"Who was it that said?

> 'It is death that makes a mockery of life. We struggle to a level of consciousness, claw our way up, as if for no other purpose than to inflict upon ourselves the excruciating pain of the awareness of its fleetingness.'

"This was a wise man who said this. This is a man who knew.

"This stock 'deal' I am told you are looking for is not what you think it is, not some pump and dump... not a swindle of any kind like you imagine... not counterfeit certificates or anything like that. With such things I would never get involved and certainly Mr. Gatsby, who is a very upright man, would never go near such a thing... not so much as touch such illegality. This is simply about information... nothing more nothing less... knowing what other people don't know. This is Mr. Gatsby's specialty, his genius... if you want to know the truth. Where he gets his information, I couldn't tell you even if I knew. This knowledge is invaluable... it's like money and must be kept scarce.... Otherwise, the stock moves suspiciously and the jig is up. The more people who know... the less valuable the information. Giving you this information is like handing you money but more than that it is giving you the power to make that very money less valuable so that others who come after you suffer. We supply the information in a very particular order to a very select few. If you are near the top of the list you have the power to ruin it for those further down on the list... if you speak out of class... shoot off your mouth. It's like giving you the keys to the bank and you set the money on fire instead of only taking a reasonable amount for yourself. If you are chosen you will be given this information in a way that can never be traced to Mr. Gatsby or myself. You must never speak directly to me or Mr. Gatsby about these matters in any way whatsoever... ever again. You may receive a telephone call from someone you don't know or have some strange person strike up a conversation with you totally from out of the blue. He'll say something very out of the ordinary with very exact words like: 'I understand you have an interest in Oklahoma oil stocks'... those words must not be different in any way... not so much as one word out of place. And you must answer 'Texas' so he knows you understand and you're the right man. But never answer with your special word unless the words you are given are exactly right.

"By your look you seem to hesitate. He who hesitates is lost.

"Jesus! I have the unquiet feeling this is the first time you've ever done anything like this? What a fine lollipop you are! What are you going to do next... get down on your knees and pray for heavenly guidance? Never trust a man who gets down on his knees for any reason. George Washington never got on his knees, especially not in church. God doesn't want you to grovel... it's unbecoming. Maybe you should talk it over with your grandmother or your old nanny. You did have a nanny didn't you Mr. Filtchcroft? Of course, you had a nanny; all you fellows had nannies.

"Nothing... but nothing... is without risk... nothing is one thousand percent. Rarely, but sometimes... just sometimes... the information is bogus. People lie, even in secret conversations, even to themselves... especially to themselves.

"I don't know Mr. Filtchcroft. Is it alright if I call you Mr. Filtchcroft or is just plain Filtchcrofth good enough? You not supposed to answer that. That's what they call a rhetorical question. Can you be trusted to keep a secret? Or do you like to play the big man... proving to people how smart you are... what a skillful picker of stocks you are... how you're in the know, privy to the inside scoop. I'm afraid, Mr. Filtchcroft, that you're going to throw a wild and unpredictable monkey wrench into the works. But what you don't understand, is that when the busted machinery comes flying apart it will take your head off first. It won't be a pretty sight... you standing there without your head. And these things that you contemplate: are they in fact wild or just downright stupid? No matter how orderly you think your existence is, no matter how well planned, death waits for you... lurking just around the corner... for you to cross the street... and you will cross the street.

"What are you going to do with all this money you're going to come into?

"You want to gamble on some stock deal...? put money in thy purse?

"If you're intent on going to hell... at least get there in a more pleasurable way.

"Chasing after money for its own sake is a kind of homicide ... more like self-slaughter, very often gory. Money must come to you by indirection without ever hunting it down... like a wild animal which you coax and which finally comes to you entirely on its own when you're not looking... and there it is, out of the blue... all of a sudden, this huge creature, scary to look at, licking your hand like a friendly dog. And if the big beast stays in the woods... sticking out its big nose for you to see between the leaves... coming teasingly close... but never close enough... That's alright too. You have a roof over your head... food on the table... clothes on your back... some good books you buy cheap from the secondhand store... maybe even a rare public library you discovered by accident... like a jewel in the forest... that's hidden away so the bums don't ferret it out... to piss on the chair cushions, blow their nose in the books and generously share with everyone some rare highly communicable disease which drops liberally from the scabs they're covered with.

What more do you really need? This is America... no one starves to death. Do your best and do what you love and the rest will follow or maybe not. I'm this way with my pearls.

To think always of money is to think the way America wants you to think... This is what the dream has become... what the country has become... This is the trap they lay... This is the way it grinds your face into the dirt... the mud... with the boot pressing on the back of your head... then you will never be your own master.

"Save your money and save your life.

"But remember what the great Roman, Seneca said: 'a great fortune is a great slavery.' Well... it doesn't have to be... not if you play your cards right. You have to learn to delegate... to find people you can trust.

"Never forget this. Money can make you free... so you never have to humble yourself to the boss man whether that boss man is an unreasonably demanding client or an overseer with a whip. Money gives you the freedom to be yourself... to create yourself... to recreate the world... With money you buy yourself out of slavery... ransom your soul, from the heavy oppression of the clock, lift it with your own hands, from off your back. With money you buy maybe a really nice house, in a good neighborhood, a strong, solid house made of brick or stone, with a full basement... the mortgage paid off, money in a protected account and you can say FUCK YOU to any man. You do a good job and they don't like it... you say FUCK YOU. You tell them honestly and reasonably what you think and they give you trouble... you say FUCK YOU. You open your heart and arms to them and they turn their back on you... you say FUCK YOU. FUCK YOU. FUCK YOU. This is the only way for a man to stay on his feet, to stay alive and breathe clean air. FUCK YOU. FUCK YOU. These two words are the free man's prayer. It is better to save your money, to live like a monk, if necessary, to pile up the greenbacks in tall stacks like armor for your soul in order to be able to say one thing and one thing only: FUCK YOU.

"I pity these poor ambitious young fellows who think they are so smart and that believe that the world is going to recognize just how smart they are and reward them... give them their due. This is bullshit. This is what the swindlers in power want you to believe. Make no mistake: it is the scum that rises to the top.

"In the classroom the most intelligent are beaten down and methodically broken by the idiot teachers who rein like despots; who deep down regard intelligence as a threat to their small brains and puny little egos. It's the ass-kissers with brown, shit-stinking noses, the shameless suck-ups who become the teacher's pet. By deciding to educate everyone we really educate no one. Where are the Shakespeares? Every single year, maybe twice a year, a Shakespeare is systematically squashed like a bug on the classroom floor. You can turn in the most keenly honed and magisterial prose and the drudge up front with terminal dandruff and the yellow teeth isn't going to give it an A... he's going to give it an F... he's going to flunk you out if he can because of the fact that you exist... can exist... and that existence threatens all that he stands for... his secure, mediocre, stupid, meaningless existence. The only thing he knows how to do is cross-out adjectives. Shakespeare loved adjectives.

It's these morons on top who want to get rid of intelligence tests. They claim that the test is not predictive of either academic or worldly success. This is absolutely true. But this is an argument against the classroom and the world. I have never met a man who tested with a high IQ who wasn't extremely intelligent and worthy of better than he got. This world is not kind to intelligent men. Many were ruined, shattered men... many criminals, some in jail. What intelligent man could live in this ridiculous world without striking out, without revolting in some visceral, violent way? "No true artist will tolerate for one minute the world as it is" I think Nietzsche said that. But not just the artist, but anyone who would call himself a man.

I have been asked why I have chosen this life for myself... but I'm not sure that I have chosen it... Perhaps it chose me. I am not sure that I am much different from the artist or the warrior... the hunter... the fanatic or the martyr for that matter... Ruthlessness, alienation is indispensable to the good writer, same as it is to the bank robber, the safe-cracker, the strong-armer. What they all ache for is to get even; for life or what passes for it; the life that gets shoved down your throat. At all cost I wanted to avoid an everyday life.

I want uncertainty and doubt... I want turmoil and fight... I don't want to live in peace... How can any man make peace with this world the way it is...? And if the world makes war on me, God help the world.

"But this is neither here nor there... I don't know why I carry on like this... it's entirely beside the point..."

Gatsby returned from his call, interrupting the never-ending narrative of Wolf, his particular one-man-show, the well-worn, well-honed wise Mensch routine that he loved to indulge so much.

There's a story of Wolf holding a gun on a man he was trying to decide whether or not to kill and speaking at very great length, not really to his target but more to himself, trying to plead the case one way, then the other; the man had finally had enough and couldn't take it anymore, blurting out:

"Are ya gonna talk me to death or ya gonna shoot me?"

Without so much as another word Wolf shot him then and there, three times in the chest. If the man had only shut up and listened, he might have lived to an old age; it would have been worth the suffering. He was a wise-guy; he liked the style of what he was saying, the quick, flippant backtalk… how it sounded in his head; and he paid for his smartass quip with everything he had or would ever have, his life.

www.ingramcontent.com/pod-product-compliance
Lightning Source LLC
Chambersburg PA
CBHW030354020726
47493CB00003B/818